# END OF THE LINE

# END OF THE LINE

## BIRTH OF MAGIC™ BOOK THREE

ND ROBERTS

MICHAEL ANDERLE

DISRUPTIVE IMAGINATION

LMBPN Publishing
PMB 196, 2540 South Maryland Pkwy
Las Vegas, NV 89109

Version 1.02, July, 2021
eBook ISBN: 978-1-64971-829-7
Print ISBN: 978-1-64971-830-3

THE END OF THE LINE TEAM

**Thanks to the JIT Readers**

Daryl McDaniel
Wendy L. Bonell
Diane L. Smith
Rachel Beckford
Peter Manis
Deb Mader
Dorothy Lloyd
Veronica Stephan-Miller
John Ashmore
Kelly O'Donnell
Jackey Hankard-Brodie

*If I've missed anyone, please let me know!*

**Editor**
Lynne Stiegler

## DEDICATION

*For everyone who waited so patiently for these answers. For hope.*

*— Nat*

*To Family, Friends and*
*Those Who Love*
*To Read.*
*May We All Enjoy Grace*
*To Live The Life We Are*
*Called.*

*—Michael*

PROLOGUE

## SAF *Enora*, Earth Orbit, WWDE+225

"Big day," Esme commented, shaking Sarah Jennifer out of her introspection about the beauty of space.

Sarah Jennifer smiled, her eyes remaining firmly on the viewscreen. "Sure is." She was almost used to being up here after months of preparation for this operation, but she was determined never to allow the wonder of the expanse to become commonplace for her. The viewscreen was split between the cotton wool clouds covering the Earth and the void of space between the BYPS satellites.

"The Gate is about to open at Lagrange Point 4," Enora announced.

"About bloody time," Esme grumbled, the twinkle of excitement in her eyes belying her tone.

Sarah Jennifer made a noncommittal sound of agreement. The arrival of the terraforming equipment was long overdue, thanks to Federation supply issues and the need for secrecy as to the consignment's final destination. Bethany Anne had been clear that this supply run had to be done without any of the companies who had supplied the components knowing that it was coming to Sol.

Sarah Jennifer and Esme turned their attention to the pinpoint of silver-green light that appeared at the prearranged coordinates. The dot spiraled as it expanded, casting a cold light that was captured by the dust blanketing the area.

The Gate shimmered as multiple containers broke the event horizon.

Sixteen hundred shipping containers in all, they hovered around the Gate while they got into formation. The Gate winked out, leaving them in darkness.

Sarah Jennifer leaned forward in her seat. "Enora, take us out."

"Arrival in six minutes, Major." When they reached the holding area, Enora spoke again. "Security protocols on the containers have been activated. Voiceprint confirmation is required to access the controls."

Sarah Jennifer had been expecting this. "Confirm: Major Sarah Jennifer Walton accepting delivery."

"Voiceprint confirmed," an EI intoned over the speaker.

"Thank you," Sarah Jennifer told the EI. "Transfer controls to Enora and treat her commands as if they were mine."

Esme grinned. "You know the EIs don't have feelings and don't require pleases and thank yous?"

"Politeness costs nothing," Sarah Jennifer returned good-naturedly.

"Next you'll be telling me good manners are the stumbling block to the robot uprising." Esme snorted at Sarah

Jennifer's blank look. "Did you miss the movie night where we watched *Terminator*?"

"I'll be back," Enora announced in an uncanny approximation of Arnold Schwarzenegger's voice before she vanished from the screen.

Esme waved a hand, laughing. "See, Enora gets it."

Sarah Jennifer gave her a blank look. "I prefer to read on quiet nights. You know that. Besides, the community center is too rowdy on movie night."

"You've got a shock coming on Samhain, then," Esme told her.

"Samhain is different." Sarah Jennifer was well aware of the crowds that were already descending on Salem for the winter festival. "It's more that the troops find it difficult to relax when they see me there. Movie night is their night to blow off some steam. They need to get rowdy once in a while. They work hard."

"You'll get no argument from me on that account," Esme agreed.

Enora returned. "I have completed the inventory of the containers. We got everything we requisitioned. There is also a message for you from the *Baba Yaga*, Major."

"Play it, please." Sarah Jennifer wasn't surprised to hear Bethany Anne knew she had requisitioned the build-your-own-planet kit. The Queen might be light-years from the Federation, but she still had an ear on the ground there.

Bethany Anne's voice filled the cockpit.

"Good luck, Sarah. Permission would have been a good thing to ask, but I forgive you." A throaty laugh came over the speaker. "I've read through the projections your engineers put together. I trust you know what you're doing.

3

Oh, and don't fuck it up. There won't be another delivery until I return to the Federation."

Sarah Jennifer smiled. That was just like the Queen. Bethany Anne did not suffer fools lightly, and they had that in common.

*This operation has been planned to the last detail,* she reminded herself.

Esme chuckled. "You know the dangers of invoking Murphy's law, Duckie. We have contingencies for our contingencies. This operation will be a success even if we have to work all the way to Plan Z to make it so."

Sarah Jennifer had given up telling Esme to stay out of her head years ago. "Only one way to find out how far into the alphabet we're going to get. Enora, let's get started. Begin recording video and scan all data and stream it to wherever Jim is currently. Habitat containers are to remove themselves to the area we marked for Habitat One. Inform me once the BYPS satellites are in position and have the EI await further instructions."

They watched while containers moved away from the holding area, remaining in formation. Sarah Jennifer took a moment to process the majesty of the spectacle as Enora turned the ship to follow the containers.

The Red Planet came into view, and eight hundred of the containers broke off to position themselves around the planet.

The doors of these containers opened, and the satellites were ejected. The remainder of the containers broke orbit and entered the atmosphere.

"I have provided the landing coordinates," Enora

announced. "Phase One of magnetosphere regeneration can begin as soon as you are ready, Major."

Sarah Jennifer glanced at Esme when their Etheric comm pinged. "It's Brutus."

"Go ahead, Lieutenant," she answered.

"How are things going up there?" Brutus asked.

"We're about to get started," Sarah Jennifer told him. "How did the operation go?"

"Lilith has the cells set up. We have Mad from three of the five groups she specified. Rory's team and Bruiser's team are expected back by tomorrow with the rest."

Esme smiled. "Good job. I bet the Venetians were happy to see you."

Brutus gave an awkward laugh. "Yeah, no. No one wanted to go to Venice again, not after last time. We got the rotters from Florida."

"As long as you got them," Sarah Jennifer told him. "Call if you need us. Otherwise, we'll be back in a few days, once we know if our efforts here have succeeded or not."

"Got you." Brutus paused for a moment. "Good luck."

Sarah Jennifer said goodbye and ended the call. Esme's face was flushed with anticipation. "You ready for this?"

Sarah Jennifer nodded. "As ready as I'm ever going to be. Proceed, Enora."

The satellites came to life, their casings unfolding to reveal what looked like huge guns.

However, the Etheric energy Sarah Jennifer sensed gathering had nothing to do with kinetic weapons. Twelve of the satellites rotated to face the planet. The rest faced outward as standard.

"Shielding is set to maximum," Enora informed them. "Preparing to engage in three…two…one. Engaging."

The ESDs on the twelve inward-facing satellites activated, lighting the void. The pencil-thin energy discharges bored straight to the core of the planet at the coordinates predetermined by Ted and Jim.

Phase One—or Attempt One, more accurately—involved passing the ESD current through the planet to liquefy the outer core and jumpstart the planet's rotation.

The expected result was that the magnetosphere, which was currently too weak for the planet to retain a viable atmosphere, would increase to a level where the rising levels of greenhouse gases would result in the planet warming, making it possible for Jim's team to begin the oxygenation process.

Baby steps, starting with the magnetosphere.

The data they had from the Federation's terraforming specialists lacked information about the use of the ESD in place of the more standard injection of fissionable materials. However, her engineers had been beyond enthusiastic about this method, and Sarah Jennifer knew when to bow to the greater wisdom of her advisors.

It didn't make this any less nerve-wracking.

She gripped the arms of her chair, offering up a mental plea that this method would work.

Esme reached over and patted her arm. "Don't sweat it, Duckie. We have a whole bunch of things to try before we have to go with the nuclear option."

# CHAPTER ONE

**WWDE+233, Mars, Reynolds Plain, Habitat One**

Sarah Jennifer, Jim, Carver, and Geordie were sitting around the table in the central hub of the twenty inter-locked shipping containers that made up the habitat.

In the eight years since Sarah Jennifer and Esme began the process, Mars' atmosphere had slowly thickened, thanks to the gradual introduction of greenhouse gases.

Outside the habitat, the land was finally greening.

Habitat One had been accessible from the start. However, Sarah Jennifer had only allowed her chief engi-neer and his two right-hand men up here once the bots had reduced the planet's toxicity to manageable levels. They still couldn't go outside without pressure suits, but the team was well-used to the inconvenience.

Everyone was snacking on creamed chipped beef and toast MREs, affectionately known to Sarah Jennifer as shit on a shingle, as they worked through the latest terraforming projections.

Jim had the map open to the area in the northwest of

the planet's eastern hemisphere that Enora had identified as having previous glacier activity and more recently as having vast underground aquifers the Defense Force could draw from to irrigate the surrounding land.

"Where are we with the lakes?" Sarah Jennifer asked.

"They're filling, for sure." Jim zoomed in on the crater that held the largest body of freshwater they'd managed to coax from the vast underground reserves beneath the surface. "As we already know, the water ice at the poles was released along with the $CO_2$ ice when we reached optimal temperature planetwide. Using existing channels with some intervention to ensure the water flowed to the places we wanted it to has been effective. Another six to eight months, and we should be ready to seed the lakes with life."

"Fish?" Sarah Jennifer took another bite of her toast and chewed slowly.

Jim laughed. "Microbial matting. Bacteria brought from the lakes on Earth. We have a ways to go before we get to the fish."

Carver and Geordie emitted identical snorts.

"Talk about understatement," Carver retorted. "It took us most of the last six years to figure the filtration system."

Sarah Jennifer wrinkled her nose. "The data Akio sent from Waterworld suggested a shorter timeline."

"That planet already had oceans," Jim reminded her. "Theirs was a cleanup operation. Ours is a tad more complex, seeing as most of our water was trapped in the aquifers and had to be 'cleaned' before we were able to use it to irrigate the ag sector."

They all groaned, recalling the voracious native microbial life that had sprung up and outgrown their first attempt to make the planet habitable to humans and their livestock.

Geordie raised his coffee mug. "Let's hear it for suppressing Martian ecology."

Sarah Jennifer sighed. "Let's not go there. Weather reports, Lieutenant."

"The important thing is that we learned from our mistakes." Jim switched to the next slide. "The climate control system is working as it should. We have initiated tropical weather systems along the equator. Breathable atmosphere will be next, so long as the arti-forests do their job."

"Oh, they'll do their job," Carver assured them. "Once we reach nominal propagation of the silk leaf trees in the temperate zones, we'll be golden."

Sarah Jennifer had limited this meeting to the four of them for the simple reason that the arti-forest had become a topic of debate among the engineering community, all of whom had their own opinions about how the planet's ecology should be structured.

She had chosen to rely on the data the Federation's terraforming specialists had given them to figure which elements they had to add to produce an atmosphere that would support Earth life, and the arti-forests were the most viable solution in the short term. They had magic, which the Federation did not, and there were dozens of witches among the teams of scientists who were waiting to come here and push the non-artificial flora to thrive.

"Geordie, your pet project is taking care of that, right?"

Geordie nodded. "I've matched production on the artificial forests that are converting $CO_2$ to methanol and oxygen to keep up with the gases released by the melt."

Sarah Jennifer grinned. "That's what I like to hear. What does that mean for planting crops? It would be good if I could tell the enlisted we have at least a tentative date for getting magic users up here to move the new growth along."

Jim smiled. "I think we're ready to begin the building phase."

"That's music to my ears, Jim." Sarah Jennifer made a mental note to schedule a logistics meeting for the day after Samhain. Everything was a half-step farther along than where it had been the last time she'd made the trip out here. "Looks like we're done. Pack it up, guys. We need to get back to Salem."

Everyone at the table turned interested gazes to her.

"Samhain," she reminded them with an exasperated smile. "You've been up here so long you lost track of the season, huh? The festival starts in two days."

All three men jumped up from their seats, talking excitedly. Jim gathered his datapad and notebooks. "Guess you're right, Major. Can't say I'm not glad to hear the winter festival has come around, though."

"You just want to see my sister," Sarah Jennifer teased.

Jim blushed. "I don't know about that. Ms. Sylvia never seems too pleased to see me."

"That's because she's crabby," Sarah Jennifer told him. "I'll meet you guys back at the ship. Make sure we don't leave any bots out here that can't run with just EI supervision until you get back."

"I'm going to bring them all in," Carver assured her. "They're too expensive to replace."

Sarah Jennifer left them to finish their tasks and took the pressurized walkway that ran along the side of the habitat to the landing site. The *Enora* sat covered in the film of red dust that coated everything out here.

She took a moment to watch the bots working the agricultural sector that ringed the habitat and stretched to the boundary of the planned city limits. Three times the size of a human, the partially autonomous bots were designed to remove toxins from the land, depositing a mix mostly comprised of nitrates, phosphates, and potassium as they churned the Martian soil.

Soon, the soil the bots were enriching would be hidden by crops.

The sky drew her gaze, the swirl of pink and blue alien compared to sunset on Earth.

Sarah Jennifer smiled, her impatience to get the Defense Force moved here tempered by the progress they were making.

### New Romanov

Esme pulled a thumb drive out of her computer and pushed back from the workstation. Her chair almost toppled when the wheels snagged on the cables snaking between her computer and Lilith's casing.

"Are you okay?"

Esme waved off Lilith's inquiry and hurried through the door leading deeper into the mountain. She neither slowed nor spoke until she reached the chamber where the test subjects were held.

"This is the one, Lilith. I feel it in my bones."

"Well, divination is always a reliable method of predicting an outcome," the Kurtherian replied with amusement.

"Less of your lip," Esme retorted with equal humor. "My intuition is rarely wrong."

The Mad raised hell when she entered the chamber. Esme walked past the sixteen cells, which were separated by six feet and barriers of transparent pink Etheric energy. Fifteen of the cells were currently occupied, the group comprised of two Mad from every group save the Weres. The Weres were less susceptible to the Madness, so the pack was hard-pressed to find very many who had been infected. They threw themselves against their cells, the resulting activation of the barriers filling the chamber with a strobe effect.

Esme ignored them as she made her way to the terminal in the center of the chamber. She plugged the thumb drive into the computer and hooked it up to the main drive.

She selected the program named >>Rotters and added the chunk of code she'd just completed to the command list. She did the same for the programs >>Nomad, >>Bitten, >>Wechselbalg, and >>Earth-Air-Water, and sat back.

"Lilith, give me some juice. It's feeding time."

"Which cell?" Lilith asked.

Esme's eyes glowed gold. "All cells. In for a penny, in for a pound."

The Mad ceased trying to get to Esme when the

machinery surrounding the cells whirred. Those who still had a semblance of a mind shrank back in fear. The rest, reduced to relying on their instincts, salivated in anticipation of the coming meal.

There was a long moment where the only sound in the chamber came from the printers producing nanocyte-infused meat.

Esme looked upon the Mad with pity. Each of them had been brought from a different population representing a different method of infection. Therefore, each would need a variant on the patch that would restore their humanity.

"This is going to hurt you more than it hurts me, but dammit, it hurts me enough to see you reduced to this, you bitey bastards." She closed her eyes. "Let this be the one."

She turned back to the monitor. The command prompt was flashing.

Esme clicked Execute.

The energy constituting the cells parted above the heads of the Mad, and a slab of bloody meat was deposited into each cell.

The mindless fell on the food, devouring it greedily.

Esme looked away, sickened by the voracity with which the Mad tore into their meals.

The two former nomads only stared at the meat, their expressions those of dogs watching their masters eat. They did not trust the food since they were able to recall the meal that had ended in pain when the previous patch failed. Some reaction between the Were nanocytes they'd ingested as blood leeches and the Madness-corrupted nanocytes had left the nomads with a ghost of intelligence. Nevertheless, they were as flesh-hungry as their mindless counterparts, and as always, instinct won out over their better senses. They too began to eat.

The nanocytes in the meat were effective almost immediately.

The Mad fell to the ground unconscious as the nanocytes began their work.

"Here's hoping this is the patch that works," Esme murmured. "The last thing I want is for the pack to have to go find replacement test subjects."

"*Again*," Lilith agreed.

The nanocytes replicated from Ezekiel's blood donations had given them the breakthrough they needed back in '215. However, his blood was not a cure-all. An outright update had proven deadly for any who received it since the existing nanocytes in the Mad reacted much the same as white blood cells did when a foreign body was introduced to the host system.

Esme and Lilith had done everything they could to refine the testing process, eventually coming up with a number of patches that worked to counter each "strain" of the corruption. The number of Mad who had died in this lab over the last ten years to reach this point was a drop in the ocean compared to the total number of Mad who had died worldwide. However, Esme was no Arthur Drake. She took every one of the deaths personally, as did Lilith.

Their fears proved unfounded. Unlike in the earliest tests, the Mad did not begin spouting blood from every orifice. This time, they fell into the sleep Esme associated with the transformation they were looking to achieve.

The nibblet of hope Esme kept close to her heart sprouted a tiny tendril as they twitched and shuddered.

"How long until we know whether this has worked, do you think?" she asked Lilith.

"It's hard to say," the Kurtherian replied. "A few days, at least. Without individual Pod-docs to monitor them, it is a waiting game."

Esme switched off the nanocyte delivery system and got up from the terminal. "In that case, I'm going to leave them in your capable hands and take my aching old behind back to Salem. The Samhain festival is two nights from now. Annie and Lenore have everything in hand, but there's not much time to prepare for my part in the ceremony."

"Go," Lilith told her. "I'll call you if there is any change in their condition."

---

The Pod sped over the Atlantic Ocean with Enora at the controls.

Esme pottered around the open compartment, making last-minute adjustments to her ceremonial robes in preparation for the one time of the year where she *had* to be in Salem.

The winter festival had grown to include traditional celebrations from the many different groups who made up the Protectorate that covered the area between Salem, Pennsylvania, and New York, but Samhain was the main event for the magic users who made up the majority of the population.

Enora watched her sewing and gluing with curiosity. "Esme, why is Samhain so important to the magical community?"

Esme paused, needle in hand. "Well, lovey, it's to do with tradition, of course. Samhain gives people an event that they feel is all theirs, one that celebrates them as witches. There's a lot of comfort to be had from coming together for the blessing."

"Are you feeling confident about such a large use of mind magic?" Enora inquired.

Esme nodded. "Yes." She glanced at the small display screen on the console from which Enora's face peered at her with interest. "The ancestor blessing is what brings people together, no matter their walk of life. It's only right that everyone gets to experience it."

Enora was well-used to Esme answering a different question than the one she'd asked. She didn't repeat herself, knowing she'd get another answer that wasn't the one she'd been seeking. "I admit, I am interested to see how it goes down since this is the first year you intend to share the magic with everyone in the Protectorate."

Esme smiled. "Me too, lovey. Me too. Lenore and Annie have worked for months to prepare. Those as knows the secrets of magic will be there to ensure everyone gets a visit from their loved ones." She paused. "Well, as long as Sarah Jennifer makes it back on time."

Sarah Jennifer's voice filled the Pod. "Don't think I'd miss this for the world. We're about done up here."

Esme's head shot up, a wry smile playing on her lips. "You were listening in?"

Sarah Jennifer's laughter came from the speakers. "Karma, my old friend. Karma. How did the testing go?"

Esme grinned. "It's looking good so far. We'll know more in a few days, Lilith says."

"And the festival prep?"

"I'll find out when I get back. Hopefully, the council won't have torn each other to shreds, and the blessing will be shared with everyone. Did you hear from Amelie? She and Eoin are planning to attend."

"Linda is coming, too," Sarah Jennifer informed her. "I think she's more interested in finding out where Ezekiel is than any ceremony."

Esme's lip curled. "She's not bringing that awful man with her, is she?"

"Play nice, Esme," Sarah Jennifer chastised, chuckling. Neither of them liked the man, but that was politics. "Adrien has been a great support to Linda since she became chancellor."

"Don't mean I have to like him," Esme retorted.

Sarah Jennifer laughed. "See you in Salem."

# CHAPTER TWO

**Salem, MA**

Brutus and Sarai walked hand in hand through the park with their three children.

Jody held the hands of his younger sisters, making sure Macey and Tori didn't get lost in the crowd gathering for the celebration.

"Don't look now," Brutus murmured to his wife. "Frank is selling candy apples."

Sarai spotted the danger and groaned. "There goes any chance of us getting the girls to sleep before midnight."

To prove her point, all three children turned hopeful smiles on their parents.

Brutus covered his mouth with a hand and whispered, "They're doing the thing with the eyes. How can I say no?"

Sarai laughed. "Go ahead. It's Samhain."

The girls squealed with delight as she gave Jody a handful of coins. Jody was more circumspect, thanking them before shepherding his sisters to Frank's booth.

Brutus swept Sarai up, his arms around her waist. "How

was I ever lucky enough to marry the most beautiful, most intelligent, most kind-hearted woman in the world?"

Sarai giggled, wrapping her arms around his neck. "Don't forget that I'm an extraordinarily talented nature witch and domestic goddess beyond compare," she teased.

Brutus kissed her soundly. "With a healthy ego to match."

Sarai nuzzled his cheek. "Why, yes. It wouldn't do to be all of those things and not recognize my own awesomeness. How would I have snagged the hunkiest Were in the Defense Force otherwise? Us mere mortals aren't worthy, my love."

Brutus' comm pinged, saving him from his blushing reply.

Sarai laughed. "My shy guy. Go take care of your duty. I see Amelie with her brood."

Sarai sashayed away to where Amelie and her children were standing, putting an extra swing in her step since she knew Brutus had his eyes on her.

"Damn, woman of mine. I hate to see you leave, but I sure as hell love to watch you go."

Sarai patted her ample rear end with a hand as she looked back to wink at him.

Brutus answered his comm, his cheeks burning.

"Took you long enough, Lieutenant," Big Ace grumbled.

"I was saying goodbye to Sarai. What's up?"

"Need you over at the gazebo. There's a problem with the setup."

Brutus had been concerned about their ability to transmit the multiple live feeds the council had requested the Defense Force set up across the Protectorate for tonight's ceremony.

"On my way." He set off. "Let the major know."

"Oh, she knows," Big Ace replied. "If you ask me, it was a stupid idea to have everyone out of town while we were setting up for such a large event."

"I don't recall asking you, Quartermaster." Brutus toned down his annoyance. "I'll be there in a few minutes."

He reached out to Sarah Jennifer as he walked.

"I already know," she answered. "Esme will be there before I get back with Jim and the guys."

"Gotcha," Brutus told her. "I'll try her now."

Esme answered the comm with a burst of colorful language. "What now? I've had an earful from the Ace boy already."

Brutus suppressed a chuckle. "Just wanted to know what your ETA is."

"Twenty minutes, so don't touch a thing!" the reply came before Esme cut the connection without saying goodbye.

Brutus sighed. "To say this is a celebration, there's not much of a celebratory mood in the pack today."

The gazebo was roped off, the inner area bustling with enlisted engineers and uniformed logistics people working to prepare for the ceremony.

Brutus nodded at the private who lifted the barrier for him.

"Got to love Samhain, huh, sir?" The Were smiled as he spoke.

Brutus couldn't help being uplifted by his enthusiasm.

He returned the private's smile. "Sure do, Jenner. You all set for the blessing later?"

"I'm on duty all through tonight, sir," Jenner informed him. "Sure looking forward to seeing my old dad, though."

Brutus caught sight of Big Ace waving him over. "As you were, Private. Enjoy the celebration."

The quartermaster's hair was out of place, and his uniform showed signs of having been worn for two days in a row. The dark circles under his eyes told Brutus that Ace was at the end of his tether.

Ace gripped the datapad that had long since replaced his ledger, stabbing a finger at the screen as he spoke. "The public screens aren't connecting. The radio is down at Hartford, and I can't get a senior engineer out here for love nor money."

Brutus steered Ace over to the mess tent. "When was the last time you took a break?" He wrinkled his nose as Ace's ripe smell hit his olfactory center. "Or a shower?"

Ace gaped at him. "With what time? We have dignitaries arriving from all over Europe. Everyone in the Protectorate is expecting a visit from their ancestors. I have requests for replacement equipment coming in every few minutes, and—" His datapad chimed three times, proving his point. "*And* I don't have the staff or the resources to deal with all of this."

Brutus eased Ace into a foldout chair. "Sit tight. We'll get this resolved. It will go easier with coffee." He left Ace there and went to get them both a cup of caffeinated goodness, returning to the table to find the quartermaster on a comm call with Sergeant Izzy Bloom.

"Sergeant, anyone who touches supplies meant for Mars will be severely—"

Brutus got on the call. "Izzy, can this wait a half-hour?"

"Sure thing, Lieutenant," the reply came. "It wasn't urgent."

"He'll call you back." Brutus ended the call and handed Ace one of the cups. "It's not like you to lose your temper with Izzy, Ace. What's going on with you?"

Ace sighed tiredly. "Cherie had her first shift this week."

Brutus suddenly understood. He and Sarai had been watching Jody for the signs of *his* first. "I get it. I'm taking you off duty for the next two weeks. Call Izzy back and tell her... Oh, wait, Sanderson could be next to have his since they were only born a few weeks apart. Remind me again why we all had kids around the same time?"

Ace dropped his head into his folded arms and groaned. "Some dumbass pack instinct driving us to continue our genetic line?"

Brutus laughed. "Yeah, that about explains it. Well, now Cherie has shifted, it won't be long until the others in her age group figure it out."

"Jody won't be far behind the others," Ace told him.

Lucy paused. She was walking by with a sandwich in each hand. "Be glad your children had nice, untraumatic childhoods. I remember how hard it was riding herd on a bunch of toddlers running around in wolf form."

Ace looked up. "Finally, someone who knows what the hell they're doing!"

"Raising Weres?" Lucy gave him a sideways glance.

"No!" Ace exclaimed. "The screens!"

Sarah Jennifer tugged on the laces of Esme's bodice, trying to persuade the recalcitrant garment to obey her.

"Easy, Duckie. You're going to crack a rib!"

Sarah Jennifer grunted and pulled harder, putting her knee in the small of Esme's back to get some traction. "That joke gets funnier every year."

Esme craned her neck to look Sarah Jennifer in the eye. "You know this mood of yours is getting into the whole Defense Force?"

Sarah Jennifer had no answer for that. Or at least, not one that didn't violate her personal preference to avoid poor language.

"Duckie…"

Sarah Jennifer finished tying Esme's stays and turned to leave the room. "You've got the rest of this. I'm going to check with the engineers to make sure that the snafu with the live links has been resolved."

She left before Esme could call her back.

Esme sighed. She knew exactly what was getting her friend down, but it wasn't her place to interfere—*yet*.

# CHAPTER THREE

Sarah Jennifer made her way to the park, then checked in with the engineers and found everything in order.

Since the witches were scattered around the Protectorate, she didn't have to worry about anyone reading her mind, but her pack knew their Alpha was silently stewing beneath her smile.

The person she was avoiding snuck up on her as she neared the gazebo.

"Sarah Jennifer! There you are!"

As always, wherever Linda was to be found, Adrien was two steps behind her.

The young man nodded tersely. "Major Walton. Thank you for inviting us. This, um, ancestor blessing is interesting…" His voice trailed off, his tone implying Salem's most sacred celebration was less than civilized.

Sarah Jennifer summoned her diplomat face. "Linda, Adrien, I'm so glad the two of you could make it. How are you enjoying the festival?"

Linda's eyes danced over the crowd. "It's beautiful. I love visiting Salem, especially during Samhain."

The question hung in the air between them.

"Ezekiel isn't here." Sarah Jennifer hated to see the crestfallen expression on the young chancellor's face.

"Oh. I was hoping…"

*You and me both,* Sarah Jennifer thought but didn't say.

Adrien put an arm around Linda's shoulders. "I saw some people playing a game with apples in a barrel of water," he told her. "I'm sure the major has her duties to attend to."

Linda looked from Adrien to Sarah Jennifer. "Yes, of course. Sorry to keep you, Sarah Jennifer."

Sarah Jennifer resisted the urge to switch to wolf form and tear Adrien's throat out. "We'll catch up properly after the blessing," she told Linda earnestly. "I really am glad you came."

Linda didn't look sure she believed her.

Sarah Jennifer smiled. "Really. Come by HQ if the night gets away from either of us. I want to hear how everything is going in the valley."

Brutus joined Sarah Jennifer as Linda and Adrien melted into the crowd. "So, no Ezekiel again. You want to talk about it?"

Sarah Jennifer shook her head. "Nothing to talk about. Ezekiel won't come home just because I get in touch with my feelings. I need to get ready to do magic. I'll catch you later."

The gazebo had been draped in diaphanous fabric for the night and adorned with holly, ivy, and yew.

Sarah Jennifer slipped inside without stopping to speak

to any of the pack and took her seat on one of the dozen cushions ringing the arrangement of candles in the center of the bleached wood floor.

To access her magic, she had to clear her heart and mind, a monumental task since her heart was full of Ezekiel. Every thought of Samhain led to a memory of the two of them laughing, working together, or, toward the end, their arguments.

Sarah Jennifer would have taken an argument over the silence between them. However, she had a duty to the people who needed her tonight. Everyone on the council had to put their magic together to assist Esme in the ancestors' blessing.

Sarah Jennifer thought back to her first Samhain when the grief she'd been holding onto had been released by the ceremony. This was different. She had no clue how to let go when Ezekiel was still alive and separated from her by choice.

She worked to push her feelings of abandonment aside and focus on the need to provide catharsis for everyone who had lost their loved ones to the Madness in the last years.

She closed her eyes, filtering out the sounds of the feast going on outside the gazebo as she concentrated on accessing the source of magic deep within herself.

Breathe in. *Take in the will to let go.*

Breathe out...

*She couldn't let it go.*

Esme entered the gazebo. Without a word, she put her elaborate headdress down, sat on the cushion next to Sarah Jennifer, and took her hand.

Sarah Jennifer bit back a sob as a wave of warmth and love from Esme washed over her.

*This is the hardest time of year for you.*

Sarah Jennifer nodded, unable to deny it.

*It's okay. You've been here before, and you'll get through it again. Feel the pain. Accept your loss as part of life.*

*I don't want everyone else to know that I'm feeling...*

*The same as them?* Esme's mental voice was full of empathy. *You are just as entitled to your grief as anyone else, Duckie. Ezekiel may still be living, but the Madness took him from you just like it's taken loved ones from everyone who has come here tonight to experience the blessing.*

Sarah Jennifer pushed aside thoughts of Ezekiel. He didn't want her in his life; that much was clear. Knowing he was alive had to be enough.

Yet...

*I feel so alone,* she admitted.

A series of explosions outside marked the beginning of the ceremony as Dinny, Linus, and Reg set off the fireworks. Multicolored lights bled through the gauzy fabric separating Sarah Jennifer and Esme from the feast occurring outside.

Sarah Jennifer pulled her hand back and wiped her eyes. "Time to put on my big girl panties," she told Esme.

Esme shook her head. "If you say so. Time for me to get out there. You'll do fine, Duckie. When this is over, we're going to track that boy down and... I suppose giving him a good hiding is out of the question, but I sure feel like it right now."

The council members came into the gazebo, ending the

conversation. They formed the circle as Esme drew back the curtain.

Projection screens around the park showed identical celebrations all over the Protectorate.

The celebrants filled the trestle tables, which were still laden with food despite the hours they had been feasting.

The youngest children sat in their parents' laps while the older ones ran wild, full of sugar and adrenaline.

Esme, wearing green and gold, stood on the steps of the gazebo holding her athame and the silver chalice that had been used in the blessing since she, Annie, and Lenore had founded Salem after the battle of New York.

Her appearance caused silence to ripple outward from the gazebo.

Esme hoisted the chalice and began the ritual. "We honor those who came before us and those who laid down their lives in the last year by raising a cup in their name. Merry meet!"

"MERRY MEET!" came the thunderous reply.

Esme drank deeply from the chalice, and everyone followed suit. "The Matriarch's blessings upon us all. We are gathered tonight to celebrate the passing of this year into the next. The Protectorate grows with each new year, and the good people are blessed to have this bounty to share with all who come to us for succor. We have lost, but we have also loved greatly.

"As the year hinges and the world moves toward the darkness, hold the light inside your hearts high so that the world can be guided through the Madness and into an era of magic for all.

"This is the two-hundredth anniversary of Salem, and it

has been twenty-one years since we opened our doors and our hearts to the UnknownWorld. Founders, please join me in the ancestor's blessing."

Esme's eyes glowed golden as she gathered the Etheric energy freely given by Sarah Jennifer and the witches inside the gazebo. The heady rush hit her, but she didn't hoard the energy, and the feeling passed as she extended her senses to the witches leading the celebrations in towns and cities all across the Protectorate.

She began the ancient Gaelic chant that was as familiar to her as the lines on her face. The speakers placed around the park relayed the harmonious voices of the witches chanting with her.

The golden light from Esme's eyes grew brighter and lighter, surrounding her in a ghostly nimbus as the mind magic expanded and unfurled.

The people's belief added to the magic, the energy entering their subconscious minds. Everyone there had lost someone, someone they wished to see with all their heart and soul.

The first shades appeared, compounding that belief. More and more ghosts materialized, filling the park. If anyone had been looking at the screens, they would have seen the same thing occurring at the other locations. Those in the know were aware that the apparitions were not really the spirits of the departed. Esme's gift was to create these projections in return for the energy the people gave. Energy she and the other witches used to replenish the barrier hexes around the cities.

Esme lifted her hands, exulting in the connection she felt to every living being attending the festival.

She reached out beyond the borders of the Protectorate, searching…

And found him, sitting on a rock.

## Potato Creek State Park, IN

Ezekiel sat on his meditation rock, considering the path that had led him here.

He missed Enora. He missed Esme and Linda, and as much as he tried to ignore it, he missed Sarah Jennifer.

His chip was still switched off. At first he had remained hidden, afraid Sarah Jennifer would come swooping down in the airship to take him back to Salem.

She never came for him.

As the years passed and the Defense Force spread across the world, then withdrew to Salem, he'd let his unreasonable anger at her fester to the point where even the thought of her made his stomach churn.

He had spoken to Lilith on a few occasions when his weakness overwhelmed him to the point where reaching out was preferable to isolation.

He'd been blocking her since he'd met Helena.

His fascination with the elderly vampire had overridden all the emotions he'd bottled up. Someday he would have to deal with them, but today was not that day.

He left his meditation spot and returned to their home.

Ezekiel sensed trouble as he approached the cabin where he and Helena lived and worked together. He loved Helena enough to trust her with the secrets of his past. She loved him enough to not make him confront it. He wished his blood was sufficient to cure her. However, short of her draining him—something neither of them would allow—there was no cure to be found there. He was able to provide small donations, which she mixed into the herbal concoction she took to stave off the change.

His vampire companion needed something to contemplate during her more lucid periods. Together, they spent their time working on keeping her alive until Esme and Lilith figured out how to reverse the corruption for everyone on Earth.

More often than not recently, she spent her days strapped to the bench they'd rigged to control her when the Madness surged within her.

He checked the traps out of habit. His barrier hex usually kept the Mad away from the house, although he had never managed to get it to stay up or make it as strong as Esme's.

Helena's cries came filtering through the trees, driving Ezekiel into a run.

He burst into their home, finding she had worked one of the straps loose and was clawing at her chest in an attempt to rip out the corruption she felt taking over.

"Hel, it's me." He took the six steps to the cabinet where her serum was stored and took the jar and a spoon.

Helena moaned, her voice eerie in the enclosed space. She lashed out as Ezekiel approached with the medicine, almost dashing the precious jar out of his hands.

Ezekiel jumped back and set the jar down before taking another approach. He held out his hand, *pushing* a wave of calming energy at the tortured vampire.

"Shh, it's all right. I'm here," he soothed, capturing her arm and pressing it down so he could retie her bonds.

With her restrained, he was able to spoon a little of the medicine into her mouth. "There...see? Doesn't that feel better?"

Helena's eyes darted around wildly for a few moments longer, then the dull red light brightened as her vampire nanocytes overtook the Madness.

She fell into an exhausted sleep.

Ezekiel watched her for a short time, opening the windows to let out the Mad scent she'd emitted during her attack.

He cleaned up the mess she'd made while thrashing around as a distraction from the traitor thoughts inside his head.

The attacks were coming more frequently. The time was coming when the medicine would no longer be enough. Taking her to Salem was out of the question. Even if he was willing to face Sarah Jennifer again, they both agreed that there was nothing that could be done for someone who already had the Madness, and Helena was vehemently against risking the innocents who lived there.

The reasoning did little to assuage his guilt. Helena's work in decoding the secrets of the corruption kept them both sane.

When she awoke, Ezekiel had a pot of soup ready, knowing she'd be starving from the expenditure of energy it took to stave off the Madness.

"Ezekiel..." Her voice was weak.

"Hey, you're back." Ezekiel forced cheer into his voice as he walked to the bench. "Let me see you."

Helena turned her head to look at him, and he checked her eyes before releasing her.

Ezekiel offered her a bowl of the thick, meaty broth he'd made. "This will help."

"I need blood," Helena admitted. "Perhaps we could hunt this evening?"

Ezekiel wasn't sure about the wisdom of her being left to roam free. They lived far from any human habitation for the simple reason that Helena forgot her vow to only feed on animals when the Madness came over her. A Mad vamp could wipe out a city with no compunction, and he wasn't fast enough to keep up with her if that happened.

Helena read his doubts as clearly as if he'd spoken them. "You don't believe it's safe."

Ezekiel shook his head. "No. I'm sorry. I will hunt at dusk. You should stay here, where it's safe."

For everyone. Neither of them needed to say it.

Helena nodded. "You're right. I have my work to occupy me. You'll put a hex around the house so I can't get out?"

"Yes."

His hunting trip was postponed when Helena felt another attack coming on just as the sun began to set.

"BLOOD!" she screeched as he strapped her to the bench.

"I'll get your blood," Ezekiel promised, knocking her out with a pulse of Etheric energy.

He raised a barrier hex around the house as he left with his sword strapped to his back. He was too worked up to create anything lasting, but it would hold for the next few hours, at least.

It was too late to find deer by this time, but he knew where he could find a herd of wild pigs. He slipped through the forest, making no noise. His senses extended, he searched for the minds of prey animals as he followed the game trails, as Esme had taught him.

There were Mad out here. A lot of Mad.

Ezekiel knew he could escape them if they swarmed him. He resigned himself to the knowledge his hunt would take him farther from the house than he felt comfortable with. Helena needed blood, and since his was not on the table, he had to find an animal she could feed from.

The night stretched on, the stars that appeared overhead lending their light to the landscape through the gaps in the canopy. That vanished an hour later when the clouds swept in and it began to rain.

Ezekiel slogged on as the dirt turned to mud. He was relieved when he finally sensed the minds of the pig herd he was seeking. He veered in the direction he'd picked up the piggy thoughts, swerving to avoid a cluster of Mad approaching from the northwest.

An almighty crash somewhere up ahead broke his concentration and scared away the pigs.

Torn between his desire to find out what had caused the noise and his need to get back to Helena, Ezekiel stopped dead.

He sensed humans, vampires…and Weres.

He had turned to head home when the sounds of battle split the night.

That was enough to make up his mind.

# CHAPTER FOUR

**Salem, MA**

Sarah Jennifer sagged onto a bench, feeling as drained as all the witches except for Esme, who was dancing with Theor as the band played a lively waltz.

Brutus brought her mead and food, which she gratefully accepted.

Esme and Linus joined them at the table, shortly followed by Linda and Adrien.

Sarah Jennifer could tell Esme was holding something in. However, the witch wasn't giving anything away just yet. Her eyes flicked to Adrien, her smile dimming for a split second. She took a deep draught of her mead, giving Sarah Jennifer a look that told her she would tell her in good time.

Sarah Jennifer gave her friend an almost imperceptible nod.

Adrien was well on his way to being drunk. He dominated the conversation, his focus on complaining about the difficulty of maintaining the protections against the

Madness they'd had in Bad Salzig since the rising sea levels had forced them to relocate the city's inhabitants inland. "We need to get the cure for the Madness," Adrien continued, oblivious to everyone's dislike of him. "Which would be a whole lot easier if Ezekiel hadn't stepped out on his responsibilities."

Linda was quiet, picking at her food. Adrien quaffed the rest of his drink and looked around for one of the townspeople who were acting as servers for the night.

Spotting Dakota, he waved his empty cup to summon her over. "Girl, I need a refill!"

"Rude," Brutus commented, but Adrien didn't hear him and Esme shook her head, mouthing, "Let him drink."

Dakota didn't appreciate Adrien's demanding tone, but he was a visiting dignitary, so she came over and refilled his cup. Esme winked at her.

Adrien put his hand on Dakota's arm to stop her from leaving. "Just leave the jug," he demanded.

Linda dropped her head, mortified.

Dakota's eyes flashed yellow as she pulled her arm away. "I'd say you've had enough."

Everyone except for Linda and Adrien noticed Esme's eyes glowing.

Adrien suddenly put his hand on his stomach. "I feel sick." He got up from the table, swaying slightly.

Sarah Jennifer kicked Linus under the table.

Linus got the message and got up to steady Adrien. "Here, I'll get you back to HQ. Looks like you need to lie down."

Adrien glanced at Linda.

"Good idea, Linus," Sarah Jennifer interrupted before

Adrien could demand that Linda go with him. "See you tomorrow, Adrien, when you're feeling...better."

Linus hooked an arm through Adrien's and steered him away.

Linda covered her face with her hands. "I'm so sorry. He can handle his alcohol just fine, usually."

Sarah Jennifer shot Esme a glance. *Subtle.*

*I had to get rid of him somehow.* Esme's mental tone was entirely unapologetic.

With Adrien gone, the atmosphere around the table lightened. Linda laughed at Katia's and Brutus' retelling of their efforts to train the newest cohort of Weres that had enlisted in the Defense Force.

Sarah Jennifer was quiet as the feast went into the early hours. Her energy had returned after she'd eaten enough to replenish what she had given to the ceremony, but her mind was still on Ezekiel.

Esme decided to spill her secret, sensing Sarah Jennifer's sadness. She got up from the table. "Sarah Jennifer, Brutus, Linda, come with me."

Mystified, they followed as Esme led them to the comm hub in Sarah Jennifer's former office.

"Why are we here?" Sarah Jennifer asked as Esme locked the door behind them.

"You'll see soon enough." Esme took a seat at the console and leaned in to type. "Enora, bring up satellite image of these coordinates."

"Of course, Esme." The AI's voice held a note of mischief.

They all stared at the wallscreen, which came on and showed them...

"A rock?" Sarah Jennifer folded her arms. "Can't say I'm too impressed."

Esme tutted. "One of these days, you're going to learn patience. Enora, go back to the timestamp that correlates with the start of the ancestor blessing."

The video onscreen wound back, then stopped.

Linda gasped, her hands flying to her mouth. "Ezekiel!"

Sarah Jennifer's heart slammed against her rib cage. The man sitting cross-legged on the rock had an impressive growth of facial hair obscuring his features, but she would have known him anywhere. "Where is this?"

"Indiana," Enora replied. "Specifically, the former state park known as Potato Creek."

Ezekiel's head suddenly snapped up, and he vanished from the rock in a flash of light.

"Where did he go?" Sarah Jennifer knew he could only translocate for short distances.

"I lost him after this," Enora informed her. "There's no way to track him unless he turns his neural chip back on."

Sarah Jennifer wished she wasn't due to head back to Mars the next day. She clenched her fists, her nails cutting into her palms as she fought to control her emotions. "Monitor that rock. Notify me immediately if he returns to it."

She bent to hug Esme. "Thank you. I really needed that."

Esme patted her arm. "Now that you know, you can focus on getting our new home built."

Linda danced around the room. "I knew he was still alive! Wait until Adrien hears about this. We'll be able to

40

expand the city in no time once we persuade Ezekiel to come back with us!"

She unlocked the door and danced out of the room, leaving the other three alone.

Brutus looked from Esme to Sarah Jennifer in confusion. "Does she not understand that guy is the definition of an asshole?"

Sarah Jennifer shook her head. "Her choice."

Esme grinned. "Maybe her choice will change once our boy is back in the picture. Seems I don't want to whip his behind raw after all."

### Potato Creek State Park, IN

The Mad were out in force, drawn by the disturbance.

Ezekiel crept close enough to see the crashed dirigible, then backed away before any of the enhanced sensed him.

He narrowly avoided being discovered by the female vampire and the Were who rushed by in pursuit of her.

The vampire's scent carried the taint of Madness. That in itself would have been enough to get him involved, but Ezekiel wanted to avoid the Weres at all costs lest they reported his location to Sarah Jennifer.

Ezekiel's thoughts were tangled as he traversed the forest.

There were still plenty of Weres who hadn't sworn allegiance to the pack, but the risk was too high for him to take a chance. He had his life out here with Helena, and nothing on this Earth could make him capitulate on his vow.

He would *not* go back to Salem with his tail between his legs.

He sensed a human nearby.

What in the Matriarch's name was going on? They hadn't had a single, solitary human being around here for almost two years, and now half the UnknownWorld was showing up?

He had little fear the vamp and the Were following her would find the house. His hex should still be holding.

Unable to repress his curiosity any longer, Ezekiel followed the mental signal of the woman, tracking her to a glade where he found her staring into a pool, talking to herself.

Her homespun clothing was in good repair, and her long dark hair was well kept. The sword she carried was impressive, telling him she had no extra abilities. He sensed...something about her; she wasn't a magic-user, however. He had met a few humans whose nanocytes gave them faster reflexes or the quick-healing of the Weres without the urge to turn furry. Perhaps she was one of those.

*Well, at least she's not Mad,* Ezekiel thought. He watched her for a while, listening to her talk to get a sense of who she was as a person.

The pool held her captive attention. "Well, it turns out the world is wider than we ever imagined. Those creatures from your storybooks? Yeah. They're real, too. Vampires, werewolves...hell, for all we know, soon we'll meet goblins and ghouls. Wizards and mummies. Witches and Frankensteins."

Ezekiel couldn't help himself. "Technically, *Doctor*

Frankenstein was the scientist. His creation was actually called Frankenstein's *monster*."

He regretted his method of introduction when he found himself at the pointy end of the woman's sword.

He smiled nervously, lifting his hand to push the blade away.

The woman didn't give him an inch. "So, the creep who's been following me can read?"

Ezekiel knew he should go easy on the snark. However, something about almost losing his head brought it out in him. "Shouldn't be surprising, really. Many survivors of the Madness can read. The two aren't mutually exclusive."

"You've seen other survivors?" The woman narrowed her eyes, her expression mistrustful. "A boy your age? Shouldn't your mommy be with you, making sure you're not talking to strange women?"

Ezekiel chuckled. Curse the youthful look his nanocytes gave him. Oh, well, he might as well play the part. "You raise two questions, there. Number one, are you calling yourself a strange woman?"

Her eyebrow shot up. "No. Not at all."

"Secondly, you don't appear to be much older than me. You must be approaching, what? Thirty summers?" Ezekiel couldn't seem to stop his mouth from running. Well, no, that wasn't entirely accurate. He wasn't looking to pick up a dependent, although there was little about this woman that said she was the damsel type.

Curse him and his propensity for being an utter gobshite, as Esme had always called him with varying degrees of fondness.

The woman huffed. "Why have you been following

me?" she demanded. "Do you just like following women in the woods?"

Ezekiel squirmed. He *had* been following her, but not for the creepy reason she was suggesting.

She continued tearing a verbal strip off him before he could defend his motives.

"I'll warn you, I've grown up around men like you, and those men don't have their goody bags between their legs anymore. You so much as touch me, and I'll—"

He couldn't help it; he burst out laughing. Matriarch, she reminded him of Katya.

She lowered her sword. "What's so funny?"

"It's just my damn luck," Ezekiel managed through his laughter. "Alone for all these years, and somehow every woman I stumble into seems to have a stick up her ass and confidence that doesn't quit. You know, my father once told me that the old world used to run as a patriarchy?"

The woman's face gave away exactly what she thought of that little nugget.

Ezekiel nodded. "Yeah. Presidents, business leaders, even the greengrocers, they were all men once. A time when your genitalia predicted your outcome in life."

He shrugged. "Now I'm surrounded by ball-busting women everywhere I turn."

"That's a problem?" the woman shot back.

Ezekiel grinned, shaking his head. "Of course not. I just find it entertaining, is all."

The woman relaxed a touch. "Where I grew up, it was all men. Men who ran the guards, men who ruled the town, men who felt they could take what they want and discard it all as though it were nothing more than trash. Those worlds still exist out there."

Ezekiel was well aware. He'd come across a few places like that on his travels. Hell, he'd met Helena when he'd rescued her from a bunch of leeches who had been intent on prolonging their lives by drinking her blood. They were all dead, but there were plenty more like them outside the protection the pack offered. "I don't doubt that they do. You escaped, though, didn't you? You broke free and now you're here. Alone in the Mad-infested woods with nothing more than a sword to protect you. Yet you remain unscathed. Even after your ship crashed into our woods."

He didn't miss the way her fingers flexed by the hilt of her sword.

"You saw that?"

He lifted a shoulder. "Come on, you don't think everybody in a ten-mile radius didn't see that? You crashed into these woods in a giant floating ship. It's hardly the height of secrecy, is it?"

She shrugged. "I suppose not."

"The Mad were driven into a frenzy." He noticed that twitch of her fingers again. She was quick to fight; that much was clear.

"You saw the horde?"

Ezekiel nodded. "Of course."

Her chin jutted in pride. "We dispatched them easy enough."

"Yet, you abandoned the ship," Ezekiel pointed out. "Why was that?"

Her gaze slipped to the tracks at the tree line. *Interesting,* Ezekiel thought. *She cares about the vamp and the Were.*

"My friends. They passed this way some time ago."

"Ah, the wolf and the vampire?" Maybe this group didn't have anything to do with Salem. His curiosity was piqued, and if he was honest, he liked this so-far-nameless woman's forthright attitude.

She tilted her head. "You saw them?"

Ezekiel nodded. "I saw them."

Her patience was running low, judging by the bite in her next words. "Which way did they go?"

He pointed in the direction of home, marked by a thin line of smoke from the chimney. "Toward the house. It's rather coincidental, really. All of this forest, and there's only one house for miles around. Well, only one functioning house, that is. The rest have long since been abandoned and destroyed since WWDE." He sighed. "Some messes are remarkably difficult to repair."

He felt a stab of guilt, knowing the mess was partially his responsibility to fix.

The woman nudged him out of his reverie. "Can you show me to this house? Is this where you live?"

"Of course, this way." His reticence about letting her in given Helena's current state was somewhat assuaged by the knowledge that one of the woman's companions was also a Mad-afflicted vampire.

He took her around the lake, avoiding the Mad crashing around the far shore.

"Though I must say in advance it's only a temporary lodging, and somewhere where we didn't expect to accommodate guests."

That suspicious nature of hers came to the surface again. "You said 'we?'"

Ezekiel thought he understood how she'd stayed alive through the apocalypse. "That's right. I couldn't live alone in the woods, you know. Much too isolating. Being alone isn't conducive to emotional and intellectual development. Can turn a person mad...the regular kind. Not the, you know." He lifted his hands and bared his teeth in a parody of the Mad. "Although, we have been living here for some time."

He continued to follow the tracks left by the two UnknownWorlders. Not that he needed to. He sensed the Etheric output from them both.

"Who *are* you?" the woman asked.

Ezekiel laughed, having the same question about her. "All in good time. Why don't we save our introductions until we've got a roof over our heads and locks on the door?"

# CHAPTER FIVE

The Were scent was accompanied by the sounds of a man struggling in pain.

Ezekiel hid his alarm at his hex failing. The man was in danger if Helena had escaped.

However, it sounded more like the Were had gotten caught up in one of the Mad traps he'd laid for exactly this situation.

The woman ran heedlessly toward the yew thicket, where they found the hapless Were caught between forms as he fought the net suspending him from a tree.

Ezekiel suppressed a smirk. He'd learned knots from Sarah Jennifer. The combination he'd used to rig the net would only constrict the Were further the more he struggled.

The man in the net was hampered by the dog jumping at him.

Ezekiel figured the dog was part of the group, given that the woman didn't pay any attention to him.

The Were quit yowling like a big baby and glared at the

woman. "Are you just going to stand there staring at me all day, or are you going to let me down?" Still partly shifted, his words came out in a growl. "If you like what you see, just let me know, and we can arrange a playdate at a later time."

Ezekiel cracked up.

The woman flashed him a look that could have cut glass and drew her sword.

Ezekiel could have told her the traps were imbued with magic to prevent the Mad from escaping once they were caught.

He chose to let her work some of that anger out.

She was stumped by the flashes of orange light the net emitted when her blade met the rope.

Ezekiel relented when he realized she was likely to turn the blade on him if he kept messing with her. He flourished a hand and removed the Etheric energy protecting the ropes.

The Were fell inelegantly to the ground on her next attempt.

Ezekiel hung back as the Were got to his feet, massaging his rear end.

He eyed Ezekiel before turning to the woman. "Smooth. Who's your friend?"

The woman ignored his interest in Ezekiel. "Did you find her? Mary-Anne? Did you get her?"

Ezekiel figured Mary-Anne was the Mad vamp. Her trail veered into the woods. She was long gone.

The Were scoffed. "I'm sorry, do you think I have the power to make a vampire invisible?" He feigned holding someone around the waist. "Oh, hey, Ma. Caitlin's asking if we found you. What? What do you mean, she can't see you because vampires are now invisible to humans? That's truly a revelation to me."

"You know what I mean!" She punched him in the arm. "What good is a sniffer dog who can't track a vampire-turned-Mad?"

"What good is a human who can't *control* her vampire?" he shot back.

Ezekiel felt the air turn cold, no magic involved. *Oh, he's for it now.* He snickered to himself.

The Were seemed to read the atmosphere just fine. He lifted his hands in submission.

"I mean... It's just... We knew this would happen eventually, right? I'm not suggesting you control her. Only..." He sighed. "We can't lose her, Kitty-Cat. She's a Revolutionary."

Kitty-Cat? That was her name? Ezekiel snorted a laugh. "Wow."

"What?" The Were wheeled on him, teeth bared and a yellow glow in his eyes. "Caitlin, who is this guy?"

Most people would have dropped a load in their pants at that snarl. Ezekiel wasn't fazed. He flashed Caitlin a cocky grin. "I've never seen a Were wilt so quickly under a human's glare. You've got a gift, Caitlin. Powers greater than I've known any human possess."

Caitlin joined in with Ezekiel's laughter. "He just knows that if he steps one toe out of line, I'm going to throw him in the doghouse." She patted her knees. "Don't you, boy? Don't you?"

The German Shepherd yipped excitedly and hopped

around her legs. "Not you, Jax," Caitlin told the dog with amusement.

"And it's 'Kitty-Cat,'" the Were corrected as he brushed the dirt off his clothing. "We've spent ages training her to answer to her name. Let's not let some strange boy be the reason she thinks she has a normal name."

"Thanks for that, Pooch," Caitlin smirked.

The Were shot her a look.

Ezekiel nodded. "I understand, although I have always made it a point of pride to call people by the names they wish to be called. So, what'll it be?"

Before Caitlin could answer, the Were jumped in. "Sir Wolfington Growlsalot of the House of the Bander Weres, at your service." He bowed in Ezekiel's direction.

Caitlin rolled her eyes. "Kain, you're an idiot."

"Pleasure to meet you, Sir Wolfington." Ezekiel dropped his hands to his hips. "I hope you realize that you have made your figurative bed, and now you shall lie in it."

Kain grinned. "Actually, I've always wanted to be nobility."

"And you can just call me Caitlin," Caitlin told Ezekiel. "Keep things simple, for once. Matriarch knows things have been complicated for far too long in this world."

Ezekiel's laughter faded at the reminder.

"And what shall we call you?" Kain asked.

Caitlin shook her head. "I've tried that. Dude likes to keep secrets."

Ezekiel made his eyes shine red. "Pleased to meet you, Caitlin and Sir Wolfington. My name is Ezekiel."

"Ezekiel?" Caitlin echoed. "That's an odd name."

Kain snorted. "Is it any odder than 'Stump?'"

Ezekiel smiled. He liked the easy banter between these two. It was clear they'd been together for a long time. "It's the name my parents gave me. I had no more choice over my name than your boyfriend had in being a Were."

Kain opened his mouth to protest. "*Not* her boyfriend!"

Caitlin cut in, "'Ezekiel.' I like it. Bit of a mouthful, though. How about I just call you Zeke?"

Ezekiel was about to argue his name being shortened when he heard Helena cry out.

"*Damn!*" Ezekiel ran for the house. Magic leaked from his pores, his heart pounding as his emotions surged. "Stay back!"

Of course, just like a woman, Caitlin ignored him.

He found Helena in the grip of the Madness, fully vamped out. The room was flooded with red light from her eyes.

"No. Fucking. Way."

Ezekiel ignored Caitlin's outburst as he worked to calm his friend. "Hel, I'm here," he murmured as he went for the cupboard with her medicine. Afraid she was too far gone, he turned his back as he tipped the medicine into a bowl and sliced his finger, adding a few drops of his blood to the mixture as he stirred it.

Caitlin and Kain looked on in horror. Ezekiel had neither the time nor the inclination to take care of their feelings right now.

Helena snapped at him, her fangs coming dangerously close to his wrist. "Hold still, old woman," he soothed. Ezekiel evaded her bite, forcing the spoon with the medicine into her mouth. Another, and another.

His guests exchanged frightened glances. Ezekiel didn't

need to read minds to know they were thinking of their Mad-vamp friend.

Outside, the German Shepherd barked frantically, adding to the unreality of the situation. Just yesterday, Ezekiel had believed his world was set in stone. Helena would recover given time, and they would continue to live here in peace until Sarah Jennifer and Esme reversed the Madness.

He cursed his childishness.

Caitlin and Kain stood by, doing the uncomfortable shuffle of strangers who had walked in on a family fight. Ezekiel continued to make soothing noises, clamping down on his magic as the medicine took effect. Finally, Helena fell into an exhausted sleep.

The moment she slipped from consciousness, the dog ceased barking.

Ezekiel's shoulders dropped. She, and they, were safe for the moment. He turned to look as Kain let the dog into the house, offering them a rueful, exhausted smile. "I suppose you're wondering what's going on here?"

Kain shook his head. "Not really. We see a lot of young men with Mad vampires strapped to benches in their houses. It seems to be the latest form of entertainment for kids. Like PlayStations or Xboxes, only this is some form of vampire torture instead."

Ezekiel flushed red. How did Kain know about pre-WWDE technology?

Caitlin's expression was full of compassion as she stared at Helena. "Who is she?"

"One of the world's most gifted women. A genius, unappreciated in her time. Someone who has been battling the Madness for more years than I care to count and who, even now, is still battling the very disease she wishes to cure." Ezekiel couldn't look at the sleeping face of the vampire. He had failed his only friend in this harsh world.

He should have taken her to Salem. He was a dumbass, stubborn, prideful—

*It's not too late.*

Lilith's calm mental voice startled Ezekiel into knocking the bowl off the table, spilling the precious medicine.

Caitlin's eyes widened as the liquid hit the floor, and she gasped. "No! It can't be…"

Ezekiel slammed the barriers of his mind down, cutting Lilith off.

"What?" Kain was kneeling with his arm around the dog. "Who is she?"

"Can't you see it?" Caitlin's face was flushed with excitement. "The mixture Zeke just gave her is the same mixture we've been giving Mary-Anne. The same drink the governor took when he was fighting the Madness?"

Ezekiel was barely there. His eyes burned, his skin felt like it was made of inside-out cacti. Every fiber of his being was focused on not destroying the house with an uncontrollable pulse of magic driven by grief and anger at himself.

Caitlin stood over Helena, scrutinizing her face. "Zeke? Is this vampire Helena Millican?"

Hearing Helena's name from this stranger brought Ezekiel back to himself. His eyebrows drew together as a thought occurred to him. "It's Ezekiel, and yes. Yes, she is. How do you know her? Are you family?"

Caitlin uttered a choking laugh. "No, definitely not family. Although, without even knowing, she has certainly shaped a lot of my life."

Kain waved his hands. "Wait, Helena Millican? The broad who wrote in the books you've been reading? *That* Helena?"

Caitlin nodded.

"The Helena who created Felicia and left a shit-ton of notes on her journey trying to cure the Madness?"

Caitlin nodded again.

Kain laced his hands behind his head and snorted. "You've got to be the luckiest sonofabitch I know. What are the odds that the one woman we've been on the track to find happens to be the woman we stumble across in the middle of the woods directly after our friggin' airship crashes?" He looked at Caitlin in awe. "There's something about you, girly. Someone out there is looking out for you."

"The world is filled with strange forces." Ezekiel almost told them everything there and then. Only long-ingrained habit prevented him. He felt the magic tingling in his hands and flexed them to stop it from escaping. "Some call it luck, some call it destiny, others call it magic. Me? I'm still trying to work out if calling this technology magic is safer than telling the truth."

They stood in silence, each digesting the information they'd just received. Caitlin said nothing for a long moment. Her gaze was still held by Helena's sleeping form, as though the vampire would vanish if she looked away.

Helena murmured as her conscious mind bubbled to the surface. Her eyes moved rapidly under their lids, then opened slowly.

Helena caught sight of Caitlin staring at her and mumbled in confusion, "Ezekiel?"

Ezekiel pushed Caitlin aside and took Helena's hand in both of his. "Helena, I'm sorry. I was gone for longer than I promised. I didn't mean to leave you unattended for that long."

He untied her, then helped her to sit up. "How are you feeling?"

Helena lifted her chin, her gaze settling on Caitlin and Kain. "If I'd have known we were going to have visitors, I'd have put something nicer on. Still, at least I'm wearing *something*." She lifted an eyebrow, and Kain remembered he was nude.

He dropped his hands to cover the goods.

Helena laughed, the sensuous sound out of place in the candlelit room. "Come on, Ezekiel, where are your manners? Get the Were some clothes."

CHAPTER SIX

**Mars Orbit**

The *Enora* much resembled a mother duck surrounded by her ducklings as she approached the planet surrounded by the Pods carrying the teams from Earth. At the rear, four hundred shipping containers packed with building materials and the majority of the construction equipment belonging to the Defense Force completed the formation.

Sarah Jennifer monitored the endeavor from the cockpit, her comm open while almost everyone else had their audio muted unless speaking to her.

The exception was Ace, the elder brother having the thankless task of making sure every Pod and shipping container landed exactly where it was supposed to within the hundred-square-kilometer boundary marked out on the western side of the Reynolds Plain.

The bots not dedicated to the agricultural sector had been busy leveling the plain and marking out the main lines for the city's water, sewage, and power since the plans had been finalized.

Sarah Jennifer had the viewscreen show the construction site as the *Enora* passed over the western plain on the final approach to Habitat One. Right now, the land looked scarred and ugly, brutalized by the bots' efforts.

The next few months would change all that.

Planning the founding of the first city on Mars had taken five long years, with Sarah Jennifer heading a committee whose job it was to approve or deny infrastructure requests from those slated to move here and then figure the approved requests into the city plans.

Sarah Jennifer's first instinct had been to wrap the rest of the city around the military installations. The planning committee had squashed the idea right off the bat, and Sarah Jennifer had happily bowed to the greater wisdom of the collected engineers, architects, and various heads of infrastructure she had gathered for the purpose of dispelling her ignorance.

The objective was to provide not only the military infrastructure needed to protect Earth but an effective place to live for the Defense Force's families and the civilians who had chosen to relocate with them. They needed roads and housing; that was a given. Hospitals, emergency services, law provision, libraries and schools, parks and playgrounds, commercial centers the civilians could run their businesses from, sporting venues, theaters, public transportation... The list went on.

Water and power were the first orders of business. The freshwater lake system had been extended and connected by bots and would act as the city's reservoirs. The water treatment plant would sit a short distance from the largest lake.

Power was no problem. The production of electricity was as simple as connecting every building to the city-wide grid, which would run on miniaturized Etheric energy supplies. All Hail Ted, indeed. His revolutionary technology meant the main building of the city's power plant would be an underground bunker no larger than Sarah Jennifer's former bedroom at Salem's town hall.

Of course, the outgoing mechanisms would take up more space, but that was to be expected.

Over the next twenty-eight cycles, which corresponded closely with Earth's days, the construction equipment brought from Earth would be added to the inventory sent by the Federation, and construction would begin in earnest. However, the immediate objective was to get the Pods unloaded, then remove to Habitat One to spend the next seven cycles acclimating to the lower gravity and temperature on Mars. While both were much closer to what everyone was used to on Earth than they had been before Sarah Jennifer had initiated Phase One of terraforming, there was still a marked difference.

Sarah Jennifer exited the airship carrying the case containing half of the precious miniaturized Etheric power supplies sent across the galaxies. Jim was right behind her with an identical case.

"How is Lucy handling her new role as head of engineering?" Sarah Jennifer asked as they entered the airlock.

"Like she was born for the job," Jim replied with amusement. "I feel good, knowing she's gonna keep the Earth division of the corps in line while I run the Mars side of things."

He chuckled. "I was always happier tinkering, you

know that."

Sarah Jennifer laughed. "It's been a long time since I first came out to your workshop by the lake, but I'll never forget how far you got just 'tinkering,' as you put it."

Jim sighed. "I'm gonna miss old Bluebird."

"You and the whole pack," Sarah Jennifer agreed. "You have the public bus fleet to build. Should keep you elbows-deep in grease and auto parts for the next few months."

"You'd think, right?" Jim explained that most of the work was going to be automated. "I'm going to be relegated to maintaining the assembly line."

Sarah Jennifer laughed, seeing that he was hiding a grin. "Let me guess: that will give you plenty of spare time to play around in your workshop."

"You got me all figured out, Major." Jim's expression was wistful. "There's going to be a thousand and one things we couldn't anticipate, and every one of them's going to need an engineering solution."

They stored the cases in the central container of the hub, then made their way to the lab/office, where they met up with the heads of division for each component of the city's planned infrastructure.

Sarah Jennifer was used to the largest area in the habitat being empty except for her, Jim, Carver, and Geordie. Today, every seat around the fifteen tables was occupied by Weres, witches, and the unenhanced scientists, engineers, and civilian specialists who had competed to be here.

The people on this committee had earned their places by becoming the eminent authorities on their specialization. Everyone who came to Mars had to bring something to the table, whether it was a physical skill or the expertise to advance their goal of creating a self-sustaining colony.

There were some familiar faces and a lot of fresh-faced idealists. The majority were still wearing their pressure suits.

Sarah Jennifer greeted everyone as she made her way to the head of the table, noting that some of the people had removed their pressure suits. "Protocol on base calls for pressure suits at all times," she told the gathered committee. "We'll wait while everyone who isn't wearing one gets theirs back on."

No one argued outright. However, some of the magic users commented that they didn't need the suits since they had the ability to manipulate their surroundings.

Esme saved Sarah Jennifer the trouble of explaining why it was a good idea to follow protocol. "If you'd like to test your theory against the very real possibility there's a breach of the habitat, feel free. Otherwise, get your damn suits on."

No one dared argue with Esme.

Sarah Jennifer used the time to set up the safety briefing. She hadn't planned on scaring the pants off the committee, wanting to trust that common sense would rule over their excitement to be here and the relative familiarity of the habitat's setup. They'd proven her wrong already. That was concerning, but she wasn't unprepared for the possibility. This environment was harsh and unforgiving. Until the terraforming process was complete, even the most innocuous activity could prove deadly, thus depriving them of the most valuable resource of all—each other.

They returned a few minutes later, suitably protected.

Sarah Jennifer gave them a moment to return to their seats. "Now that we're all settled, welcome to Mars. I know everyone is eager to get going, so we'll keep this short and sweet. The next six months are going to be grueling. For many of us, it's the second time around. Those who weren't involved in the rebuilding of the Protectorate, you're going to wonder what in damnation you signed up for before we're ready to start shipping people out here."

A murmur of agreement went around the room. Sarah Jennifer smiled; the newbies to committee life thought she was making a joke. "I'm not kidding. Expect to realign your definition of exhaustion. This is our first briefing. There will be many more, but none more important. It is your responsibility to ensure the people working under you survive. The next thirty minutes will give you the knowledge you need to perform your duty."

She picked up the control panel for the lab and dimmed the lights. "Enora, run the video, please."

The back wallscreen lit up, and the title *How Not to Die on Mars* came up.

By the time the video ended, even the committee veterans had lost their worldly attitudes. The idealists looked somewhat green around the gills.

Sarah Jennifer was satisfied they'd had good sense scared into them. Everyone there was now fully aware that they weren't in Salem anymore.

She brought the lights back up and gave Jim the nod.

The chief engineer, still wearing his pressure suit, made his way to the front of the group.

"You all know Lieutenant Jim Johnson," Sarah Jennifer

told them. "If you have any questions about safety, direct them to him now."

Jim's eyes scanned the sea of raised hands and pointed at one of the newbies, the nature witch in charge of getting the crop cycle in order. "Go ahead, Stella."

"We can't plant without a breathable atmosphere," Stella stated.

"Not exactly a safety problem, but I'll answer. The oxygenation process is still ongoing."

"But I saw a huge forest out there. I'm supposed to have my people work the agricultural sector," Stella pointed out.

Sarah Jennifer cut in. "The forest is artificial. You visited the manufacturing facility outside of Boston, right?" Stella nodded. "The artificial leaves gather the $CO_2$ emissions from the ice cap melt. The $CO_2$ is converted to oxygen, among other things, some of which is being stored in preparation for your division's needs. Everyone here has tailored access to the database. Your datapads have a welcome message waiting for you. If you switch them on, you'll find that Enora connected your individual accounts while the safety video was playing. Check the entries for your division's responsibilities and make sure you're fully cognizant of the tech we've put in place to assist you in achieving your goals."

There was a rustle as the division heads pulled out the datapads they'd been issued on the way here.

Sarah Jennifer gave them time to access their messages. "For those who aren't aware, the day/night cycle here is thirty-seven minutes longer than Earth's. The ground-breaking ceremony will be starting at 0700, so make sure you get something to eat and some rack time after you've passed what you learned here on to your teams. If there are no other questions, we'll wrap this up."

There were a few more minor inquiries about the emergency protocols, and then the committee broke up and headed out to pass the information on to their teams. Esme left with them, intending to make sure the magic users took the briefing seriously.

Sarah Jennifer held her senior officers back. Jim, Big Ace, Brutus, Katya, Linus, Ozzie, and Bruiser remained at the circular central bench while the rest of the pack moved to sit at the surrounding tables.

"Grub's up." Sarah Jennifer retrieved a case of self-heating MREs from the cupboard under one of the lab benches. "We have choices."

"Ooh, choices," Katya snarked, looking through the packaging. "Cardboard-tasting pasta, cardboard-tasting pot roast. Anything with some flavor?"

Linus snagged one of the packages. "How about spicy cardboard-tasting tacos?"

Katya shrugged. "Why not? Hand it over."

Linus tossed the taco package across the table to her. "All yours. I'm going with the marinara meatlessballs."

Katya wrinkled her nose. "It's not right for a Were to eat veggie."

"It's all the same to me," Linus countered.

Sarah Jennifer chose the chicken parmesan and pulled the tab to trigger the rehydration and heating functions. "You're all spoiled. There's nothing wrong with these. Did I ever tell you about the time TH had us eating—"

"Hundred and fifty-year-old MREs he found in a bunker?" Brutus joined in with a singsong voice. "Yeah, cuz." He tore into the packaging to get the pizza out. Unlike earlier iterations of MRE pizza, the pie was already constructed. "They know how to do things right in the Federation."

"I'm just playing," Katya admitted, sniffing her food as she peeled back the foil. "These smell pretty good."

"How is everyone feeling about getting started with construction?" Sarah Jennifer asked as they ate. "Any major concerns?"

"Not on my end," Linus answered. "VR training took care of my guys learning how to operate the excavators. Everyone is ready to start digging out where the bots marked."

Sarah Jennifer turned her attention to Bruiser and Ozzie. "Pipework?"

"All set," Bruiser assured her. "We're gonna work out timing after dinner so's we're following Linus' teams."

"Power lines will be just fine as long as Rory's team figures out the insulation before we get rained out," Little Ace added.

"We're not going to see rain for a few weeks," Geordie assured them. "Plenty of time to get the groundworks done and dusted."

Rory pointed at him. "Not much to it besides point and shoot. Operating foam dispensers isn't exactly rocket science."

"Then my guys will lay the roads." Katya crunched into her taco. "Mmm, 's good."

Sarah Jennifer nodded. "Brutus, Big Ace, and I will be circling the sectors to keep on top of manpower requirements."

"Carver and I will be there when the dust gets to be too much for the equipment," Jim promised. "You all know there's gonna be breakdowns. Report them immediately so we can get a crew to you soonest."

The conversation turned to lighter things.

"Is it weird I'm not mad about us being crammed into barracks again?" Linus asked. He ducked as everyone pelted him with the balled-up foil from their packaging. "Well, screw you assholes," he complained.

Sarah Jennifer pointed at the empty space between the benches. "You're going to regret doubling up on those meatballs, Linus. Get to kissing the floor."

"Worth it," Linus grumbled as he got into push-up position. "You guys *suuuuck*."

---

After dinner, Sarah Jennifer made her way to the room she was sharing with Esme.

The witch was already there, unpacking her belongings. She smiled when Sarah Jennifer walked in. "There she is."

Sarah Jennifer hugged her on the way to her bunk, collapsed on the bare mattress without taking her boots off, and yawned. "What a day."

"Lilith called," Esme told her. "She got hold of Ezekiel."

Sarah Jennifer sat bolt upright. "And?"

"And nothing," Esme answered. "He blocked her out soon as she spoke to him."

Sarah Jennifer let out a grunt of frustration.

"She got something before he did," Esme offered. "He

was thinking about a vampire. She said he was dealing with some emotional turmoil."

Sarah Jennifer didn't know what to make of that. "You think he hooked up with the vamp?"

Esme shrugged, resuming her unpacking. "Could be."

Sarah Jennifer wanted nothing more than to curl up in a ball and sleep for the next six hours, but she had to know what Lilith knew.

"I'll be in the comm room if you need me."

Sarah Jennifer left the residential hub and made her way through the habitat to the container where the long-range comms were set up. It took a few moments to connect to New Romanov, then she heard Lilith's voice.

"Esme told you?"

"She told me you managed to contact Ezekiel, and he was thinking about some vampire," Sarah Jennifer replied. "I came straight here to get the details from you."

"I don't think you'll like what I have to say," Lilith cautioned.

"I'd rather know." Sarah Jennifer sighed. "Lay it on me. What situation has he gotten himself into?"

"I saw many memories of a female vampire. He has been with her for a while."

Sarah Jennifer frowned. "You think since he dropped off?"

"It looked that way. You can never be sure with the human brain. Sarah Jennifer, there's something else. The vampire is Mad."

Sarah Jennifer almost dropped her headset. "What, like, *Mad* Mad?"

"Yes."

69

CHAPTER SEVEN

Ezekiel felt Lilith's probing presence as he dug out some clothing for Kain in his room. He didn't have much that wouldn't look like Kain had borrowed it from a child, but those were the breaks when a Were didn't know to bundle before they shifted.

He had an overlarge tunic that could be easily modified, but the fleece-lined trousers he'd made to go over his winter clothing would at best look like capris on the muscular Were.

He returned to the main room in time to hear the end of Caitlin's story. Kain gave the shirt Ezekiel offered him a pained look.

"It's all I have for you," Ezekiel apologized. "We're not exactly compatible in build. Do what you need to. I don't want them back."

"Can't be helped. Thank you." Kain took the knife Caitlin offered and cut the sleeves off the shirt, then slit the sides a little to give himself a chance of fitting into it.

"The real question," Helena continued, eyeing Kain appreciatively, "is where did you learn my name?"

"I was given your journal by a man named Stump," Caitlin answered. She relayed the circumstances while Kain fought to squeeze into the trousers.

"*That's* where I left those notes." Helena smiled. "I spent days looking for them but couldn't find them anywhere. It's lucky my memory is so good. Otherwise, I'd have…"

She broke off as pain wracked her body.

Ezekiel was by her side in a second. "Helena, are you okay?"

Helena made her fangs drop. *I'll be fine,* she told him, using their blood bond to speak mind to mind. *Play along. I need to talk to you.*

*Maybe give me some warning next time?* Ezekiel knelt beside her and murmured soothingly as he poured healing energy into her body.

*You're a terrible actor,* Helena replied. *Can we trust these people?*

*I'm not sure yet,* Ezekiel admitted. *They seem to be on the level.*

*We don't tell them a thing until we know for sure.*

*They already know enough,* Ezekiel countered. The nanocytes in the blood he'd given her earlier responded to his command, pushing back the rising tide of Madness that was always threatening to consume her.

*Then we dance around the truth. Bethany Anne wouldn't be very pleased if she knew we spilled her secrets to any hunky man who walked through the door.* Helena clutched her stomach, letting out a groan that was only half-faked. She plastered a smile on her face as she forced her fangs to retract. "This doesn't get any easier."

Caitlin and Kain were too concerned to notice the surreptitious exchange.

Kain was the first to speak. "What happened?"

Ezekiel answered, "The Madness. Every time we feel as though we're finally in a place where we understand the patterns, it throws us a curveball."

Kain narrowed his eyes, smiling in appreciation. "Baseball analogy? Nice."

"What's baseball?" Caitlin asked.

Ezekiel didn't reply. He left Helena's side and walked over to add the time to the tracking sheet they used to monitor the frequency of Helena's episodes.

Helena cast off the blanket that covered her, drawing Caitlin's curiosity when she uncovered the bandage on her ankle.

Caitlin nodded at the injury. "How did it happen?"

"An unhappy accident," Helena informed her. It was almost true. "Curse me for getting caught in a rainstorm and surrounded by hungry Mad. I knew I shouldn't have risked searching the university, but we needed equipment that I just didn't have."

Kain tilted his head. "The university?"

Ezekiel returned to the seating area. "Chicago State, a few kilometers west of here in the main city."

Kain's eyes lit up. "We're near Chicago? Kitty-Cat! We nearly made it. We're near the other Weres!"

Caitlin was more circumspect. "What were you looking for?"

Ezekiel's head snapped toward the door, sensing the vamp just before she appeared.

"Nanocytes, of course," Mary-Anne told Caitlin.

Ezekiel pushed away his initial reaction. The vamp was beautiful despite her tangled, bracken-mussed hair and the angry welts that covered her skin wherever the mud didn't.

Helena flowed to her feet, her welcoming smile tinged with concern. "How in the name of the Queen Bitch and the Dark Messiah did you make it through all that sunlight?"

Mary-Anne gripped the doorframe, her breath coming in heaving gasps. "It wasn't easy, I'll tell you that much. There's only so much shade beneath the trees before you've got to cross in the open, and no amount of vampire speed can combat the pain you feel when sunlight hits your skin."

She was already healing. She refused the chair Helena offered, walking over to the sink to wash the mud off. "Please, don't let me be a distraction from your conversation. This is real talk about real problems, and I need your help to purge this shit from inside me."

Caitlin turned her attention back to Helena. "The nanocytes? You were looking for nanocytes?"

Helena looked at Ezekiel, who nodded.

*I don't think they're the bad guys,* he reasoned. *Maybe we don't dance. Well, not too much.*

*This would be much easier if we could get some of your blood into Mary-Anne,* Helena told him.

Ezekiel's mental snort was loud. *Yeah, I'm not down with offering myself up to a vamp I just met. We do this the hard way. Trust has to be earned.*

Helena inclined her head. *Very well, but I still think a little misdirection is necessary. We can always correct their assumptions later.* "Esme Proctor said it best. 'Nanocytes are the secret to it all.' Bethany Anne blanketed the Earth with the Kurtherian technology, which used to be exclusive to Weres and vampires. It is the code—the instructions—inside these tiny machines which has become corrupted, and the infected are acting as vectors for the Madness to spread even wider."

Kain's brow furrowed in confusion. "But how? How is that even possible? *Humans* have nanocytes now, too? How do you know this?"

*And the dance begins,* Helena sent to Ezekiel. "Extensive testing. You think decades of experimentation hasn't yielded *some* answers?"

"How did it happen, though?" Caitlin asked. "How did the Madness begin?"

"And how do we end it?" Kain added.

The dog yipped. "Easy, Jaxon," Caitlin murmured.

"One thing at a time." Ezekiel wasn't comfortable dissembling. "The truth is, *we* don't know what caused the event. What we do know is that something cataclysmic happened way back when it all began. Some event that kicked everything off at once and caused the world to degenerate and devolve."

Kain wrinkled his nose. "Like, a pulse of energy or something?"

Helena jumped on his misconception since it was close to the truth. "Yes! Exactly like a pulse." She pulled a clean sheet of paper off the board and scribbled a quick diagram of the BYPS. "As far as I can figure, it was something big. Something powerful enough to affect everyone at once and cause the corruption. What is one of the only things in the world that can scramble every machine in range, but that humans and other sentient beings cannot feel when it happens?"

Mary-Anne turned from the sink, a towel in her hands. "An EMP?"

Helena pointed at Mary-Anne. "Bingo!"

Ezekiel frowned. *Helena, they're going to figure out we're not telling the truth.*

*Then we plead ignorance,* the vampire told him. *We have a duty to protect the UnknownWorld, even from itself.*

Jaxon launched into another frenzy of barks, putting an end to Ezekiel's argument.

"Woah, woah, woah." Caitlin calmed the dog with a touch. "An EMP?"

"Electromagnetic pulse," Helena supplied.

Caitlin frowned. "Electro mag... *What?*"

Mary-Anne gave Helena an exasperated look. "She's not from our time."

"Or mine!" Kain chipped in.

Ezekiel suddenly understood how the Were knew about things that hadn't been around since before WWDE.

"An electromagnetic pulse," Helena repeated. "See, our ancestors were the gods of technology. We came to a point in time where tiny computers people carried in their pocket had more power in them than the rockets that first sent a man to the moon."

Caitlin's skepticism was clear to see. "People went to the moon?"

"Yes," Helena replied. "So much technology existed that we were able to put computers into space. We called them 'satellites.' These computers gave us images of the Earth, helped the internet bring the world together, and gave us information on storms, weather patterns, and so much more."

Helena continued, "Great technology that had the power to unite the world and keep signals bouncing invisibly across the globe. There are satellites up there now that belong to—"

Ezekiel cut in. "Don't start praising Sarah Jennifer. I won't hear it."

Helena gave him a knowing look. "She was the one with the original knowledge. Without her and Esme, we wouldn't know anything about the BYPS. The Baba Yaga Protection System, or BYPS, had only one flaw; it is connected to someplace on Earth. My life's work has led me to believe a pulse was sent to the BYPS from this place, a pulse that somehow corrupted the nanocytes the Queen had intended as the solution to all of humanity's ills."

That was as much as she was willing to share. "However infinitesimal the probability, I can only conclude that we are the victims of fate's capricious nature. All it would take is a slight surge in a faulty circuit. A single error in one circuit, leading to a cascading failure. The consequent ejection of the failing satellite from the system would be powerful enough to—"

Caitlin interrupted. "I'm sorry, a circuit?"

Ezekiel took over the explanation. "Think of it as a minuscule highway over which the electricity would run to make the machines operate."

Caitlin looked at Ezekiel blankly.

"As I was saying," Helena continued, "a slight surge in a

circuit would be powerful enough to destroy it. To fry it and cause it to malfunction, which would set off the safety measures. Whoever designed the system made sure to build in enough redundancies to ensure the BYPS could run without maintenance for centuries. Magnetic pulses could do unspeakable damage to machinery across a vast range, potentially the world over. Much better to lose one satellite than the whole network."

"That can't be right!" Caitlin exclaimed. "Why would anyone do something like that?"

"Maybe it wasn't intentional?" Kain had his attention on the tray of scientific instruments Helena had left out. "Maybe somebody did it by accident. You know, tripped over a wire, or mashed the wrong button, and sent the wrong signal to the satellites?"

"It really doesn't matter how it happened, and this is all just my theory." Helena sighed. "All that matters is that we find a way to fix it. We find the cure and set the world to rights."

Her next words sent chills through Ezekiel.

"And now, the baton can be passed over to you."

Caitlin looked at Ezekiel. "I'm sorry, what is she talking about?"

Ezekiel didn't answer her. He grabbed Helena's hand in both of his. "You need to stop talking like this. You can't give up now. We will fix you before it's too late, I promise."

*Are you going to speak to Lilith?* Helena shot back.

*If I have to!* Ezekiel stated hotly. He dropped the mental link, too emotional to maintain it. "She knows the way, I'm telling you. If we just listen to her and go now, we can make it together. All of us." He was desperate. He would do anything to save her.

Helena cupped Ezekiel's face in her hands. "I'm already too far gone, my boy. You've seen what happens when I'm left alone. I won't make it five minutes before I go Mad and turn on you all."

Ezekiel wrenched free and looked away. His magic surged again as he fought to contain his fear of losing her.

Helena smiled softly. "Don't think of it as a sad occasion. Think of it as though we're turning the chapter on what has come before. I still have some fight in me, so I can help you prepare, but you know as well as I do that we've done as much as we can do here. It's time to go to Lilith and discover what she knows. It's the only way we'll make everything right once more."

Ezekiel released his grief, hot tears flooding his eyes. "No, Hel. No. I need you."

"It's time to let me go," Helena told him, her voice gentle but firm.

# CHAPTER EIGHT

**Mars, Reynolds Plain**

The next morning, Sarah Jennifer woke with the resolve to put Ezekiel from her mind for the time being. The knowledge he was alive had to be enough until either Lilith or Enora was able to glean enough information for her to act on. In the meantime, she had a behemoth construction project to manage.

She arrived at the site to find someone had set up a stage, complete with a ribbon to be cut.

Of *course*, she was expected to give a speech. She had prepared one, and for once, she was even looking forward to it. She smiled. The ribbon was a nice touch.

Brutus handed her a pouch with a long, bendy straw attached. "Plug it into your water feed," he told her. "I know you didn't stop for breakfast."

Sarah Jennifer thanked him and plugged the pouch into her suit. The sweet sugary coffee hit her tastebuds, and she felt almost human again. "Gold star, cuz," she told him.

"No one expects a rousing speech pre-caffeine," he teased. "You ready for this?"

Sarah Jennifer nodded. "More than you know."

She waved at Linus, Dinny, and Reg in the excavators as she contacted Enora through her comm chip. "Play me a few soundbites from appropriate occasions," she requested, wanting to feel connected to other leaders who had been in the same position.

Bethany Anne's voice, the Colonel's, and others she didn't recognize spoke into her mind while she walked the red-dust path to the stage. Their voices lifted her up, her mood soaring.

Grinning from ear to ear, she took the stage to raucous applause.

Everyone had come out for the groundbreaking ceremony. There were some bleary eyes; not everyone had been to sleep yet. Overhead, a number of camera drones controlled by Jim zipped around recording the event. The footage would be sent to Salem to show everyone what was happening up here.

Sarah Jennifer tapped the microphone to test it. "Good morning, teams. Nice to see no one slept in."

"As if!" someone heckled.

Sarah Jennifer laughed. "Before we get started, I'd like to say a few words to mark the occasion. To quote my grandfather's reaction when he found out this was my plan, 'Mars is every science nerd's wet dream.'" That raised cheers and laughter from the crowd, three-fourths of whom were science nerds. "The Colonel has his particular way with words, but this is no dream."

She lifted a hand to the east, where the sun was making

its ascent. The sunrise would soon give way to the yellowy-brown that reminded Sarah Jennifer of caramel or pudding, but for now, it was robin's-egg blue, pale and clear. "We're here, and we're about to break ground on the first human colony in the Solar System. Everyone here today has earned their place by being the best at what they do. Whether your specialty is construction, engineering, civil planning, agriculture, or magic, you have outshone everyone on Earth to make it onto this project. Those who have read the pre-WWDE texts we have in the Salem library are well aware that humanity has always looked to Mars. The ancients sent all kinds of robots here, hoping to gather as much data as they could without the ability to set foot on the planet."

She choked up, thinking of the hopes those ancient scientists had held. "We honor those who came before us by making the most of this new world. We have found the rovers, and they will take pride of place in the museum. We are the first humans to build here. It's kinda special. You will be remembered as the founders of this world. That's a responsibility as well as an honor."

The people received her words with solemnity, everyone having their own personal reasons for pushing themselves to heights they still didn't believe possible to qualify for the teams. Sarah Jennifer knew. She was as familiar with every person standing before her as their own mothers. They had been handpicked, not just for their expertise in their individual fields, but for their steadfast adherence to those qualities she'd had drummed into her since the moment she could walk.

Honor. Courage. Commitment.

"Enough talk. Sergeants, start up your excavators." Sarah Jennifer took the scissors Brutus handed her as Linus, Dinny, and Reg switched on the gargantuan machines. She walked to the ribbon and held the open scissors over it. "I declare this project to be commenced. Welcome to Promessa."

The cheers were deafening as she cut the ribbon.

The excavators moved in, their gigantic buckets scooping out the first plugs of Martian dirt. Below the regolith, the soil was rich and dark, altered by the bots to remove toxins.

Sarah Jennifer opened her datapad and checked the schedule for the day's work as the sleepy scientists extracted themselves from the crowd to return to Habitat One in the Etheric-powered roamers they used for everyday travel.

She was standing on the site of the city park, modeled on Central Park in New York in both shape and size to account for the planned grid layout of Promessa. She already saw the completed city in her mind's eye.

There would be other parks and recreational areas, but this one would be the most easily accessible by everyone in the city and the one they used for community events. Sarah Jennifer imagined children playing hide-and-seek in the arti-forest, couples taking romantic strolls along the walking routes, families and friends picnicking on the rolling green spaces—all the things that were at present not doable by the citizens of Earth.

Esme joined her. "That's some imagination you have."

"I'm seeing the future," Sarah Jennifer told her, smiling. "This is going to be our home. We've had enough heartache to last ten lifetimes, and once you and Lilith are ready to roll the patch out to humanity, we'll be able to focus on building."

"That's what I came to see you about." Esme's eyes twinkled. "We're almost ready. I have to get back to New Romanov."

Sarah Jennifer's eyes widened. "Really?"

Esme nodded. "Yes, really. The latest patches were a hundred percent effective at rewriting the corrupt code in most of our test subjects."

"Meaning?"

"Meaning, we have the cure for everyone but the nomads."

"The Were nanocytes they inherited from their blood-leech parents are still causing issues?" Sarah Jennifer didn't like it, but they had to work with what was achievable, and they'd held off long enough.

"Unfortunately, yes. Lilith is reporting that the subjects aren't Mad, but they're not fully regaining their humanity, either. There's some remnant of the desire to consume flesh in them, she thinks because there's an interaction between the disabled Pricolici code all Were nanocytes have and another line that bastard Arthur Drake added that can't be erased."

Sarah Jennifer sighed. "They won't be able to infect anyone else with it or spread it to others?"

"No," Esme confirmed. "We were able to remove that part of the programming without killing them all. The nomads are only a tiny percentage of the global population anyway. Everyone else will be cured. All we have to do is get the patches out to everyone." Esme explained that the process was two-step. "First, we have to distribute a blanket of nanocytes over Earth, much as Bethany Anne did, to replace the corrupted nanocytes saturating the planet. Then, we use the BYPS to keep the nanocytes in Earth's atmosphere. Once the saturation process is complete, we activate the new nanocytes and send out the patch code."

"How does that account for the different variants?" Sarah Jennifer asked.

"The nanocytes will go out with the generic patch, and the BYPS will introduce whichever patch the host needs. It's an if/then situation. Lilith has the printers working overtime to produce Madness-resistant nanocytes. How'd you feel about leaving all this in Brutus' capable hands? The BYPS won't take commands from me."

Sarah Jennifer's heart soared at the prospect of moving on from the Madness. "Give me thirty minutes and meet me at the *Enora*."

### Earth, New Romanov

Lilith was fully occupied with preparing for Sarah Jennifer and Esme returning and doing what she could to assist Olaf with taking care of the recuperating men and women who had been released from their cells after waking up confused but Madness-free.

They were weak from the battles waged inside their bodies and needed to rest while their repaired nanocytes worked to rebuild them from the inside out. Lilith intended to talk to Sarah Jennifer about how they were going to provide support worldwide once the patches went out.

Olaf entered her cavern from the side cavern they were using as the recovery suite, his expression thoughtful. "Lilith, I need to go into the town for supplies."

"Very well," Lilith replied. "Give my regards to Mayor Kuznetsova. Sarah Jennifer and Esme will be arriving within the hour."

That was news to Olaf. The Were pushed his hair out of his eyes. "Yeah? What about Mars?"

"Sarah Jennifer's access to the BYPS is required for us to distribute the nanocytes I am printing," Lilith explained. "She has left Lieutenant Timmons in charge of the construction project for the time being."

Olaf nodded. "Fair enough. Did you hear from Amelie yet? I know she wanted to be here when we made a real breakthrough."

"I sent her a message, but she has been dealing with a request for assistance from Marrakesh."

"How long until the fleet is due back?" Olaf inquired. "Maybe I should requisition a Pod from Boston and fly over to pick her and Eoin up."

Lilith laughed. "You have enough to take care of, bear-warrior. Didn't I hear you invoked the anger of one of the Urai warriors?"

Olaf reddened. "I wasn't cheating, which would have been clear to everyone there if they weren't weed-addled."

"That's what you have to say," Lilith teased. "You forget I have access to the communication network. All of Urai is talking about you. Mika especially."

Olaf cursed under his breath, rubbing his jaw where

Mika had broken it. "That woman…" Still, Mika hadn't left his mind since the fight in the dive bar. Her ice-goddess looks and her ferocious right hook left quite the impression on a man. "Okay. I won't leave to find Amelie right now. But if Mika comes here looking for me, you tell her I'm *far* away from Siberia, you hear me?"

Lilith's laughter followed him out of the mountain.

The Kurtherian busied herself with checking on the patients while she waited for the *Enora* to arrive. She was monitoring the ambient Etheric energy when she felt a mental "knock" she'd had little hope of.

*Ezekiel?*

*Hey, Lilith.*

The silence stretched out. Lilith didn't speak, afraid to scare him off. She could feel he was as ready to bolt as a small mammal that saw the eagle's shadow pass overhead. Still, she had to say something.

Ezekiel spoke first. *My friend is going Mad, and she can't fight it anymore. Have you and Esme found the cure yet?*

*I'm sorry,* Lilith put all the emotion she could muster into her words. *We can't reverse the Madness in a vampire at this time.*

*Fuck. Fuck, fuck, fuck, fuck, FUUUUCK!* His mental voice was torn with anguish. *I love her, Lilith. She's been there for me. Filled the void I created when I left Salem and Sarah Jennifer. She's one of the smartest people this world has ever known, and I'm going to lose her to the damned Madness just like I lost my parents.*

Lilith was silent while Ezekiel raged.

*There's another vampire. She's infected, too. Do I have to tell her people that she's got no hope of beating it? I've only just met them, but they're good folks.*

Lilith didn't know what to say. *Ezekiel, come home. Bring the people you've bonded with along with you. All I can promise is that we'll do what we can for your friends.*

*Helena doesn't have that long,* Ezekiel told her. *The journey will kill her if the Madness doesn't take her first.*

*Then make her last days on the Earth memorable,* Lilith advised. *Spend them together. Cherish what time you have remaining, and then* come home.

Lilith registered a spike of anger and fear, then Ezekiel was gone from her mind as suddenly as he'd arrived.

She tried to reconnect, but the link had vanished.

The Kurtherian fretted for a long moment, but she knew there wasn't anything she could do. "Sarah Jennifer isn't going to like this."

---

The *Enora* broke atmosphere over the Pacific.

Sarah Jennifer radioed Salem to let HQ know she was onworld for the next few days.

"Good to know," Izzy told her. "We've had increased Mad activity here. There's been a surge of outbreaks in the nomad populations on the West Coast running all the way into Central and Southern America and an outbreak along the coast of Africa. Something has the Mad riled up. Annie says it could be a ripple effect from Samhain, magic spreading out from Salem."

Sarah Jennifer had assigned most of the Defense Force to

watch over the world while the Mars project got underway. "Are we stretched?" she inquired, a frown creasing her brow. "We can divert from New Romanov if anyone is in a jam."

"We've got the Americas covered. Amelie has taken the merchant fleet to the port at Marrakesh," Izzy informed her. "They're carrying warriors and mages from all over Europe to answer the SOS."

Sarah Jennifer muted Izzy and waved to get Esme's attention. "You hearing this?"

Esme nodded. "I'm inclined to agree with Annie until we get better information."

Sarah Jennifer unmuted the mic. "What about Siberia?"

"Mostly in the southern regions. Arkhangelsk hasn't been affected so far."

Esme's expression was severe when Sarah Jennifer finished taking Izzy's report. "This was an unexpected turn of events."

"And you're the queen of understatement." Sarah Jennifer wanted to assist with the outbreaks, but she knew the best way to overcome the Madness was to keep on track with the plan. "It sucks not being able to do anything for them, but I trust everyone to do their duty. We need to get to New Romanov and start the process of getting the patches out."

"Couldn't agree more," Esme replied.

Sarah Jennifer couldn't shake the feeling their time to turn the tide was running short as the *Enora* passed over Siberia. Mad were visible even without zooming in, huge groups of them bunched together in the snow, moving north. "A mutation of Mad," she murmured.

When they arrived at Lilith's mountain, Sarah Jennifer

gave Enora instructions to do a sweep of Siberia to get a better idea of the number of Mad roaming the tundra before following Esme off the airship.

Esme scrutinized her as they walked into the mountain. "You're concerned they're going to head this way?"

Sarah Jennifer shrugged. "I'm just plain concerned. I have this feeling something is hanging over our heads, waiting for us to take our eyes off the ball before it drops."

Esme patted her arm. "We're about to take the final steps toward rescinding the apocalypse. You're feeling doubt, but that's all it is—a feeling."

Sarah Jennifer appreciated the comfort. "All we can do is keep moving forward."

"How are the patients doing?" Esme called as they entered Lilith's cave.

"Well enough," Lilith answered. "I heard from Ezekiel."

Sarah Jennifer almost dropped her pack. "You got through his mental block?"

"He reached out," Lilith clarified and relayed their conversation.

"He was sure it's too late for Helena?" Sarah Jennifer asked.

"She's in the final stages," Lilith told her. "I saw her through his eyes. She's held on for a long time, but she's beyond help. All he can do is be there for her."

Sarah Jennifer listened with her heart sinking. "We don't have a patch for Mad vampires. I didn't know there *were* any vampires left on Earth besides Royland." She broke off. "We should call Prince Edward Island and see if he'll give us a blood sample we can work from."

"I wouldn't care to see Cammie's reaction if he said no," Esme called after her.

Sarah Jennifer ran to the control room and put the call through, but Cammie and Royland weren't there, and their seconds couldn't say more than the couple had gone off with a bunch of strangers on a dirigible. She ended the call and reached out to Salem to have Izzy send a unit to Indiana to pick up Ezekiel and whoever was with him.

"I'll send someone as soon as we have someone to send," Izzy promised. "Best I can do, I'm afraid, Major. Everyone is out west dealing with Mad incursions."

"Thank you, Sergeant. That will have to do." Sarah Jennifer didn't like it, but Ezekiel wasn't going anywhere until his friend had crossed the boundary into full Madness.

She returned to the main chamber, somewhat crestfallen.

"What's to do, Duckie?" Esme asked.

"Neither of them are there," Sarah Jennifer told her. "It's bad enough Ezekiel is going to lose the woman who's been there for him so close to us resolving this. I wanted to do something for his new friends."

"I can take care of it," Esme assured her. "Soon as Ezekiel gets here with his new friends, I can take a blood sample from the infected vampire and work from there."

Sarah Jennifer had to be satisfied with that. Her urge to act resurfaced. "Okay. I'm going to visit with the patients in the recovery room."

"Sounds good to me," Esme told her. "I'm going to go down to the lab and get the nanocytes we already have printed ready for transport."

Olaf had returned by the time Sarah Jennifer emerged from the control room. He dragged his sled behind him, the simple platform on skis piled high with food and other supplies. He was surprised to find her there. "You're already here? I could swear I just saw that airship of yours coming in from the east."

"Nice to see you, too, Olaf." Sarah Jennifer accepted his handshake. "Enora is surveying the Mad in the area."

Olaf snorted. "Could have saved her the trouble. They're everywhere."

He began unpacking the sled. "Lilith tell you how well the patients are doing?"

"I'm about to go visit them," Sarah Jennifer told him. "Coming?"

# CHAPTER NINE

Sarah Jennifer wasn't sure what to expect when she walked into the recovery suite.

The walls were lined with the same metal as the rest of the complex, creating a sterile environment that contained sixteen fully equipped hospital beds. Thirteen of them were occupied by people in various states of consciousness.

Olaf noticed her scrutiny of the still forms in eight of the beds. "Not everyone is awake. Some are sedated while their bodies heal the damage they took when they were made Mad."

Sarah Jennifer didn't suppose she'd like to be awake while her internal organs were rebuilt, either. She recognized signs of water damage in two of the people asleep in the beds. Not so affectionately named "rotters," their skin was still mottled with bruises and pruney from long-term immersion in swamp water.

"Olaf!" one of the men sitting up in bed exclaimed, his

voice hoarse from disuse. "We were beginning to think you weren't coming back!"

Olaf laughed. "Not a chance, Marlon." He smiled at the interest everyone who was awake showed in Sarah Jennifer. "This is Major Walton. She's the one who had you brought here."

"You can call me Sarah Jennifer," she told the patients. "It was my men who brought you here. How are you all feeling after your ordeal?"

"Hungry, mostly," one of the women replied.

"That goes without saying, Fabrice," Olaf chipped in cheerfully as he turned on the oven in the kitchen at the far end of the room. He unwrapped a crock and put it in the oven to heat the contents. "Irina sends her regards."

"Smells like she sent her goulash, as well," Marlon enthused.

Olaf laughed. "Dinner will be ready in an hour, which gives us time to see to your wounds."

"Let me help," Sarah Jennifer offered. She followed Olaf's finger to a woman whose arms and chest were covered in bandages, then grabbed a tray with medical supplies, walked over, and asked the woman's name.

"I'm Gretel." Her voice was croaky. "Thank you for saving us."

Sarah Jennifer smiled. "The world is going to thank you. You're the first people we've been able to reverse the Madness in. Matriarch knows we've been working long enough to make it happen. You're miracles, all of you. Let me see those wounds, please."

Gretel bore the pain of her bandages being removed with only a wince. The skin beneath was a mess of scabs, surrounded by scarring in the shape of bite marks. "Lilith says we have tiny machines in our blood that will heal this mess."

Sarah Jennifer nodded as she unwound the bandage on Gretel's right arm. "That's right. Everyone on Earth has them. Have you felt anything else..." She wasn't sure how to explain. "Like a buildup of energy?"

Gretel shook her head. "No. Nothing yet. The bear-man says we'll get some warning before we set anything on fire."

Sarah Jennifer glanced at Olaf. "You explained they could start manifesting magical abilities?"

Olaf pointed at the ceiling. "Lilith did."

Lilith's voice came from the speaker overhead. "I am monitoring the Etheric energy level in the room. If anyone begins to manifest magic, shielding will activate around their bed while we wait to see what ability emerges."

Sarah Jennifer glanced up and saw the shield emitters in the ceiling. "Good enough." She finished dressing Gretel's healing wounds and moved on to the next patient, a man attached to an IV who introduced himself as Pietro.

"What can I do for you, Pietro?" Sarah Jennifer asked, unable to see a visible wound.

The man lowered his sheets, exposing his bandaged torso. "It's itchy as hell."

"Growing a new kidney will do that for you," Olaf quipped from the next bed. "We're lucky to still have you with us."

"The luck's all mine," Pietro responded. He peered thoughtfully at Sarah Jennifer. "Olaf and Lilith say you're going to save everyone from the Madness. Too late for our kin, but not too late for humanity."

He had an ancient look in his eyes despite his relatively youthful appearance.

Sarah Jennifer felt drawn to him. "You're the Were."

Pietro nodded. "Once upon a time. No magic for me. I just want my wolf back, as impossible as that is."

Sarah Jennifer smiled. "Now *that* I can do. How did you get infected?"

Pietro colored red. "I failed, that's how. I was employed as a guard for a caravan of human traders going east from Petersburg when the Mad attacked. None of us made it."

Sarah Jennifer eyed the extensive scarring over his body from dozens of bite marks as she ripped a strip from her roll of medical tape. "You were one Were. You didn't fail." She held the tape between her teeth as she grabbed a fresh pad.

"My conscience says different," Pietro countered. "The people I was sworn to protect were torn to pieces."

Sarah Jennifer put the pad over the site of the wound on his stomach. "The Madness has taken my pack over thirty years to contain, and we are almost a hundred thousand strong at this point."

Pietro's eyes widened. "A hundred thousand Wechselbalg? *How*? We lost the ability to shift…well, decades ago."

Sarah Jennifer shook her head. "I have the Queen's assistance in reversing the Affliction. I accept every Were who is loyal to Bethany Anne into my pack and repair their ability to shift. They have the choice between military service or becoming part of the civilian community."

"Where do I sign up?" Pietro asked, sitting up. He groaned as the movement sent a bolt of pain through his body.

Sarah Jennifer laughed and gently pushed him back onto his pillows. "You get better first. Then we'll see about getting you enlisted."

Enora checked in shortly after all the conscious patients were settled with bowls of goulash and hunks of rustic bread. Sarah Jennifer answered the comm. "How's it looking out there?"

"Not good," Enora replied, concern tingeing her voice. "There are approximately twenty thousand Mad traveling up the banks of the estuaries south of here. They're split between a number of groups at the moment, but they're heading this way."

Sarah Jennifer put down her bowl. The estuaries were fed by the lake a few kilometers from the mountain. "How long until they converge?"

"I did what I could to create physical boundaries to slow them down. Maybe a couple of weeks?"

"Okay. We have time to get some extra defenses in place." Sarah Jennifer relayed the information to Olaf in a low voice so as not to alarm the patients.

The werebear stopped eating. "We have time to prepare. I will go to town and ask Irina to come up here and look after the people in my absence. There are many warriors in Arkhangelsk who will fight to defend the Oracle."

"I'm not convinced it will be enough," Sarah Jennifer told him. "I'm calling in reinforcements."

As Olaf set out into the snow, Sarah Jennifer settled into the comfy chair in the comm room and got to work contacting her allies, starting with Reika.

The Thane of Agatha's Mountain got straight to the point. "What do you need?"

Sarah Jennifer smiled. "Never one to beat around the bush, are you, old woman?"

"Call me old again, and I'll see how you like the flat of my blade on your ass the next time I see you," Reika retorted without malice. "You're twice the age of me and not a gray hair on your head. Now, I know you wouldn't be calling if you weren't in some need. The dew falls on both dirt and lily. How can I be of service?"

"I need bodies."

"The live kind or the other?"

Sarah Jennifer snorted. "Preferably living, if you don't mind. We have a situation in Arkhangelsk—twenty thousand-plus Mad converging on New Romanov and the mountain."

Reika let out a low whistle. "Situation, you call it. I call it trouble. I can send my warriors. No problem. Well, one small problem. Transport."

"I have that covered," Sarah Jennifer told her. "Amelie is next on my list. How many swords do you have?"

"I can give you three thousand," Reika told her. "I will send two-thirds of my warriors and hold back the rest to protect my mountain."

"Fair enough. You have my eternal gratitude, Reika."

"Knowing what eternity is for your kind, I expect that gratitude to be passed along to my daughter's daughter's daughters."

"And then some," Sarah Jennifer vowed. "Thank you, Reika. I'll make sure Amelie radios when she's in range of Bråviken, and you will get first dibs on the next cocoa crop."

"Now you're talking, my friend!" Reika exclaimed with a lusty laugh.

Sarah Jennifer said goodbye and reached out to Amelie.

The trade mistress was moved by the situation. "I have the main fleet headed for the Baltic Strait. We need to resupply at Upinniemi, and then we'll set out for Arkhangelsk."

"Can you make a stop at Mount Bråviken?" Sarah Jennifer asked. "Reika has promised three thousand warriors, but they need transport."

"You don't have any Pods?" Amelie's reply was colored with surprise.

"Not that I can spare," Sarah Jennifer admitted. "Most are on Mars. The rest will be running Weres here from the Americas."

"The outbreak there is contained?"

Sarah Jennifer wished it was. "I'm splitting my forces. We have some twenty-odd thousand Mad moving north. It looks like they're being drawn here somehow. The mountain must be protected at all costs, or everything we've worked for will be for nothing."

"Consider it done," Amelie assured her. "We'll be there in a week, eight days at the most if Reika's people aren't ready when we arrive."

"They'll be ready."

Amelie covered the mic with a hand while she shouted an instruction to her first mate. "I'll have my people meet us with supplies, so we don't need to go into the harbor. You know what it's like when you've been away for a spell. The administrators seem to save the knottiest problems until I return, always."

Sarah Jennifer laughed. "I feel that, my friend. Smooth seas."

"And the same to you," Amelie replied before signing off.

Sarah Jennifer felt marginally better until she spoke to Izzy.

The acting lieutenant gave her a grim recounting of the Defense Force's efforts to quell the rise of Madness from Guatemala to Panama.

"How many magic users do they have with them?" Sarah Jennifer asked. "More importantly, *which* magic users?"

"David is down there, Paula Simmons, Harriet Grandin, Marc Karlov, Snorri Karlson, Nicky Jakes, and Farah Hadid."

Sarah Jennifer counted off the available magic power. "So, two rock mages, three physical magic users, two nature, and one water. Okay. Keep the magic users and a unit each to protect them down there. They're going to have to seal off all the routes into North America. I need the ground troops here."

Izzy sucked in a breath. "Major, that's a huge ask."

"I know, but it's necessary." Sarah Jennifer sighed. "The Mad are amassing, and we have to protect our base at New Romanov or lose our ability to reverse the Madness for everyone. Reika has given me three thousand swordsmen and women and Amelie has the warriors who travel with the trade fleet, and all of those could go Mad before the battle is done. I need Weres."

"Understood," Izzy told her. "I'll get to work on the

reassignments and send you everyone I can. Can we get some Pods back from Mars? I have twenty."

Sarah Jennifer hesitated to remove resources from the colony. "No can do. If the habitat is compromised, every one of them will be needed there."

"Why are we always caught between a rock and a hard place?" Izzy complained.

Sarah Jennifer let out a humorless laugh. "That's easy. No military gets to operate in ideal circumstances. We'll manage. We always do."

## Potato Creek State Park, IN

Ezekiel's connection to Lilith was broken when a bunch of newly-turned Mad ran into the clearing where he and Caitlin were meditating.

Baby Mad were nothing to sniff at. They were driven by the insatiable, instinctive desire to consume whatever flesh they could sink their nasty teeth into, and some still retained a warped version of the ability to think.

Ezekiel's preferred method of disposal was a tsunami of flames. However, before he had a chance to react, Caitlin had that damn sword of hers drawn and ran at them, blocking his line of fire.

"Ezekiel, run!" she yelled through clenched teeth.

Not a chance. He watched her go, admiring her form. This woman knew how to move, her sword an extension of her being.

Ezekiel took cover, giving himself space to get his magic under control. The problem wasn't a lack of ability.

It was that he risked burning the forest to ashes if he didn't regulate his emotions.

The way Caitlin moved had him somewhat hot under the collar.

He couldn't take his eyes off her. He supposed it had something to do with her being the first attractive woman he'd encountered in a long time. However, she was not for him. He hadn't been entirely honest with her, and his moral compass wasn't set that way.

Caitlin fended off a Mad who leapt at her from a tree, her blade flashing in the early morning sunlight as she carved a chunk from its shoulder.

She pivoted to avoid a sloppy haymaker from the next to charge. Unfazed by the partial contact the huge sono-fabitch made, she ducked and tossed the one who grabbed her from behind, spinning in the same movement to drive her blade into the Mad's skull.

Ezekiel heard her murmur, "One down," and forced himself to concentrate.

Instinct drove him to react when the rest moved in, overwhelming her with their numbers. The fire sprang to his hands unbidden as she went down, her sword knocked from her grip.

He flung the fireball with accuracy, no longer caring if he eradicated the forest. Caitlin's life was more precious than the trees.

The Mad was thrown into a tree in flames. It screeched, dropping to the ground as the pain of being burned alive overtook the desire to feed.

Caitlin gasped, her eyes flicking to Ezekiel as she reached for her sword.

He ducked back behind the rock, clenching his hands into fists as the magic threatened to overwhelm him.

The Mad on fire rolled around on the grass while the others got over their fear of the flames and closed on Caitlin again.

She was ready. She ducked as she twisted her wrist to gut the Mad nearest her. She swore loudly as she realized that wasn't enough to stop it and stepped back, withdrawing her blade, then swung for its throat.

That Mad fell to the ground unmoving, opening a space for the big bastard who was still set on eating Caitlin for breakfast.

Ezekiel sensed help was coming. Not a moment too soon.

Caitlin was no match for the Mad's strength and size, not that it stopped her. She lifted her sword, her eyes alight with anger.

She growled low in her throat. "Can't you learn to take a hint? When you get knocked on your ass, just stay down. It'll be better that way."

Ezekiel let out a strangled laugh. The fire inside wanted to be let free. He worked to contain it as the Mad came at her again.

Caitlin took a stand and prepared to eviscerate the Mad.

A blur shot out of the trees and took the Mad out before Caitlin had a chance to swing her sword.

Ezekiel didn't recognize the vamp, but he didn't smell like a Forsaken.

The vampire pulled his dagger out of the Mad's heart

and flashed a devil-may-care grin. "Captain Royland, reporting for duty."

Caitlin looked relieved. "About time."

The other Were Ezekiel had sensed at the crash site bolted out of the same spot where Royland had emerged from the forest. Seeing the immediate danger was over, she bent, her hands on her knees as she drew heaving breaths.

Ezekiel's magic receded with the Mad all dead. He stood straight, his snark returning unbidden. "I thought Weres were supposed to be fit?"

Royland snickered. "Sure, aggravate Cammie. I mean, you just escaped death…"

Cammie shot daggers at Ezekiel. "You try keeping up with a vampire." Her nose twitched, her enhanced sense of smell registering that he was no ordinary human. She turned her attention to Caitlin. "Who's your friend?"

Caitlin stared at Ezekiel, her clear gaze questioning.

Ezekiel cut in before she had a chance to voice her thoughts. "You're the same Royland and Cammie who live on Prince Edward Island? I've heard a lot about you."

Cammie dropped her hands to her hips. "Can't say the same, sunshine. What the hell do you smell of?"

"Magic," Ezekiel answered simply, turning to tell Caitlin, "We need to get back to the house."

Caitlin looked down at her blood-spattered clothing. "I need to wash this shit off me. Let's go."

# CHAPTER TEN

Inside the house, Helena and Mary-Anne were awake.

Mary-Anne had made clear what she thought about being strapped to an identical bench to the older vampire's. However, the concession had to be made. She was Mad or approaching Madness, and it wasn't safe for her to be loose with Kain asleep and Caitlin sneaking out to follow Ezekiel.

Mary-Anne had eyed Helena skeptically the whole time they'd been talking. Helena became introspective for a long moment, her gaze drifting to the ceiling. Mary-Anne concealed her impatience for answers, waiting for the other vampire to gather her thoughts.

Helena sighed, coming back to the conversation. "We were given a gift. Vampirism is the greatest thing I could ever have asked for. No matter what happens when the Madness finally claims me—and I feel that that time may be sooner than anyone realizes—I was given more time than any human to do my work and get us to where we are now. The culmination of all that's yet to come."

Mary-Anne's eyebrows drew together as her restraints chafed her body. "And what's that?"

Helena offered her a beatific smile. "A journey. A journey to parts of the world that no one outside the UnknownWorld has visited in a long time."

"How will we get there?" Mary-Anne asked.

Helena laughed.

Mary-Anne cursed herself. *Of course.* She already knew the answer. "The boy?"

Helena flashed her fangs at Mary-Anne's tone of disbelief. "Don't underestimate him. There's a lot more to him than meets the eye. He may be young, but he's wise beyond his years. He's been through a lot, and he's more doggedly determined than anyone I have ever met." She caught her anger before it spiraled into another episode. It wasn't the younger vampire's fault that she and Ezekiel hadn't been forthcoming about his connection to the heart of the problem. "Even me."

"What is it?"

Helena barely heard her. Her mind was slipping again... "Did you know that the Queen Bitch—or the Matriarch, as many call her—always had a team by her side? Dozens of humans, Weres, and vampires fighting to help keep justice in the world."

"Team Queen Bitch—TQB. Of course." Mary-Anne was losing her patience despite her understanding of Helena's fight to retain her mind while the Madness ate away at her. "What does that have to do with this?"

"They weren't the only ones fighting." Helena turned her head to meet Mary-Anne's eyes. "I suspect they had

Kurtherian aid. Possibly even machines that were intelligences in their own right. I believe there are sentient beings who had been trapped or were hiding across Earth, beings who are waiting for someone with enough of an understanding of the Kurtherian race and the threat they posed to find them and help revive them to functional use."

Helena drifted for a long moment before continuing, "I believe it because it's true."

She registered the look of suspicion on Mary-Anne's face. "Mary-Anne?"

Mary-Anne remained quiet, her expression shifting from suspicion to fear.

"You there?" Helena asked.

Mary-Anne returned to herself. "Sorry, I'm not used to people calling me by my real name."

Helena wondered where Mary-Anne had come from and what her experience was that the mention of Kurtherians roused such a strong reaction in her. "You've heard the stories, haven't you?"

"But what has that got to do with the Madness?" Mary-Anne's tone became strident. "What has that got to do with the boy? What has the Queen Bitch and her history got to do with *anything*?"

"It's got *everything* to do with it." Helena fought for control as the Madness surged inside her. "Forget the story I spun earlier. I know you know better than to believe the Queen's technology could be subverted by something so primitive as an EMP. Don't you understand? It's *because* of the Kurtherian nanocytes that all this has happened. Without them, the world would be ticking by right now.

Humans would be holding hands in a world where no Mad roamed the land looking to eat people's faces."

Mary-Anne scoffed in disbelief. "I doubt it. Someone pushed the red button to start WWDE. Somehow the world would have fallen to shit one way or another. If there's one thing I've learned about humans, it's that they don't like to look after the things they can't fix."

Helena had to convince her, otherwise her plans to use Mary-Anne's predicament to get Ezekiel to go back to Sarah Jennifer would come to nothing. "I've spent over seven decades looking for a cure. Reading everything I could find. I even stumbled across entries from diaries and journals written by Frank Kurns."

That got Mary-Anne's attention. "*The* Frank Kurns?"

"The very one," Helena told her. "A member of TQB himself, and the one rumored to have inducted Bethany Anne into the UnknownWorld all those years ago. I studied everything I could about the history, everything I could about the nanocytes. Anything I could find that might suggest the answer. I traipsed across the country. I made friends, and I lost them. I killed, and I healed, and you know what all of that added up to at the end of the day?"

Mary-Anne shook her head.

"Squat!" Helena growled in frustration. "Nothing more than a formula for a concoction that can slow the damn thing down. A formula that two vampires lying in this very room are now taking in the hope that they may be spared a few more precious days to fix this mess."

"I don't understand," Mary-Anne countered in confusion. "If all of that was wasted time, why are you telling me all this?"

Helena squirmed to turn on the bench so she could face Mary-Anne. "Because the boy knows one of the beings, a sentient entity trapped inside a machine who may have all the answers we've been looking for."

Mary-Anne gasped. "How? What is it?"

Even now, Helena found it hard to betray Ezekiel's confidence. However, her love for him and the fear that he would fall back into the dark place he'd been in when they'd found one another won out. She gave Mary-Anne a modified version of the truth. "She calls herself Lilith. She speaks as though she's met Bethany Anne, and seems to know all there is to know about the nanocytes."

Mary-Anne pulled at her restraints. "Well, let's get going, then. Let's go to her. Do you know where she is?"

Helena lay back, to Mary-Anne's surprise. "Ah. There's the rub."

Mary-Anne stopped struggling. "What? You can't be telling me you don't know where she is? You realize we're both dying? Let's go find her before it's too late!"

Helena sighed. It *was* too late for her if only everyone else would accept it. "I can't. But you all can."

Mary-Anne resumed her attempt to free herself, to no avail. "What are you talking about?"

Helena took her time answering. "Lilith lies across the sea. Across the Atlantic, in Europe. We've had no means to fly to her," not strictly true, "nor am I sure I would even have lasted the journey." That part was no lie. She felt her end growing closer with every minute that passed. "You have to promise me you'll find her. Take Ezekiel, and swear you'll keep him safe. You have to go on your way without me. I saw your dirigible. A marvelous piece of technology, and something I thought I might never see again. You can fly there, right? Fly to Lilith and find the answers we need."

It was Mary-Anne's turn to be silent.

"How do you know this Lilith even exists?" Mary-Anne eventually asked. "If she's thousands of miles away across the Atlantic, how can you possibly know?"

Helena smiled, relief and hope blossoming despite her knowledge that this was the end for her. "Because she speaks directly to the boy."

Exhaustion stole over her and she lapsed into sleep, leaving Mary-Anne to process everything she'd learned.

---

Helena awoke to the smell of Mad blood. She started, then realized the smell was coming from Caitlin, who had returned with Ezekiel.

Ezekiel came over and released both vampires, starting with Helena. "There was an incursion, and I didn't have a hex up."

Helena pulled herself to a sitting position, rubbing her chafed wrists. "I take it you dealt with it."

"Actually, Caitlin did," Ezekiel told her.

"What am I, chopped liver?" Royland exclaimed.

Ezekiel was grateful for the distraction. He didn't want to tell Helena that he'd almost destroyed the whole forest. "Helena, this is Royland and Cammie."

Helena's eyes widened with surprise. "It's my honor to meet you both. Your part in the battle of New York hasn't been forgotten. Not by me, at any rate."

That won Cammie over. She smiled at Helena, waving off the praise. "Aw, it was nothing. Gotta take care of our own, right?"

"Speaking of," Kain cut in as he exited the bedroom. "How are we for dinner? Did anyone hunt?"

"Is your stomach the only thing you care about?" Caitlin called from the bathroom. She emerged, her hair wrapped in a towel. "There will be time to eat when we've talked through what we're going to do next. Our ship is damaged. How do you suggest we continue the search for the cure without our ride?"

Mary-Anne looked at Ezekiel. "Magic Boy has the answers to where the cure can be found, apparently."

Ezekiel reddened under the scrutiny when everyone turned to look at him.

"Truth time, Ezekiel," Helena murmured.

Ezekiel sighed. "Okay. I'm not a century old. I'm thirty-three. I come from a town called New Romanov in Siberia, where Lilith lives. I was brought up by Sarah Jennifer Walton after my parents died, and she is the one spear-heading the resolution to the Madness."

"Walton?" Royland blurted.

"As in, the Alpha?" Cammie was awed.

Ezekiel nodded.

"Why would you hide that from us?" Cammie asked. "Wait, we were looking for you! Everyone was!"

Ezekiel's blush deepened, his embarrassment driving

his magic dangerously close to the surface. "I'm not talking about my relationship with Sarah Jennifer."

Helena cut in, "Pack politics isn't the question here. The only thing that matters is how you're going to get to New Romanov before it's too late for Mary-Anne."

Kain snorted. "Okay, so let me get this straight. You're suggesting that the six of us—"

Caitlin coughed and nodded at Jaxon. The dog turned intelligent eyes on the Were, his stare accusatory.

Kain rolled his eyes. "Sorry, Kitty-Cat. Can't forget the dog, now. That the *seven* of us fix up the flying ship which we crash-landed into the trees thanks to a superstorm. Then we blindly set out on a mission thousands of miles across the ocean, where there's literally zero places to land safely if anything goes wrong, and search for a place none of us have ever visited. All to go and find some kind of machine which may or may not hold the answers to fixing the Madness once and for all." He looked around the room. "Does that about cover it?"

Kain's mouth dropped open when he was met with a round of determined nods.

Cammie and Royland offered him zero support.

Kain threw up his hands. "Okay, I'm not saying I'm not eager to help put an end to all of this shit—particularly with Ma pushed even closer to the brink of batshit crazy herself—"

Mary-Anne glared icy daggers at him. "Thanks for that."

"You're welcome. But can we stop and think about this for a minute?" Kain's eyes flashed yellow, his voice dropping to a growl. "This is suicide. You know that to get to Europe would take days? Maybe even weeks? We traveled a couple of nights and got smacked by lightning. What are we going to do if we crash into the ocean? I can't swim, and I doubt Jaxon will be happy acting as a life raft for everyone, do you?"

Caitlin interjected, "Kain…"

He ignored the warning, getting up to pace off the concern driving his energy. "What's going to happen when we get there? We're just magically going to find this robot and ask it to click its mechanical fingers and fix everything? How do we even know that it exists?"

"Not a robot," Ezekiel murmured.

No one heard him.

"Kain," Mary-Anne tried.

Panic colored Kain's voice, and his energy changed as his wolf rose in response to his fear. "And don't you think that *if*—and I'm talking the extremely unlikely case that this thing actually exists, because how the hell do we really know it's real?—*if, if, if, if, IF* this thing exists, don't you think it'll be protected? Don't you think that forces across the pond are already aware of it then they'll already be protecting it? Maybe this machine is the reason for all of this in the first place. Did—"

Caitlin planted herself in his path, her hands on her hips. "*Kain!*"

He turned, his bared teeth beginning to elongate. "What!"

The dog whined.

"Shut. Up. And. Listen." Caitlin stared him down, her fiery gaze daring him to argue. Seeing she'd snapped him out of it, she turned to Ezekiel. "Zeke, it's over to you, buddy."

Ezekiel nodded. "Lilith isn't a robot. She is a Kurtherian, an alien from the species that has visited Earth on a number of occasions. The Kurtherians fall into two groups. There are the Five, who are genetically incapable of violence of any kind, and the Seven, who are hellbent on enslaving any species they see as inferior—which basically means any species but their own—and using them to force their religion on the universe.

"When I was a boy, I only knew Lilith as 'the Oracle,' an entity whose motivation was protecting the people in my hometown. When I was fourteen, my parents were killed by a Mad. I was adopted by Sarah Jennifer, and I met Lilith...in person for the first time. She taught me about magic and the true history of the world. The Unknown-World. The Madness is not a virus, not like we would think of one, anyway."

Everyone in the room was silent as he continued.

"When the Matriarch left Earth the last time, she placed a satellite network in high orbit and blanketed the planet in nanocytes meant to push humanity into the next stage of evolution—magic. Her people also placed climate control technology all around the planet. A man by the name of Arthur Drake messed with the Queen's technology, causing the Madness and plunging the northern hemisphere into eternal winter."

Ezekiel sighed. He didn't want to tear the scab off his wounds. "The Defense Force reversed the winter. They've been all over the world, containing the worst outbreaks of Madness. I left. I needed to do more. I needed to do things my own way, not the military way. I argued with Sarah Jennifer about her intention for the Defense Force to leave Earth. I have to admit that what I did was wrong." He looked at Helena. "But if I hadn't left, I wouldn't have met you. I can't regret that."

Helena took his hand. "I wouldn't have had things any other way. You are my family."

"What does any of this have to do with Lilith?" Caitlin asked.

Ezekiel sighed again, deeper this time. "The Defense Force has two branches. One is made up of the pack, the other is made up of magic users. I was the first person born with magic, but there are thousands of others who have learned the ability. Their leader Esme worked for TQB back before WWDE. She's the one who has worked with Lilith to decode the Madness, and it's her we need to ask to help Mary-Anne."

Helena spoke into the stunned silence. "Imagine how I felt discovering yet another hidden layer to the UnknownWorld."

Caitlin fixed Ezekiel with her shrewd gaze. "You can communicate with Lilith? How?"

"When I quiet my mind, I can connect to her," Ezekiel told her. "She has begged me to come to her for weeks now. She tells me there is great danger and that time is short."

Royland had questions. "Why didn't you go, then? Why didn't you heed her call yourself?"

Cammie threw a hand back, slapping him on the stomach. "Because he had no means to cross the ocean. He's just one boy, and she's just one woman."

Helena had to argue that. "Excuse me, I'm a vampire."

"You won't be for long," Kain muttered. He shrugged at the look Mary-Anne gave him. "What? I'm just saying. If we're really considering this absolute fuckfest of a mission, then shouldn't we all be really honest about what's going on here? She's going to go into full Mad-mode in the next few days." He pointed at Mary-Anne. "*She's* a few weeks behind on the timescale, but with the unpredictability of the damned thing, she could turn at any moment, as we've seen." He moved his hand to point at Ezekiel. "And this *boy* thinks he can hear voices from halfway across the world. How do we know that *he's* not going Mad?"

Ezekiel had heard enough. He focused on his breathing, controlling the well of magic he'd been holding in.

Kain eyed him with concern. "Um, what's the kid doing?"

Assured he wouldn't accidentally burn the house down, Ezekiel released the magic, shaping it to match the image in his mind. His eyes glowed red as he manifested a fireball.

Helena gasped, realizing he didn't have the control he was aiming for.

Ezekiel was aware. Fire was the easiest magic to manifest but also the easiest to lose control of. He launched the fireball at the window. It shattered the glass before scorching the grass outside where it landed, lighting up the night.

Kain darted to the broken window and peered out at the guttering ball of flames. He whirled, his eyes wide as he stared at Ezekiel. "Magic? It's real?"

Helena interjected, "It's not magic."

"Not true," Ezekiel countered. "Esme always told me that once a technology is sufficiently advanced, it appears to be magic." The glow from his eyes faded. "I'm paraphrasing. What I mean is, if everyone believes it's magic, who's to say any different?"

"Yes, well." Helena's face made her feelings clear. She had gone around and around this debate with Ezekiel over the years, and while they had never fallen out over it, she'd always sided firmly with Sarah Jennifer's opinion. "You know whose side of that argument I agree with. There's no such thing as magic. What you've just witnessed is the full potential of the Kurtherian nanocytes, an unlocked version of the very same technology that lives within me, and you, and you, and you. Even the dog may have them, for all we know."

Ezekiel couldn't argue that.

Helena's expression was fiercely protective. "We don't know exactly what's going on here, but what we do know is that the boy possesses a gift none of us understands or knows the limits of."

Ezekiel frowned. "Esme understood."

Helena chose to ignore him and turned her attention back to Kain. "If you're telling me that in a room filled with Weres, vampires, and humans in a world where the Madness exists that you can't believe another form of this technology could also exist, then I ask you to leave my premises. These doubts are not conducive to progress. However, if you wish to save your friend any time soon, then you best get your big-boy believing pants on and prepare for a fucking voyage because there's no other way this damn thing will end. Of that, I am sure."

Kain was clearly unused to being told what to do. However, even a vampire at the end of her life—and especially a vampire who could go Mad at any moment—was a dangerous person to aggravate. The energy Helena put out subdued his instinct to dominate.

He very wisely closed his mouth.

His silence wasn't enough.

# CHAPTER ELEVEN

Helena's gaze was locked on the Were, her chest rising and falling as the drive to feed took over. Her eyes began to shine dull red.

She clasped her head with a hand, trying to push away the desire to kill.

Ezekiel saw the change come over her. "Helena. Is it happening?"

"Take me to the table," she murmured.

Kain got out of Helena's line of sight, moving to stand by Royland and Cammie, who were both unnerved by the sudden change in the vampire's demeanor.

Cammie whispered to Caitlin, "Is she okay?"

Caitlin nodded. "She will be. It's just an episode."

"Help me out here, Kain," Ezekiel asked.

Kain didn't hesitate. He took one of Helena's arms, and the two of them guided the vampire to the other room, where the twin benches were.

Helena's fight began almost as soon as they started strapping her down.

ND ROBERTS & MICHAEL ANDERLE

Her grunts turned to growls and screams as they left her to wait out the episode.

Mary-Anne turned inward, ignoring the concerned glances they sent her way as they hesitantly talked about what would happen next.

Ezekiel found it hard to concentrate on the matter at hand. He heard Lilith's advice over and over in his mind and wished he could do more to help Helena through this. However, he knew from experience that his presence would only cause her to become more frantic. He couldn't help but feel for Caitlin and Kain when Mary-Anne's time came.

The thought of them having to suffer as he was brought out a determination to get Mary-Anne whatever help he could.

He wondered if this had been Helena's plan from the moment they met Mary-Anne. He didn't care. He liked her as well, and he would bleed himself dry before he allowed another to go through the torment Helena was in right now.

She screamed again, and the sounds of her agony tore Ezekiel's heart in two.

She broke off, her exertion too much for her body to handle.

Royland spoke into the sudden silence. "We should be able to fix her."

Ezekiel started. What did the vampire know?

"The ship. The dirigible, I mean," Royland continued quickly. "The crew was making great progress on the hole, so it should be airborne by morning."

Cammie shot Royland a look that told him he was an

122

idiot. "Sure. Airborne, but not prepared for the long voyage you're all talking of taking. We've added a band aid to a cut. We need to put on the antiseptic, bandage that baby up, and have the whole thing checked over before we can even think of heading to Europe. The last time anyone voyaged that far..."

They smiled, recalling their glory days.

Kain, the voice of reason, cut into their nostalgia trip. "Where do you expect to fix her up? It's not like there's a mechanic nearby where we can just drop her off for a quick once-over. It's hopeless. We've got nothing. A suicide mission and a ship that won't make the voyage."

Ezekiel was silent. He was very close to reaching out to Lilith to ask her to pass a message to Sarah Jennifer...

Kain's eyes flashed yellow. "How about it, Ma? Shall we just call it quits and submit to the will of the Madness? Helena's doing it. How about you bite me in the neck right here, and then maybe I can just get it over with. It's not like you're going to survive the journey, is it?"

Mary-Anne refused to meet his stare. She turned away as she felt the Madness creeping inside her.

"See?" Kain's fear for her manifested as anger. "Even Ma thinks the whole thing is stupid. Just admit it, Caitlin. We've hit a dead end. It's over. We'll never make it—"

Cammie slapped him.

Kain's hand shot up to his face. "You hit me!"

"Somebody had to," Cammie snarled. "Do you realize how crazy you sound?"

Kain's mouth dropped open. "How crazy *I* sound?"

"That's right," Cammie told him bluntly. "Do you realize what this world's been through? Do you realize the struggles, the trials and tribulations that have brought about each age that has come before ours? When the Nazis rose to power, people thought they couldn't be defeated and that the world as we knew it was over. It wasn't."

Kain stammered, "B-but..."

Cammie waved off his weak protest. "When technology was brought into the world and people thought that the year 2000 signaled the end of all things as we knew them, we survived. I've known Weres who have wandered through the apocalypse and rebuilt the land. I've known vampires who have overcome their own families and fought off evil to make the world a better place."

"That's not what I'm—"

Cammie cut across his argument. "I know one vampire who came into the UnknownWorld with less knowledge than a newborn has of algebra, and she tackled everything that came her way. She overcame age-old feuds, she learned to harness Kurtherian technology, and she's out there right now battling to keep our tiny shithole of a planet safe."

Kain had no recourse for that. Everyone knew Bethany Anne's story.

Cammie continued in the same angry tone, "And now our small band of fighters has a chance to restore the world to rights. To help rebuild the world one more time, and you're shaking in your boots, cowering before the job at hand? Well, let me tell you something. There are only a few moments in our life where we get to choose what truly defines us. Moments when life asks you who you want to become, and you get to make your choice."

Kain hung his head. She was right; he knew it.

"Your choice is now, Kain," Cammie stated. "Mary-Anne. Caitlin. Zeke—"

"*Ezekiel*," Ezekiel corrected.

"Whatever." Cammie stabbed a finger in Kain's direction. "So, what choice do you want to make?"

Ezekiel was stung to the core by her rant. She was right, of course. It wasn't about any of their individual needs beyond the urgency to get Mary-Anne to Lilith's mountain before her Madness progressed past the point of no return.

Before he had the chance to tell them he would reach out to Sarah Jennifer, Caitlin spoke up.

"Well, I don't know about the rest of you, but I'm ready to go kick this Madness in the ass." She gave Cammie and Royland one of those shrewd looks. "If you've got the balls to give a speech that rousing, that must mean you've got a method to repair the ship?"

Royland wiggled his eyebrows. "Oh, we've got some friends nearby. If we can get the ship in a position to fly a short distance, we can get the rest of it patched up and ready to go."

Caitlin nodded, her expression resolute. "Great. The moment Helena snaps out of her episode, we'll bid our farewells and set out to the sunrise."

Royland sucked in a breath. "Oooh, the sunrise?"

He preened when that got a laugh, which had Cammie rolling her eyes.

"What about it, brother?" Caitlin asked Kain. "Are you in?"

Ezekiel was flooded with relief at dodging the reunion he'd been avoiding for so long. This way, they could avoid Salem altogether. It brought his sense of humor back. "Oh, come on," he teased. "Don't tell me Sir Wolfington is afraid of a little adventure?"

Kain let out a playful growl. "*Fine*. We've come this far. What's an extra thousand miles?"

Caitlin paused as she returned to her seat, realizing something was off.

She wasn't the only one. Now that the heated discussion had come to an end, the house was silent.

She caught Ezekiel's eye. "Erm, Zeke?"

Royland whined, "How come *she* can call you that?"

Cammie placed a hand on his arm. "Let it go."

Ezekiel and Caitlin had bigger concerns.

Ezekiel dashed from the room.

The bench where Helena should have been secured was empty.

His heart rate skyrocketed as he rushed back.

Caitlin groaned, understanding immediately. Kain was half a step behind. "What is it?" he asked. "Is she..." He couldn't bring himself to say, "dead."

Ezekiel shook his head, dread contorting his features. "Helena's gone."

Not for long.

She burst through the door with the Madlight in her eyes.

---

Ezekiel knew this was it. Helena was gone, and all that remained was a Mad with vampiric strength and speed.

He heard Caitlin whisper, "Nosferatu," and couldn't deny it.

Helena's strength sent her crashing through the furniture and into the wall, unable to pull back from her frenzied charge.

Still, Ezekiel was loath to kill her.

The others had no emotional bond to hold them back.

The room suddenly bristled with weaponry as everyone but Ezekiel pulled their blades. Royland had a pistol, of all things. Even Mary-Anne, in danger of turning Mad, vamped out.

Ezekiel panicked. "Don't hurt her! It's just an episode. We can calm her. Tie her back down. This isn't the end."

He knew that wasn't true, yet he still held a child's hope that she could be saved. If they just subdued her. If they bound her and...and...

Helena threw a table at Kain.

The Were ducked, avoiding the makeshift projectile. "Has she ever escaped from your contraption before?" he yelled as the Helena-Mad stalked the room, eyeing each of them as if trying to gauge the weakest and therefore prime target.

Ezekiel hesitated to answer, knowing it would seal her fate. "No," he answered eventually. "She's never been strong enough."

His mind churned, caught between loyalty to a person who no longer existed and the living.

Caitlin lifted her sword, holding the growling Jaxon back with her foot. "It may be time to accept that Helena is gone."

The dog let out a loud bark and the Helena-Mad zeroed in on him with a starved look, saliva dripping from her mouth.

Madness-fueled, Helena blurred across the room, her sights set on the noble animal.

Jaxon leapt in front of Caitlin, his instinct to protect his human overriding his sense of self-preservation.

Before the two met in the center of the room, Mary-Anne took the Helena-Mad out at the waist, flinging the Mad vamp across the room. The rest were unable to keep up as the two vampires went fang and claw against each other. Even Royland was hard-pressed to make out who was going to come out on top.

Still, he did his best when Mary-Anne took a blow that sent her reeling, leaving the Helena-Mad free to go for Jaxon again.

His eyes flashed red as he tackled the Helena-Mad to the floor, screaming, "Run!"

Cammie dragged Caitlin out of the house as the sounds of the vampires battling it out tore the night apart.

Caitlin pulled free of Cammie's grip when she realized neither Kain nor Ezekiel had emerged from the house.

Cammie took her hesitation for fear. "Keep close, Caitlin. I'll protect you." Her eyes shone yellow in the dark as she called her wolf to the surface, ready to shift in an instant if necessary.

"No!" Caitlin told her. "You can't shift. Don't risk it!" She felt Jaxon bump against her leg and was glad at least the dog had made it out safely. "Kain's still in there. I can't just leave him."

They paused by the tree line as an almighty crash came from the house and the Helena-Mad sped through the wreckage of the door.

The Madlight shone from her eyes, casting a corrupt halo around her in the gentle drizzle that was falling.

Cammie hunched, preparing to shift, when a bloodcurdling howl rent the air and Kain made himself a door where the wall had been.

Standing almost eight feet tall in his Pricolici form, his claws tore up the ground as he bounded across the clearing in pursuit of the Helena-Mad.

She stalled, the howl speaking to some primal part of her psyche deep below the Madness corruption that drove her to seek sustenance from the living.

That gave Mary-Anne and Royland an opening. Together, the Pricolici and the two vampires triple-teamed Helena, wrestling her to the ground.

Cammie shoved Caitlin toward the trees. "Go." Caitlin didn't move. "GO!" Cammie yelled, her voice torn with fear for her lover. "Royland! Get away from her. Remember, you can't touch her blood!"

Royland backed off, and Mary-Anne took his place. "Just go! Get Caitlin to safety, *now!*"

Caitlin still refused to move. "Where did Ezekiel go?" she yelled. *"EZEKIEL!"*

She made for the house but only managed two steps before Royland scooped her up and flung her over his shoulder. He snagged the German Shepherd with his free arm and ran at vampiric speed through the trees.

Caitlin screamed in frustration at being forced to leave her family behind and losing the only link to the cure. She beat at Royland's back in vain. "Let me down, you ass! Ezekiel is more important than me!"

Royland gave no sign he heard.

Back at the house, Ezekiel watched helplessly as Mary-Anne and Kain fought Helena. He wouldn't risk unleashing a wall of flames as much as his instincts were screaming at him to do so. Not with them all so close.

He was reduced to waiting on the sidelines, hoping they would subdue Helena, when Lilith touched his mind.

*Not now, Lilith*, he begged.

*You are in considerable distress,* the Kurtherian told him. *You reached out to me.*

Just like that, the urge to burn everything vanished, replaced by a crashing wave of grief. Magic poured from him, and the heavens opened in response.

Lightning came from the clouds obscuring the dawn, and thunder crashed.

The pouring rain turned the ground to slick mud.

Ezekiel wept, the salt of his tears getting washed away in the storm. Lilith's voice was balm for his soul.

*You will do what you have to, child. What would your friend want?*

Ezekiel thought back to when Helena had first realized she was infected. Her words, which he had brushed off as frightened talk, came back to him.

*"We will go far from here. Far from any humans. When my time comes, don't let me hurt anyone, Ezekiel. I couldn't bear it."*

He had run to avoid his duty. To forge his own path, free of the restrictions he'd seen in Sarah Jennifer's way.

"Duty has a way of catching up with you," he murmured in a broken voice. "Whether you want it or not. It's not fair."

*Life seldom is,* Lilith told him in the same calm voice.

*However, you have the strength to get through this and anything else your destiny sets before you.*

The talk of destiny made him think of Sarah Jennifer again. How many times had she been forced to make decisions that affected people the world over? "How does Sarah Jennifer cope with it?"

Lilith's reply surprised him

*She feels much as you are feeling now, that no one person should be faced with the responsibility for the life of another. She saves her tears for when the hard work is done, and she holds herself accountable for every living being lost to the Madness in the meantime.*

The scales fell from Ezekiel's eyes. *I know what I have to do.*

# CHAPTER TWELVE

The Helena-Mad had escaped in the downpour.

Ezekiel followed the trail she and the others had left to the dirigible, his heart heavy. Despite his grief, he felt better control over his magic than he'd had in a long while. Perhaps it was because the event he'd been fearing for so long was past. Helena was gone, never to return, and now all he had to do was obey her final wishes.

He heard frantic shouting up ahead at the crash site.

Slipping through the trees, he saw that the dirigible had been repaired well enough to get them airborne. It was no *Enora*, but it was a sight to behold all the same.

He felt no sense of Helena's mind in the clearing. The dual stench of Madness and fear filled the air.

There she was, still attempting to get at Caitlin's dog.

He hesitated, wondering if the fixation on Jaxon was the last vestige of sanity clinging to her mind or just her long-ingrained habit of only feeding on animals surfacing like some macabre muscle memory.

He heard Caitlin's voice drifting toward him as he

inched closer, calling on every bit of magic he had in his effort to replicate Esme's ability to control the Mad.

It was in the blood.

It was always in the blood.

Caitlin had her hands up in a conciliatory gesture. Her left foot was back, her body held in a ready stance should it come to a fight. "You can't have him. He is not yours to have, Helena. Nor are any of us. You are a vampire under the influence of the Madness. Hear me, if you can, and give us some kind of sign that you are still in there."

Ezekiel's heart hurt. He wanted to believe he saw recognition flaring in the Helena-Mad's eyes.

"Helena?" Caitlin repeated. "If you're in there, give us some kind of sign. Anything…"

Ezekiel hung back, his entire focus on calling to the nanocytes running through the Helena-Mad's veins.

She growled, baring her teeth as Caitlin took a step toward her.

Even from a distance, Ezekiel saw the Madlight in her eyes, the dull red outshining the early morning sun filtering through the breaks in the clouds.

Jaxon snarled as Caitlin continued talking in that low, persuasive voice.

"Helena? Are you in there? Come back to us."

She reached out, breaking the spell.

The Helena-Mad snarled and lunged at Caitlin, tossing her into the crew standing as if frozen on the deck of the dirigible.

She darted toward the dog, and Ezekiel knew it was now or never.

Something clicked in his mind, and he found the bridge

he needed through the remnant of his own blood that was still in Helena's system. He reached for the nanocytes coursing through her veins and sent out a single thought.

*STOP.*

The Helena-Mad froze mid-strike.

Ezekiel ignored the people staring at him as he advanced toward the dirigible, his hands glowing with white light.

The light extended, surrounding the Helena-Mad.

Ezekiel broke out in a sweat as pain wracked his body, the magic threatening to tear him apart. He refused to give in. Refused to believe he would fail.

This was Helena's last wish, and by the Matriarch and all the stars above, he meant to make sure the woman this Mad had once been got the ending she deserved.

He focused, his hands trembling with the effort of holding her in place.

"Bind her," he called to the other UnknownWorlders. "Tie her up while I can still hold her. Hurry! I can't hold her for long."

They obeyed without question, restraining her from head to toe in ropes and chains. Just in time, since Ezekiel's nose began to bleed as his effort became too much for his body to handle.

He released his magic, bending almost double as the recoil of it snapping back hit him like a punch to the gut. He waved a hand to indicate they should move her off the dirigible.

Tentatively, since she was snapping at them, they removed her to the edge of the forest, hardening their hearts against her plaintive cries.

"Here," Ezekiel told them as they reached the foot of a mighty pine.

Caitlin looked at him like he was a taco short of a combination plate. "What? Why are you stopping?"

"We need more rope," was his only reply.

He directed them to lash Helena to the trunk of the pine and asked them to leave.

Caitlin took a few steps back. "Of course. We'll wait here."

Ezekiel turned sad eyes on her. "No, go back to the ship. This won't take long."

When they were out of earshot, he knelt just out of Helena's reach and looked into her eyes. "You were there for me when I needed a friend. Now it's my turn to be there for you."

His hands glowed white again as he renewed his connection to Helena's nanocytes. This time his command was simple, yet they were the most painful words he'd ever had to say.

*"Self-destruct."*

He waited until the light in her eyes had faded before leaning in to kiss her forehead. "Goodbye, my friend. Know that you left this world loved. I'm going back to my home. Where I belong."

He sat back on his haunches and opened his mind to Lilith. *I'm coming home, Lilith, and I'm bringing my friends with me. I don't think Cammie and Royland will stay with us, but I have Caitlin, and Kain, and Mary-Anne.*

Lilith's mental voice was layered with sadness and compassion. *I'm so sorry for your loss. I hope her passing was peaceful.*

Ezekiel got to his feet and gazed at Helena's face for the last time. *In the end, yes.* He filled her in on the events of the night as he walked back to the dirigible.

*How will you get here?* Lilith asked.

*We have a dirigible. We'll make it somehow.* Ezekiel's heart lurched as he considered the difficult journey ahead. *Tell Sarah Jennifer I'm coming home.*

## New Romanov

Sarah Jennifer had not stopped for more than a couple of hours' rest here and there since Enora had brought the news that the Mad were on their way. Enora had reported in after returning from her regular flyover, telling them more Mad had joined the hordes slowly making their way toward the mountain.

Olaf roamed Siberia, radioing in from each village and town he came to. His army grew at each stop, and every day the ring of camps forming a barrier around New Romanov grew in number and size.

Esme came up from the cavern in the roots of the mountain twice a day to tend the recovered Mad, all of whom were awake and out of their beds thanks to her healing energy.

Lilith spoke into her mind. *Sarah Jennifer. I have just spoken with Ezekiel.*

Sarah Jennifer straightened in her seat. "And?"

*He asked me to tell you he is coming,* Lilith continued. *His vampire friend has passed. He is bringing his group here, including the other vampire who is infected.*

Sarah Jennifer swallowed hard. At last, the crack in her

heart could be mended. She let out a long breath as she assimilated the idea of having her adopted son home again. "That's… That's big news."

*You already know two of his present company.*

"Who?"

*Cammie and Royland.*

"From Prince Edward Island?"

*Yes.*

Sarah Jennifer frowned. "Royland is the infected vamp?"

*No, they don't intend to stay with Ezekiel's group past Chicago. The infected vampire is called Mary-Anne. From what I gathered from Ezekiel, his group consists of Cammie and Royland, a human named Caitlin and her dog, a Were named Kain, and the vampire I just told you about, as well as the crew of the dirigible they're flying in.*

"Well, damn." Sarah Jennifer sat back. "They're going to have a hell of a welcome when they get here. Can you stay in touch with him as much as he'll allow?"

*Of course.*

"Thank you. You know, you'd think after all this time I'd have dealt with my feelings about his choices."

*You see yourself as his adoptive parent. My experiences with humans have shown me that logic is often pushed aside when it comes to your children, no matter their age.*

Sarah Jennifer folded her arms. "You're saying I'm illogical?"

*I'm saying I think you have done well to allow Ezekiel the space to make his mistakes, however you felt about the way he left. You haven't rejected him despite the hurt he has caused you emotionally.*

Sarah Jennifer sighed. "Why would I reject him? I knew from the start he was going to hurt me. It's what kids do. It's what I did to my family when I left them at Alameda. If anything, I wish I'd been more open about my past so the kid didn't feel like he had to cut himself off to go find himself, or whatever."

Lilith returned to her work, leaving Sarah Jennifer to get on with hers.

Diverting the Defense Force had been no easy decision. Neither was choosing to allow Ezekiel to make his own way here. However, Lilith had assured her that his present company was more than capable of protecting him, not that he needed it, and that they had transportation in the form of the dirigible.

As her grandfather had often said, perfect was the enemy of good enough. She knew better than to fall into *that* trap.

She was about to make the second of her twice-daily calls with Theor, who was running point for her on the defensive line, when she heard Esme's footsteps heading her way from the lower levels. She looked up from her battle plan as the witch walked in. "You look happy."

Esme headed straight for the coffee pot. "The printing is finally done."

Sarah Jennifer let out a huge sigh of relief. "Then let's get the airship loaded and get up there. The sooner we get the saturation done, the better."

Esme looked askance at her, then extracted her cup from the machine. "I don't know about you, but I need to eat before we get to work. I think you skipped a step or two. We do need to get up to the BYPS, but we won't be starting the saturation today."

Sarah Jennifer realized it had been almost eight hours since she'd crammed in a quick bite before settling down to work on the logistics of defending the mountain from the hordes of Mad. Working into the early hours tended to warp her perception of time. "I'm sure you'll tell me why. But we eat fast. There's not much time left and I'm not comfortable leaving the mountain unguarded."

"It's hardly unguarded with half of Siberia camped out down there."

"You know what I mean," Sarah Jennifer responded. Her stomach growled, putting an end to the conversation for the moment.

They headed for the mess and prepared their food in companionable silence. Sarah Jennifer gratefully drained a large mug of hot, sweet coffee while the cooking was happening and refilled it before going to sit down with her laden tray.

"You have your math face on," Esme commented wryly.

Sarah Jennifer pushed her hair back and sighed. "Yeah. I like having Ace around for logistics planning. I've gotten lazy."

"What's the problem?" Esme asked.

"I got the numbers from Izzy late last night, and I've been working on the plan for the battle since then. It's not adding up for me."

Esme nodded. "Okay, break it down. You have one hundred thousand Weres, right?"

Sarah Jennifer seesawed a hand. "Thereabouts. A little less, but I like to round off."

"How many on Mars? Fifteen, twenty thousand?"

"I'm only counting available combatants who are on active duty." Sarah Jennifer's orders were to save lives, not take them. So close to getting the patches out, it would be a travesty to deny so many the chance to reclaim their humanity if the Madness got into those peaceful communities scattered around the globe. "I'm not moving units from around Europe or the Protectorate, where they're needed to protect vulnerable civilian populations."

Esme's forehead wrinkled. "You're making this harder than it needs to be."

"Did I mention I hate math? You can't hit it, for a start." Sarah Jennifer grinned at Esme's pointed look. "I'm getting there. I have fifteen thousand coming in from Central and South America, and another six from California now the outbreak there has been suppressed. Olaf has mustered around eight thousand, maybe closer to ten by the time he finishes his tour of Arkhangelsk. I have three thousand from Reika, plus another two coming in with Amelie, but those are mostly weather and water mages."

"Sounds to me like you have it under control," Esme told her.

"I have to feed and quarter all those people," Sarah Jennifer reminded her. "Izzy is working with the trade alliance to procure supplies, but again, we're running into transport snafus."

Esme grimaced. "Ah, the heart of the problem, as always."

Sarah Jennifer nodded. All the technology in the Federation couldn't make up for time and her need for people power. "I will get it resolved, one way or another. We have enough competing for the top spot on the objective in the meantime."

Esme continued chatting as they breakfasted on sausage links and scrambled eggs fresh from the town. Sarah Jennifer hardly heard her, too focused on the mental playbook she had running, shifting resources to fill the coming need.

Esme waved a hand in front of her face. "Did you hear a word I just said?"

Sarah Jennifer blinked. "Um, no. Sorry. What did you say?"

"I was asking if you'd checked in with Mars," Esme repeated. "Transport to and from the colony isn't going to be possible for the next six months while the BYPS is activated to prevent the nanocytes we seed in the atmosphere from being lost to space."

"What?" Sarah Jennifer frowned in confusion. "This is the first I'm hearing of this. Why do we need to activate the BYPS defensive measures?"

Esme dropped her fork onto her empty plate and reached for another slice of buttered toast. "Easiest way to make sure we get the nanocytes to where we need them. We used up all our reserves of biomass to print them. It's no good if we lose them to space."

"And the laser grid is the solution?" Sarah Jennifer wasn't getting it. "Surely any we lose will be destroyed by the grid?"

Esme shook her head. "I sent you a report."

"When?"

"Six months ago."

Sarah Jennifer didn't recall it and told her friend so.

"That explains your confusion. And why you didn't prioritize the task." Esme groaned. "Okay, it's like this. The laser grid emits an energy field we can use to repel anything escaping Earth's atmosphere."

"You mean, destroy it?" Sarah Jennifer was familiar with the operating parameters of the BYPS.

Esme shook her head. "That's why we're going up there. I want to see if we can tweak the system to make it produce something more along the lines of a static barrier that will push back instead of obliterating anything that comes into contact with it."

Sarah Jennifer's shoulders slumped. "So, we won't be releasing the nanocytes today."

Esme shook her head. "No. Especially since we need to make sure everyone building Promessa is adequately supplied for the time we're going to be cut off from Mars."

Sarah Jennifer got to her feet and went over to the sink to take care of her tray. "More supply issues. Fantastic. I need to get hold of Brutus."

Esme joined her at the sink. "We can do that from the airship."

Sarah Jennifer paused to look at the camps as they made their way out of the mountain. Thousands of tiny fires lit the predawn, the gently curving line evidence of her efforts to reconnect the world.

She reached out to Olaf first when they got to the cockpit.

"What can I do for you, Major?" the werebear asked.

"Esme and I need to go up to the BYPS," Sarah Jennifer informed him. "I need you back here. We're going to be gone a few days while we fix a supply run to Mars."

"No problem," Olaf replied. "Theor is keeping things together in the camps, right?"

Sarah Jennifer confirmed the Icelandic Were was doing a more than satisfactory job of managing the various bands of warriors Olaf sent their way.

"The man is Matriarch-sent," Olaf admitted. "I couldn't ask for a better second."

"I think he might consider you *his* second," Esme cut in.

Olaf laughed, the sound rich and deep. "One of these days, we'll have to settle that."

"It had better wait until we don't have the Mad breathing down our necks," Sarah Jennifer told him. "We have no room for leadership challenges right now."

"I'm just playing," Olaf assured her. "Theor and I have a good relationship."

"Amelie will be at the Petersburg Estuary by now," Sarah Jennifer reminded him. "Enora counted an additional seven or eight thousand Mad on her latest scouting mission."

Olaf cursed.

"Don't think I won't find a way to teach you some manners," Sarah Jennifer told him, unimpressed by his poor language. "We need to extend the defensive line to the east to cover the towns out that way."

"I'll get on it as soon as I get back to New Romanov," Olaf promised.

Sarah Jennifer closed the radio link and opened the Etheric comm to get hold of Brutus.

There was a short wait before he picked up. "How's it, cuz?" she asked.

"Pretty good!" came the reply. "You sound a bit…stressed."

Sarah Jennifer snorted. "Yeah, missing a memo that puts us back will do that. I need to check on your inventory status. What will you need to get by for six months?"

Brutus laughed. "I see. You're getting ready to activate the BYPS around Earth."

Sarah Jennifer was pleasantly surprised. "You know already?"

"Well, yeah. Esme told us about it months ago."

"See, *someone* read my report," Esme grouched.

"Give it a rest, Esme," Sarah Jennifer retorted. "I missed one report. It's not like I don't have all of Earth and Mars to be aware of. Brutus, supply status?"

"We're good. We're already planting the modded wheat, rye, and corn in the ag sector. Hydroponics is up and running without any issue. I won't lie, the coffee is gonna run short at the rate the scientists are slurping their way through it, but Ace has us covered otherwise."

Sarah Jennifer shot Esme a look. "Thank you for picking up my slack," she told Brutus. "I'll get a shipment of perishables sent up before we do anything with the BYPS."

"Hey, are comms gonna be down while the grid is up?" he asked.

Sarah Jennifer looked at Esme for the answer.

"No idea," Esme told him. "Could be."

"Give me twelve hours before you switch it on?" Brutus requested. "Give everyone time to call home if it's gonna be our last chance for six months." He paused. "Damn, six months. Didn't seem like such a big deal in theory, but now

I'm wondering how much my kids will have grown by the time I see them again."

"You won't be cut off from your children," Sarah Jennifer vowed. "I'll approve Etheric comms for the families of everyone on Mars."

"Might want to give him his twelve hours just the same," Esme suggested. "That many comm sets will take a couple of weeks to source components for and produce."

"Of course," Sarah Jennifer agreed. "It's probably going to take us that long to figure out what we need to do to adjust the BYPS, anyway."

"I'll pass on the word," Brutus told them before signing off.

Sarah Jennifer paused for a moment before getting up from her seat. "We're spread so thin."

Esme put a hand on her shoulder. "I know, Duckie. But our allies have answered the call. We're not alone in this."

Sarah Jennifer didn't know what she would do without the good friends who had her back. "Come on. We need to get out there and get started."

They made their way to the drop bay and pulled on EVA suits over their clothing before getting into the roamer they'd kept back from the consignment sent to Mars.

The small vehicle was rated for all environments and handled like an ATV—if the ATV was AI-controlled and had a bubble of transparent alien polymer instead of a roof.

Enora opened the drop doors and guided the roamer to the primary satellite.

Of all the Queen's technology, the BYPS was the most

intimidating. The roamer was dwarfed by the satellite, adding to the feeling Sarah Jennifer had of being in the presence of something far beyond her understanding.

Truth be told, her usefulness ended at being the only one with clearance to access the system, even if she *could* follow Esme's instructions to work on it.

Esme sensed her thinking, as always. She tapped Sarah Jennifer's arm. "You're woolgathering again. Helmet on, Duckie. Time's a-wasting."

# CHAPTER THIRTEEN

The satellite admitted them after Sarah Jennifer confirmed her identity. They unclipped their tethers once they were inside the airlock, and the hatch closed without a sound.

Air rushed in and sound returned, and a thousand tiny hisses and clicks filled Sarah Jennifer's hearing as she and Esme eased through the inner hatch into the small space beyond, where the controls for the entire system were mounted on large panels wrapped around a single high-backed stool.

Esme clucked in approval. "Now, *this* is fancy."

Sarah Jennifer had no clue what all the dials and switches did. "Where do we start?"

Esme bumped her out of the way and claimed the stool. "Don't touch anything until I say. Last thing we want is another great big mess on Earth."

"Have at it. I have enough to do," Sarah Jennifer told her, extracting her datapad from her suit pocket. She fired off a quick message to Izzy requesting the perishables she'd promised Brutus to be prepared for pickup within the next hour, then opened the app she was using to plan the defense of New Romanov.

A few minutes later, a question occurred to her. She glanced over Esme's shoulder at the monitor the witch was working at. "How exactly do you alter the system, anyway?"

"I'm downloading a copy of the operating system. I'm going to work on altering it to adjust the frequency of the output when activated. The plan is to convince the system to produce the same kind of shielding we used to keep the Mad contained in the lab." Esme's fingers flew over the keyboard as she answered. "Plus, Enora has written a program for the climate control modules that needs uploading. That's going to take a while. We're using the prevailing winds to propagate the nanocytes. We need to be in control of the weather systems around the globe."

"What are we supposed to do if Bethany Anne's war spills over to Earth while the defenses are down?" Sarah Jennifer asked.

"Are we expecting it to?" Esme returned.

"Well, no, but there's always the chance someone out there figures out Earth's location. I wouldn't be any kind of guardian if I didn't at least consider the possibility."

Esme laughed. "The laser network will be activated. Anyone trying to attack Earth is going to find themselves playing with fire." She pushed the keyboard back into its recess. "I'm done here. We'll have to come back so I can upload the changes before we start the saturation."

Sarah Jennifer nodded. "That's going to go as I expect, right?"

"That depends," Esme told her with a laugh. "Did you read the brief?"

"I can confirm I did, that one at least." Sarah Jennifer closed her datapad screen and put it away before picking up her helmet. "Let's get the run to Salem out of the way. Then Mars, and then we'll see if your plan worked."

"Of course it'll work!" Esme retorted. "Cheeky sod. I'm not a bloody amateur. I've memorized this system back to front, which is more than I can say for anyone else."

Sarah Jennifer laughed as she sealed her helmet. "Why would anyone else need to know when we have you?"

Esme snorted as she sealed her helmet. "Hmmph, absolute liberty! I won't be around forever, you know."

"Yeah, right," Sarah Jennifer shot back. "You've outlasted Twinkies, concrete, and probably cockroaches. You're not getting away from us anytime soon."

They continued their easy banter while the airlock cycled and the roamer took them back to the *Enora*.

They left the airship at the landing strip on the edge of town and walked to Defense Force HQ. The center of Salem felt like a ghost town despite the bustle of administrators and committee members. Sarah Jennifer put it down to the dearth of uniforms around the place. That changed once they entered the military complex around the former town hall.

Izzy met them at the requisitions depot. She had her back to them, too busy yelling at the men and women loading a truck with crates to notice their arrival. There was another truck that was already loaded off to the side.

"Move your sorry asses! If the major gets here before

we're done, it's going to be shit duty for you all for the next forty-eight hours!"

"Should we wait?" Esme murmured so only Sarah Jennifer could hear.

Sarah Jennifer shook her head. "A healthy fear of the QM is a good thing. They look to be almost done. We'll walk slowly."

The last crate was loaded as they reached Izzy's position in the yard.

The acting lieutenant whirled when her underlings snapped to attention. "You heard that? I apologize for my language, Major."

Sarah Jennifer waved the apology off. "There are situations where it's called for. This is one of them. I take it this is our consignment?"

Izzy nodded. "Yes, Major. All loaded and ready to go. I'll have the trucks taken out to the airstrip and get the crates loaded before you're ready to leave."

Sarah Jennifer tilted her head. "We're leaving right away."

Izzy's reply was cut off by a familiar voice.

"Sarah Jennifer!" Sarai called. "You're here! *Good!*"

Sarah Jennifer wasn't sure she liked her cousin-in-law's tone.

Sarai ran down the steps of the main building with all three of her children in tow. "You're heading to Mars?"

Sarah Jennifer couldn't miss the backpacks she and Jody had slung over their backs. "Yes. Why?"

Sarai flashed a bright grin, her curls bobbing in the breeze. "We're coming with you."

Sarah Jennifer's jaw dropped. "You're *what*, now?"

Izzy stepped away from them in an attempt to make herself scarce.

"Stay right where you are, Acting Lieutenant," Sarah Jennifer snapped. "You knew about this?"

"Well, they were hardly going to get their belongings loaded without my knowledge," Izzy replied sheepishly.

Sarai breezed by them, ushering Macey and Tori into the waiting truck. "Don't take it out on Izzy. Six months is too long to be separated from Brutus. Jody needs to be with his father. I'm not leaving any of my children, so we're all going."

Esme chuckled. "I don't think you're getting a choice, Duckie."

Sarah Jennifer had a hundred reasons why this was a bad idea. And two in the balancing column that outweighed them all. Unlike Cherie, who had a grand-mother who had already raised two Were boys to take care of her, Jody really did need his father, and Sarai's affinity for agriculture would be invaluable in the terraforming effort.

Still...

She caught Sarai's arm. "You know the city isn't going to be habitable for months? You'll be living at Habitat One. There will be no time without suits. Cramped quarters and rations. You'll be stuck with the pack around the clock, and you'll be working twice as hard as everyone else with three children to take care of alongside your duties."

Sarai laughed. "I know exactly what I'm getting into. I spoke to Brutus—who doesn't know about this yet, so don't tell him. Six months is too long for us to be apart. Jody is getting closer to his first shift. I can't deprive him of his pack right now. As a mother, I know it's the right thing. Besides, don't tell me they couldn't use me up there. The only witch better with nature than me is my mother. We won't be on rations for long."

"What does Annie have to say about this?" Esme cut in.

Sarai shrugged, fleeting sadness obscuring her smile for a moment. "She's going to miss us, but she understands. I have Jana and Janie covering the hospital. Everything is arranged."

Sarah Jennifer dropped a hand to her hip. "You thought of everything, huh?"

Jody stuck his head out the truck window. "Aunt SJ, we *are* going, right?"

Sarah Jennifer saw the gleam of yellow in his eyes, a sure sign his wolf was going to make an appearance soon. She sighed. "Yes, Jody. You can go."

He whooped with joy.

The girls peered out the window at them with big eyes. They were too young to understand the changes that were coming, but they would soon adjust. Children had the resilience most adults strived for.

Sarai hugged Sarah Jennifer. "Thank you," she whispered. "I'm sorry to spring this on you, but I didn't see any other way you'd agree."

Sarah Jennifer huffed. "Well, you got your way. You can drive that truck. Acting Lieutenant, you can drive the other. I'm not feeling especially fond of either of you right now. I'm going to walk to the landing strip. I expect the crates to be loaded by the time I get there."

"Yes, ma'am," Izzy mumbled.

Sarai hopped into the truck and drove out of the yard after Izzy.

Esme chuckled. "I can't wait to see Brutus' reaction."

Sarah Jennifer shook her head. "I'm going to call him as soon as we're airborne. Sarai might want to surprise Brutus, but the pack needs to make arrangements for their arrival."

### Mars, Reynolds Plain, Habitat One

Brutus and the elder Ace waited for the *Enora* at the landing site with a trio of general-purpose bots.

Ace watched Brutus pace the walkway without offering a comment. The news that Sarai and the children were on their way had hit Brutus hard. Ace supposed he would have been just as agitated had Tamara decided to bring Cherie up here, seeing as they were still living out of the shipping containers that made up Habitat One.

At this moment, Linus and Dinny were clearing out one of the containers previously assigned to storage since they were the only spaces large enough to fit a family, while Reg and Katia scoured the base for furniture.

The speaker over the hatch crackled. "Lieutenant, I have just received word from Enora. The ship has just broken atmosphere over the northern plain."

Brutus quit pacing at the EI's announcement. "Thank you, Galileo. Initiate airlock procedures and inform Enora we are waiting."

"Airlock cycle initiated," Galileo intoned. "Transfer tunnel extending in fifteen seconds."

"I'll get out there, then." Ace sealed his suit and stepped

out of the access hatch. The bots followed him across the packed dirt as the transfer tunnel snaked out on its runners beside them.

The *Enora* came into sight a few moments later, her body catching the light of the midafternoon sun. She swooped in, looking as magnificent as the day she was launched.

Brutus sealed his suit, then resumed his pacing until Galileo had connected the transfer tunnel to the drop bay doors. He hurried along the tunnel, eager to hold his family in his arms again despite the thought of his *very* active children running loose around the habitat giving him gooseflesh.

The girls ran out in their tiny pressure suits, squealing, "*DADDYYYYYY!*"

"How are my preciouses?" Brutus scooped them up, one in each arm, as Sarai and Jody followed.

"We went in space!" Macey squealed.

"I gotta spacesuit, Daddy!" Tori blurted.

Their faces were flushed with excitement inside their hoods. Brutus swung them around. "That's my girls. Let me see your brother." He put them down. "No running wild now, you hear?"

He took a knee to greet his son, putting his hands on the boy's shoulders. "How you doing, kiddo?"

Jody shuffled in that awkward way preteens have. He met his father's eyes, revealing the yellow shine that was there most of the time now. "I'm okay. Missed you, Dad." His voice slid around as he spoke.

Brutus' eyes stung with the emotions welling up. He pulled Jody into a hug, all his misgivings washed away by the gratitude in his son's expression. "You're here now, son. *I'm* here. We stick together, okay? Linus is getting our quarters ready. Go find him. Galileo will help." He smiled. "Did your mom tell you we wear our suits at all times?"

Jody nodded. "Yes, sir. Hoods ready to deploy, no helmets while we're inside. Helmets on while we're outdoors."

They heard Linus' voice up ahead and the girls squealing happily.

"Looks like Linus heard you arrived," Brutus commented wryly. "He gets too much joy out of being the fun uncle."

"Make sure your sisters don't get into a pickle," Sarai told Jody, putting a soothing hand on his shoulder. "I want to talk to your father."

"Stay out of the labs!" Brutus added as Jody caught up with the girls, and the three of them vanished into the habitat. He waited until the children were out of earshot. "I'm not mad at you."

Sarai dropped her defensive pose. "You sure?"

Brutus took her hand, and they walked into the habitat together. "All honesty, I was scared at first. It's hard living out here."

Sarai laughed. "Bethany Anne's people lived in containers when they first went to space. If they could get along, so can we."

Brutus pulled his hood off to kiss her. "I'll be in as soon as SJ has gone. Linus will show you our quarters."

Sarai cupped his face in her hands. "I'll just follow the sound of our noisy children."

Brutus released her reluctantly and resealed his suit

before heading out the hatch and walking over to where Sarah Jennifer was supervising the unloading.

Sarah Jennifer offered him a wry smile. "Hey, cuz. What, no coffee?"

Brutus snorted. "You don't deserve coffee after springing this on me."

Sarah Jennifer laughed. "Springing it on *you?*" She recounted Sarai's method of getting her permission to transfer here, to Brutus' amusement. "But enough of that. I brought coffee, tea, sugar, chocolate, milk powder—"

"The sooner we can get cows here, the better," Brutus grumbled.

Sarah Jennifer smiled. "That reminds me. Izzy cleared out the freezers at HQ, too."

"Steak?" Ace asked hopefully.

"I have no idea," Sarah Jennifer admitted. "Whatever was in there before harvest, she had it packed up."

"I miss steak," Ace murmured as he got the bots moving.

Brutus had a hankering for lamb. He'd hidden a few shanks at the back of the freezers, knowing his favorite meat would get scarce before winter arrived. "You and Esme going to take a look around the construction site before you leave?"

Sarah Jennifer shook her head, explaining the situation at New Romanov. "We need to get back sooner rather than later. Is there anything that needs my attention?"

"I've got everything running mostly to schedule," Brutus told her. "There were a few snags with the appliance printers, but they'll be resolved before the build gets that far. Thought you might wanna take a look at the park, though. Carver's team got the arti-forest outside the city up and running a couple days ago. Jim's projections have us breathing the air as soon as four weeks from now, and that was before Sarai got here. Stella might actually get off my damn back about increasing her team's share of the oxygen once Sarai does her thing."

Sarah Jennifer chuckled, patting Brutus on the arm. "You can deal with Stella. We'll do a flyover of the park on our way out."

Brutus nodded. "Then I guess I'll see you in six months."

Sarah Jennifer pulled him in for a hug. "You call me if you need anything, and I'll figure a way to get here."

She returned to the cockpit and took her seat while Enora went through the preflight checklist. "I want to fly over Promessa, Enora. Adjust our exit route to account for it, please."

"Done," Enora confirmed. "I would like to see the city take shape."

"You and me both," Esme concurred.

"That makes three of us." Sarah Jennifer leaned forward and slapped the console. "Let's go already."

Enora vacated the viewscreen and turned it over to an external camera view as they lifted off. The three of them were quiet as the landscape of Mars opened up beneath the ship.

The rolling red plain ended abruptly as they flew over the agricultural sector, barren sands replaced by rows of raised mounds in the Hügelkultur style that were interlaid with Stella's oxygen delivery system. Similar to the air diffusers used in hydroponic systems, the pipes fed a continuous mixture of gases that approximated Earth's air into the ag sector and made growing possible in the low-oxygen environment.

Sarah Jennifer saw the agricultural teams hard at work in the fields, maintaining the mounds and monitoring the water reclamation stations. Every thirty feet, the fields were broken up by the stations that were simply made from a plastic box, a Perspex sheet, and a small tarp. Jim refused to claim credit for the technique, which he'd told Sarah Jennifer was handed down by Alaskan homesteaders from before WWDE.

More than ever, waste was not something they accepted. Their environment had to be made to work for them, and they had to make the most of every gain on the road to Mars being made habitable.

The city came into sight a few minutes later. They had opted to forgo walls since the threat level was practically zero. Instead, the edge of Promessa was closed in by the arti-forest. Beyond the tree line, the city was beginning to take shape.

Enora banked and slowed to get the best view of the buildings and open spaces set out on a grid below. Most of the partially completed buildings were the same blush color as the Martian soil. The pale mud plaster protected the metal sidings and printed fab-wood frames from the weather. In the sectors that were close to being completed, the walls contrasted pinkly with the green areas.

The park was everything Brutus had hinted at. Tall faux-oaks jostled for space with artificial pines, alders, sycamores, and a dozen other models Carver's team had produced and "planted." Real grass grew everywhere that wasn't paved, brushing up against the banks of the water-ways and ponds.

Already, the open park was providing a place for people to come together during their time off. People lay on blankets, just as Sarah Jennifer had imagined the day they'd broken ground on the project.

In short, Promessa was shaping up to its name.

Sarah Jennifer smiled as Enora turned her nose to the stars. The trials on Earth aside, the future was looking as rosy as the city below.

# CHAPTER FOURTEEN

**New Romanov**

Olaf and Theor were in the command tent in the center of the camp, which stretched in a continuous line for three kilometers on either side of the mountain.

Most of the Weres had arrived from the Americas, and their camps filled the spaces between the Siberian, Finnish, and Swedish warrior bands.

Olaf had burned a few bridges to secure the cooperation of some and had called in every old favor and leaned on every obligation going back to before WWDE. He had pleaded, cajoled, and outright threatened where necessary to get the warriors here. Even the communities who traditionally remained cut off from the outside world had offered up their warriors to hold the defensive line against the encroaching Mad. Everyone in Siberia owed Olaf or Boris for one reason or another.

What they were facing was no skirmish. As well as the Mad they could track, Lilith had learned from Ezekiel that more were coming from the west, seemingly following the dirigible he and his company were sailing. Amelie was out on the tundra to the west, working with her mages to bring a snowstorm in from the estuaries that would delay the ravening hordes for a few more hours. The Defense Force was out with Reika's warriors and rock mages, shaping the land and laying mines and other nasties to further slow the progress of the Mad heading their way from the south and east.

A steady stream of scouts had been reporting to the tent where the two Weres bent over the table spread with maps and tokens representing the various groups who had come through snow and hail to make their stand against the destruction threatening Arkhangelsk, Siberia, and the entire world.

The most recent scout to report in left to get a good meal before she went back out into the snow. Olaf and Theor remained to contend with the final battle plans as sent by Sarah Jennifer.

Theor's brow was creased in concentration. "We can hold them off until dawn, perhaps."

"Perhaps," Olaf agreed. "Still, we should—"

The tent flaps were flung back, and a statuesque blonde woman with cheekbones that looked like they could cut diamond stormed in, her blue eyes flashing with anger. "There's a disturbance in the Etheric west of the Mountain. *That's* what's drawing the damned Mad here!"

The news knocked Olaf for six. "What do you mean, Mika? What kind of disturbance?"

The ice maiden flung out her sword arm. "Come see for yourself. It cannot be described."

The Weres exchanged concerned glances before shifting. Olaf had the forethought to snag a radio in his mighty jaws before pushing his way out of the tent.

Theor howled, scenting sickness not of this world coming from north of the mountain. Olaf smelled it too. He roared and grabbed Mika in his paws, tossing her up onto his back.

Mika, to her credit, didn't stab him. She grasped his thick fur and leaned into the wind as Olaf and Theor ran for the source, backtracking her path through the forest, flinging up the snow as their paws ate up the distance.

They reached the Urai warriors' camp on the western flank of the defensive line and pulled to a stop, spraying snow in a wide arc.

Mika dismounted, and the Weres shifted back.

The first thing they noticed was the lack of sound from the forest. The taiga was normally full of creatures of the night competing to be heard over one another.

There was nothing, not even an insect.

Mika didn't need to point out the anomaly. Olaf and Theor looked up without saying a word. Neither of them had ever seen anything like the crack in the sky. It crackled with spitting energy, spilling dark, loathsome light that pushed away the night.

"What is it?" Mika asked, her voice cutting through the silence.

Olaf had no answer. Neither did Theor.

"What do we do?" Theor murmured, a chill that had nothing to do with the temperature running down his spine.

Olaf's skin crawled as the utter *wrongness* of the

anomaly seeped into his bones. "This is beyond us," he told them.

Without warning, a mental scream tore through their minds.

"The Oracle!" Mika exclaimed.

Olaf tossed the radio to Theor and dashed back the way they'd come, calling over his shoulder, "Call the major. I need to get to Lilith."

***

Inside the mountain, Lilith's connection to Ezekiel was cut suddenly and without warning, leaving him alone to navigate Amelie's storm.

Lilith felt pain for the first time since she had been wrenched from her body and stuffed into the machinery that supported her consciousness. She cried out as the sensation of being pierced by icepicks penetrated her entire being.

Every attempt to reach out to Sarah Jennifer, Esme, and Ezekiel was crushed by another wave of crystal-sharp pain as the entity attacking her severed her mental connections with brutal efficiency.

Lilith had no idea where the pain was coming from or how she could escape it. She was helpless, her consciousness pinned and bound. Each second stretched out into eternity. Her efforts to break free only tightened the trap she was in.

All she could do was scream.

The cavern reverberated with feedback from the speakers as her voice ratcheted up in agonized octaves.

Somewhere in the needle-sharp constriction of her mind, she heard familiar laughter. Barely able to think, she couldn't pinpoint who the voice belonged to, only that she recognized it.

Lilith screamed again, barely aware of the humans entering her cavern. A sudden memory sliced through the barrier of pain as her attacker laughed again.

Her attacker was Kurtherian.

As she had the realization, she heard a voice.

*Too late, Peace-Through-Superior-Genetics. Your heresy has earned you death.*

---

Olaf bounded up the mountain on four paws, his heart pounding as Lilith's screams cut through the night. He barreled past the guards at the main entrance and pounded down the tunnel, still in bear form.

Reaching the central cavern, his first reaction on seeing Pietro and the other recovered Mad surrounding the casing that held Lilith was that they had relapsed and were responsible for the Kurtherian's suffering.

He roared, rearing up on his hind legs to tear them limb from limb.

They fell to their knees, faces upturned, and he saw through his rage that their eyes were not red and they were just as scared as he was.

He pulled back his attack just in time, shifting on the spot. "What happened here?" he demanded, his tone sharp with anger.

"We don't know!" Pietro swore. "We heard her

screaming and came up, but there is no enemy that we can see."

Olaf vaguely understood how the Etheric engine worked. He rushed to the wall and tore off the panel hiding the manual connections to the machine. Whatever was going on externally, this would give him a connection to her innermost psyche. "Get me a headset!" he commanded. "The drawers to the left."

Marlon was closest. He rummaged in the drawer to find one and handed it to Olaf. "Save her, please," he begged. "She's done so much for us. She doesn't deserve this."

Olaf jammed the headset jack into the control panel and fumbled the headset on. "Lilith, can you hear me?"

The cavern shook with her screams, but Olaf heard her voice, small and exhausted.

"Help me. Laughter is killing me."


## Over the Petersburg Estuary

Ezekiel had lost his connection to Lilith suddenly.

He knew his way home from here; that wasn't a concern. However, he was left wondering what could have wrenched the Kurtherian out of his mind so abruptly.

Below, the Mad surged toward the mountain in their thousands, drawn by the Etheric disturbance that felt to him like wearing wet socks on his soul even from this distance.

He remained in place at the helm, sitting cross-legged as he had done since Lilith had contacted him to guide them over the storm Amelie and her people had created to slow down the hordes.

His attempts to reconnect to Lilith had failed. Again he reached out, and his mental connection had all the efficacy of a grappling hook tossed two feet too short.

"Did we lose them?" Kain called.

Ezekiel left the answer to Caitlin. His stomach lurched as she abruptly dropped the dirigible twenty feet into a break in the storm.

They weren't losing the Mad. He hadn't told the crew what they were heading into, trusting that the evidence of their eyes would inform them of the severity of the situation.

Caitlin and the crew believed they were drawing the Mad, but even without the temptation of an easy meal should the dirigible land, the infected would still be moving inexorably toward Lilith's haven.

Ezekiel was wracked with fear for the people preparing to meet the hordes head-on. His hope was that Mary-Anne would be lucid when they arrived and that Esme would have the fix for her Madness ready so the vampire could join them in the coming battle. He heard Caitlin and Kain conversing quietly.

"Do you think he's okay?" Caitlin murmured.

"He's gotten us this far, hasn't he?" Kain was not the voice of doom for once. "He's even managed to keep Ma in check. Do you really think that now is the time to start doubting him?"

Hope was a slender thread, fraying with the weight of reality.

Ezekiel had expended untold amounts of energy

keeping Mary-Anne under control, even going so far as to share his blood with her in an attempt to hold back the rising Madness after she had escaped from belowdecks and almost killed Caitlin.

Luckily, he had pulled himself out of his mental connection with Lilith just in time and taken control of her the same way he had Helena.

Matriarch, the pain of losing Helena was a fire consuming him from the inside out. It gave him the determination he needed to keep pouring his energy into pulling Mary-Anne back from the brink each time she teetered on the edge of no return.

The vampire was currently belowdecks, strapped to a bench since they'd passed over the former Danelaw. Every now and then, he heard the tinkling of the little bell Caitlin had given her to get their attention when she was lucid.

The only thing Ezekiel could concentrate on was his fear for Lilith and the growing pull of twisted energy he'd picked up coming from his homeland.

Caitlin took the dirigible back up above the clouds, cutting off their view of the Mad below.

Ezekiel swallowed his pride and reached out. The connection he sought was faint, as though his mentor was farther away than he'd thought possible. He faltered, unable to say anything.

*Is that you, laddie?*

Esme's no-nonsense burr warmed his heart despite his misgivings. *Yes,* he managed. *It's me.*

*Well, it's about damn time you got in touch! Are you in New Romanov yet?*

Ezekiel frowned. *I thought* you *were in New Romanov?*

*I'm not even on Earth right now.*

Ezekiel was quiet for a long moment. *Esme, something is wrong with Lilith. I think she's in trouble. There's something going on there. I can sense something bad in the Etheric.*

There was silence, then Esme returned, concern coloring her voice. *You're right. She's in grave danger. We're on our way. How far out are you?*

*Still a few hundred miles,* he told her.

*Get there as fast as that bucket of bolts will take you,* Esme instructed. *We'll meet you there.*

Ezekiel spent the remainder of the journey with anxiety twisting like snakes in his stomach.

He forgot that Caitlin had his radio, not that it would help unless he put the insides back together. He spoke only to give her course corrections, guiding the dirigible toward the malignant energy he felt coming from New Romanov.

The hordes of Mad thinned as they crossed into Arkhangelsk, but Ezekiel knew appearances were deceptive. He felt them advancing on Lilith's mountain in huge numbers, hidden by the taiga.

His companions had no connection to the Etheric to tell them differently.

Caitlin leaned back with her hands still on the wheel, looking over her shoulder at Kain. "Can you see any?"

Kain was leaning over the rail. "No more than usual. A small smattering here or there. I think we may have finally shaken off the bulk of them."

"Good." Caitlin's relief was clear to them all. "Good."

There was a moment of danger when they passed over Amelie's position at the head of the estuary.

Ezekiel sent a quick mental greeting to ensure the water mage didn't have her storm take them out.

Amelie's reply was laced with laughter. *Talk about good timing. You're getting here just in time for the battle. There are Mad coming from the East and the South.*

*There are more following behind us,* Ezekiel warned. *Don't let up just yet.*

*Good to know,* Amelie told him.

*You could give us a favorable wind,* Ezekiel returned. *Lilith is in danger. She needs my help.*

"Whoa!" Caitlin called as the wind shifted.

"Go with it," Ezekiel told her. "We're getting some help."

*Thank you, Amelie,* he sent.

The tailwind provided by the trade mistress drove the dirigible on. They passed over the Northern Dvina and he had Caitlin adjust their heading again, turning them north-northwest and into the mountains.

All too soon, the abandoned towns south of New Romanov were to their rear, and the peaks began to rise around them. Ezekiel opened his eyes. He knew this land by heart. It spoke to his soul. The snow and pines were the landscape that filled his dreams.

In the near distance, Lilith's mountain loomed over the rest, its purple-black body topped by a snowy cap that grazed the heavens.

The dirigible sailed over the valley, getting ever closer.

Ezekiel jumped to his feet. "Lower!"

Caitlin obeyed, bringing the dirigible down as she steered over the foothills.

"*Lower!*" Ezekiel commanded, his eyes blazing red as the urge to get to Lilith increased. He felt the Kurtherian's pain but was still unable to connect from this distance.

New Romanov was a speck beneath them.

"Down!" Ezekiel roared as the reason for the pain that was wracking Lilith became clear. He sensed an alien entity in the malignant energy blanketing the mountains.

The entity also sensed him.

"Where?" Kain retorted. "It's uneven as hell down there! Where are we supposed to land?"

Ezekiel didn't answer. He was fending off the alien entity, which was trying to gain access to his mind and magic.

"Ezekiel!" Kain's voice rose in frustration. "Can you hear me?"

The storm suddenly cleared as they broke the wall of Amelie's defenses.

Below, Kain saw the vast army gathered behind huge icy ramparts in preparation for meeting the Mad coming their way. "What the…"

Ezekiel didn't hear him. He was concentrating on fighting off the entity. His attention only returned to what was going on around him when the wind, no longer controlled by Amelie's people, battered the dirigible.

"Down!" he yelled, the gale stealing his voice.

Caitlin dropped the dirigible lower, narrowly avoiding crashing into the side of the mountain.

Jaxon ran loose, barking as he darted from one side of the deck to the other. The faithful animal sensed the Mad.

Kain caught the German Shepherd as the dirigible lurched under Caitlin's inexpert control. "Slow down, Kitty-Cat! We can't take this!"

Ezekiel knew there wasn't a moment to waste. "*Down!*"

"*BRACE!*" Caitlin yelled as the wheel pulled out of her grasp.

She caught the spinning wheel, almost being flung over the rail in the process. Somehow, she tamed it, bringing the dirigible back under her control before they crashed.

She knew they weren't going to get much farther. Something had given in the controls, and steering was not as responsive. Caitlin felt like she was wrestling with the dirigible rather than piloting it. She lashed herself to the wheel even as Kain tied himself and Jaxon off with a length of rope.

They were losing altitude rapidly, and Ezekiel wasn't doing much besides providing a red light on the deck as his eyes shone with expended magic.

Whatever the magic was, it wasn't being worked to save them from crashing.

Caitlin heaved on the wheel, forcing the nose of the dirigible to point at a frozen lake in the valley below as Kain moaned with the nausea rolling his stomach.

The dirigible hit the ice, and the sound of wood splintering filling their ears.

Everyone was thrown to the limits of the ropes tethering them to the deck. Everyone but Ezekiel.

The crew swarmed out from belowdecks as the dirigible began to sink.

Ezekiel remained in place, his eyes still shining red as he redirected his magic and froze the surface of the lake before they could be sucked into its icy depths.

He made his way to the deck, where he found Caitlin, Kain, and Jaxon.

"We're here," he told them.

Caitlin pulled her cloak tighter around herself. "What now?"

Ezekiel pointed at the mountain. "We go save Lilith."

Without further explanation, he vaulted the rail and set off running across the ice.

Caitlin looked at Kain in dismay. "How are we going to get Ma there without his magic?"

"I'm not baggage," the vampire snarked, emerging from the gondola. "I'll walk."

Caitlin and Kain whirled at the sound of her voice.

Mary-Anne smiled. "I'm not Mad. Not completely. Not yet." She took a running leap over the railing. "What are you waiting for?" she called over her shoulder. "Let's go!"

They caught up with Ezekiel just before he reached the road at the foot of the mountain.

"Why the rush?" Caitlin asked with more than a little annoyance.

"Can't you feel it?" Mary-Anne answered with a shiver. "Something freaky is going down here."

Ezekiel waved them on. "We need to hurry. Lilith is under attack by whatever is causing the Etheric to feel so...wrong."

Having learned more about the Kurtherian on the journey, his companions were puzzled by what could attack her.

"I don't know either," Ezekiel told them. He pointed out a group of people dressed in black uniforms at the foot of the mountain. "The Defense Force. Don't do anything stupid. They have guns."

"Like Royland's pistol?" Kain inquired.

"No," Ezekiel answered. "Weapons you couldn't imagine existed in this world. But try to, knowing they can fire three rounds per second might persuade your wolf that getting into a dominance match with these Weres is a bad idea."

Before Kain could argue, the area was flooded with light from above.

They all looked up as the *Enora* swooped overhead.

"What the fuck was that?" Caitlin demanded.

"A *real* airship," Ezekiel told her, his anxiety doubling as the thought of facing his past became unavoidable. "The *Enora*. Sarah Jennifer and Esme are here."

# CHAPTER FIFTEEN

"I picked up Ezekiel's Etheric signature as we came in," Esme informed Sarah Jennifer as they exited the airship.

Sarah Jennifer's heart lurched. *Don't yell at him when you see him,* she told herself sternly. "Enora, be ready to bring Amelie and her people in, please."

A tortured scream echoed from the belly of the mountain, cutting off the AI's reply.

"Lilith first, Esme. Ezekiel can wait." Sarah Jennifer set off across the plateau at a run, heading for the tunnel.

The two of them hurried to the main chamber, where they found Olaf and the recovered Mad surrounding Lilith's casing. Olaf slipped the headset off and offered it to Sarah Jennifer with a severe expression creasing his features. "I can't hear her anymore."

Esme shooed everyone out of the way and got to work opening the casing. Her eyes glowed golden and the bolts holding the casing closed spun in place and fell out, landing with soft pings that were lost beneath the screams coming from the speakers.

Sarah Jennifer rammed the headset on as Esme laid hands on the Etheric engine.

"Can either of you reach her?" Olaf fretted. "She spoke only once, and she wasn't making much sense."

Sarah Jennifer couldn't hear Lilith even with the headset. Her friend was too far gone, her mind unreachable. She pulled the headset off and pinned Olaf with a hard stare. "What did she say? Tell me exactly."

"That laughter was killing her," Olaf replied with confusion. "Like I said, she wasn't making any sense. She's not laughing, she's being tortured in there."

Esme's eyes flashed as she forced a connection to the Kurtherian's psyche and was thrown back by the interloper, but not before she caught a mental glimpse of their enemy. She crashed into the wall, breaking her ribs. "Not laughter," she gasped. "*Laughter*. Laughter-Brings-Meaning-To-Life."

"What?" Sarah Jennifer almost dropped the headset when she heard the name of Lilith's old rival. "The Kurtherian? *How?*"

"I don't know how," Esme grunted, pulling herself to a sitting position as she healed her injuries. "I just know she's in there, hurting our Lilith, and I mean to force the bitch out before she kills her."

Sarah Jennifer's eyes flashed red, and her wolf threatened to take over as anger flooded her. "Does this have anything to do with the Etheric energy we felt as we came in?" Her words came out in a low growl. "What can I do? I can't reach her!"

"You can go to the disturbance and stop Laughter there. She must have torn a rift between here and whatever hell-planet she's on," Esme answered, picking herself up off the floor. "I've got this. Take Olaf and get over there. Send the boy in. He's dithering outside."

"Olaf, let's go." Sarah Jennifer pelted from the cavern with Olaf hard on her heels.

They almost collided with Ezekiel's group at the mouth of the tunnel.

Sarah Jennifer's senses tingled when she scented the Were in the group. There was something different about him. She was drawn to every Were since it was part of her magic, but this was...something else.

Kain stepped forward, his head lowered in respect for the aura of power that surrounded her. "You're the Alpha. I'm Kain."

Sarah Jennifer realized what was different about him. "You're a Pricolici."

Kain was taken aback. "That's right."

Sarah Jennifer shook her head to clear the distraction his scent was causing her and turned to Ezekiel. "Ezekiel, you're needed below."

Ezekiel nodded. "Sarah Jennifer—"

She cut him off with a wave. "Not now, Ezekiel. Esme needs you down there." She turned her attention to Caitlin and Kain. "You two, with me. Vamp-lady, you have a Pod-doc waiting for you."

Mary-Anne opened her mouth to argue, but Sarah Jennifer pointed at the entrance, her face set in determined lines. "If you go Mad, my men will kill you, and we won't have a vampire in the fight. Pod-doc *now*, or I'll shoot you myself and have them drag you down there."

The Weres standing guard at the entrance tensed, their hands moving to their rifles.

Caitlin and Mary-Anne looked at Ezekiel, who shrugged. "Meet the major. Come with me, Ma."

"You don't know me well enough to call me that," Mary-Anne snapped. Then she sighed. "Fine. Lead the way, *Zeke*."

Ezekiel narrowed his eyes at the vampire before turning to put his hand on Sarah Jennifer's arm. "I'll be here, waiting. It's good to see you."

Sarah Jennifer swallowed the lump in her throat as she returned the gesture. "You too, kiddo. Now, scram."

Ezekiel took Mary-Anne's arm and they darted into the tunnel, leaving Caitlin and Kain standing uncomfortably.

Jaxon sniffed Sarah Jennifer's hand and licked it.

Sarah Jennifer petted the dog's head. "You're a good boy, huh?"

Caitlin looked at Kain and shrugged. "If Jax likes her…"

"People, we do not have time for waffling," Sarah Jennifer told them sternly. "Get your behinds in gear. We have a situation here. Olaf, lead the way."

Olaf was in the process of stripping. He shuffled out of his pants and bundled his clothing before shifting.

"Whoa…" Caitlin's eyes widened as the werebear rose to his full height before leaping off the side of the road into the snow-covered undergrowth.

Sarah Jennifer paused only to relieve one of the Weres standing guard at the tunnel entrance of his rifle and ammunition belt before following Olaf without so much as a glance back at Kain and Caitlin.

Jaxon plowed after them, barking spiritedly.

"What has the kid dragged us into?" Kain asked. Internally, his wolf growled at him, unhappy Sarah Jennifer was out of his sight. He'd never had this reaction to another Alpha. Maybe she was just *that* powerful.

He wondered what her wolf looked like and if she was a Pricolici like him.

Caitlin nudged Kain, dispelling his daydream. "Only one way to find out," she told him as she hopped down from the road.

Kain was slow to respond.

"You coming?" Caitlin asked, looking up at him from the ditch.

Kain caught himself and laughed. "Sure thing, Kitty-Cat."

Ezekiel and Mary-Anne ran toward Lilith's cavern with the Kurtherian's screams rebounding off the walls around him.

Esme looked the worse for wear when he entered the main cavern.

Bruised and bleeding from her nose, the witch turned from the Etheric engine as Pietro reacted to his presence. "It's okay," she told the Were. "This is Ezekiel. Laddie, am I glad to see you! Help me, here."

Ezekiel knelt by Esme. "What's happening?"

"She's being attacked by another Kurtherian," Esme explained. "We have to force the enemy out of her mind, or she's going to die."

All the pain Ezekiel had been holding in since Helena's

death surfaced in a torrent. His eyes blazed red as his tenuous grip on his magic was lost.

Mary-Anne yelped in surprise as the energy surged out of him.

Esme noticed the vampire for the first time. "You're the Mad one. Go." She pointed at another exit. "Third exit off that tunnel. You'll see a room with a silver box inside. That's the Pod-doc. It's ready for you."

Mary-Anne nodded. "I know what a Pod-doc is." She edged around Ezekiel, suddenly wary of the power she hadn't understood he wielded. "Good luck saving the Kurtherian."

Ezekiel heard none of the exchange. His mind was focused on Lilith, on his determination that he would not lose another person he loved. *Not on his watch.*

His entire world shrank down to his effort to connect to Lilith. There was another entity blocking him, a cold, evil presence preventing him from reaching her.

Pain bloomed in his head as the entity split her—he sensed she was female—consciousness between him and Lilith.

He felt Esme's hands on his shoulders, her mind wrapping around his to insulate him from the attack.

*Get her,* she murmured into his mind. *Get her good.*

Ezekiel found himself in a battle for his life. He didn't care. His need, his desire, his entire focus was centered on freeing Lilith from the spiderweb of Etheric energy permeating the circuits of her life support system.

*You'll never defeat me,* a cackling alien voice declared. *You are weak. Insignificant. I am Kurtherian. You are nothing compared to me. I am superior to you in every way.*

*You are going to die.* Ezekiel ground his teeth and redoubled his will to sever the mental chains the alien entity had flung around Lilith's psyche. He had anger on his side. More, he had faith. Everything Esme had taught him about strength of will had been in preparation for this moment.

The laughter faded. The alien's voice cut into his mind. *Give up. You will fail, and I will kill you along with the heretic. Earth will be mine, and it will burn at my command.*

*You can fucking try it,* Ezekiel snarled, feeling Lilith still fighting to break free despite her pain. *You are losing against one human. What do you think you're going to do against a planet full of us?*

*Surrender,* the Kurtherian told him, her voice seductive. *Surrender, and live. You are powerful. I will grant you a place by my side, and you may rule Earth as my vassal. This is your alternative.*

Visions of destruction raced through Ezekiel's mind, placed there by the Kurtherian. New Romanov on fire. People dying by the millions. He saw himself on a throne, his eyes dulled by cruelty and the people of the world bowing at his feet while the Madness raged unchecked.

Ezekiel ignored the sickening visions. *I am human,* he ground out. *I don't give up. I don't give in. I might fall, I might fail, but I will never, ever surrender!*

*Fool!* the Kurtherian crowed. *Then die with the rest of your pathetic species!*

Ezekiel heard the note of fear in her voice. He saw that her weakness was arrogance and that in her arrogance, she had not bothered to protect herself against having her attack turned back on her.

He followed the psychic attack to the source. Suddenly,

he saw the enemy in his mind. He'd often wondered what Lilith had looked like before her body had been stolen from her. This Kurtherian was frail-looking, with gray skin stretched tight over a bony frame. Her face was round, with a pair of mandibles protruding in place of an upper lip.

*What are you doing?* Laughter screeched.

Ezekiel rebuffed her attempt to remove him from her mind and extended his reach to get a look at her surroundings through her eyes.

The Kurtherian cried out as he took control. She was inside something like a Pod-doc. The design was different from any he'd seen, but he knew the technology when he saw it.

Seizing his opportunity, he sent a pulse of Etheric energy through the connection. The shockwave sizzled along the bonds she'd put around Lilith, burning them away.

The laughing Kurtherian screamed.

*I'm free!* Lilith exulted. *It's not over, Ezekiel. Don't let Laughter escape!*

Too late, Laughter flung open the Pod-doc, severing the connection.

Ezekiel collapsed to the floor, drained. "Lilith, are you okay?" he mumbled, his head spinning.

Esme yelled with relief when the Kurtherian spoke.

Lilith's voice was weak but steady. "I will be fine, but Laughter-Brings-Meaning-To-Life is not done with us yet. She has opened a rift in the Etheric and means to send her soldiers through. I saw her plans. She has genetically modified aliens—huge, wild beasts—under her control. If they get through to our side, all will be lost."

Esme and Ezekiel looked at each other in dismay.

"Sarah Jennifer is out there with your friends." Esme pulled Ezekiel to his feet, pushing a wave of healing energy into his body. "Suck it up, my boy. We're not done fighting."

"Who will protect Lilith?" Ezekiel asked.

"Laughter will not catch me unaware a second time," Lilith vowed. "My only concern is for the nanocytes we have stored below."

"You can count on us to protect this mountain with our lives if necessary," Pietro swore. "Send the soldiers down from above. We'll protect Lilith and the nanocyte stores with our lives."

Esme nodded. "The vampire will be done with her Pod-doc treatment within the hour. She will be weak on completion, but a weak vampire is still twenty times deadlier than even the strongest Were. We need to get to the rift, Ezekiel. The mountain will be safe."

The radio crackled as they prepared to leave the cavern.

"Dammit, what now?" Esme swore loudly but answered, "Go ahead."

"Esme?" Theor sounded stressed. "We have contact with the Mad along the east boundary."

"You're going to have to deal with them without us," Esme responded. "We have an alien invasion to take care of."

Theor cursed. "Has this got anything to do with the split in the sky on the western line?" he asked.

"Smart man," Esme told him. "You've seen the rift?"

"Right before I was called here to deal with the Mad."

Esme closed her eyes and reached out to check the positions of the magic users along the line of defense. "Call Amelie. She has twelve mages with her and should be on the *Enora* any minute now. Block the Mad; do whatever you need to do to hold them back. I have to get out to the rift. Sarah Jennifer and Olaf are there without any magical support."

Esme's assessment of Sarah Jennifer's position was not strictly true.

Sarah Jennifer's grasp of magic had never been the strongest.

*Until now.*

She, Olaf, and the newcomers had arrived just as the rift birthed its first monster. Bright red, ten feet tall, and angry as hell, it had emerged horns-first and charged them. Almost simultaneously, the Mad had erupted from the forest in their hundreds.

Caitlin and the Urai warriors had formed a circle, while Kain had shifted into his Pricolici form and joined Olaf in defending the humans from the worst of it.

Those who have never seen real war are often misled into romanticizing it. There was nothing romantic about the ensuing chaos. The open space was filled with the screams of the dying. The Mad had no sense of self-preservation, and the living were attacked on both fronts. The dual stenches of blood and shit soon overcame everything else. Death abounded on all sides as the alien monster tore into the melee, uncaring whether those it killed were infected or not.

Sarah Jennifer emptied her rifle twice before realizing the monster was impervious to her bullets. She tossed the rifle aside and opened herself to the Etheric, necessity and her pragmatic nature taking over.

She *had* to believe.

And she found she did.

Unlike her failures in training, this moment, when all that mattered was her continued ability to protect the unenhanced and with the cold heat of battle upon her, the magic flowed.

Sarah Jennifer leapt over the rising rocks, drawing the monster out of the way of the warriors. Her eyes blazed red as she threw everything Esme had endeavored to teach her over the years at it.

The monster turned to her as if sensing the Etheric energy she was pulling.

"Come and get me, you big red bastard!" she screamed, pouring her energy into the command.

The monster roared and took a lumbering step toward her, unable to resist the compulsion. It lowered its head and splayed its jaws, emitting a bloodcurdling shriek that shook the ground.

Then it charged.

It was almost effortless. She taunted the monster with continued attacks as she backed up the slope, drawing it away from the battlefield. She shifted the rock beneath the alien's feet, pelted it with icicles the size of spears, and unleashed torrents of fire that sent the Mad around its feet running for cover.

The more energy she pulled from the Etheric, the more it offered her. She didn't have the finesse of Esme or Ezekiel, but she was never one to insist on a scalpel when a hammer would do the job just as well.

This monster—this *alien*—had no right to be on her planet. She had no compunction whatsoever about ending its existence.

The monster was bleeding from her sustained attacks; thick, dark blood streamed from its torso and limbs, staining its red skin black. Still, on it came, the claws on its feet scoring the earth as it advanced on her, ignoring everyone else.

Sarah Jennifer wished Esme were here to see that she had finally freed herself from the restrictions she'd placed upon herself in the name of a fair fight. She laughed bitterly as she realized the only thing that had prevented her from wielding magic on this scale before had been her reticence to take the lives of her fellow human beings.

The monster lowered its horns and charged again, its sudden burst of speed cutting her reverie short.

No matter. Sarah Jennifer was almost to the place she'd chosen as the monster's gravesite. She threw more fire and drew great shards of rock to fling at it as she continued her strategic retreat, slaloming around tree trunks as the land rose around her.

The monster gained speed, crashing through the ancient trees like they were matchsticks.

Sarah Jennifer reached her goal, where the sharp incline culminated in a sheer drop-off. The ravine beyond stretched almost a mile wide, cleaving the mountains. There was no way of knowing how deep it went.

The land on the other side rose sharply, the mountainside covered in loose scree and jagged boulders. She called to the rock, shaping it to her will as she ran to the edge of the cliff. The rock responded to her command, extending from the cliff edges on both sides to meet in the middle.

Sarah Jennifer ran across at full speed, knowing the bridge was strong enough to take her weight but not the monster's. She reached the other side and prepared to drop the bridge she'd created the moment her quarry had taken the bait.

"Just a little farther," she murmured as the monster charged without awareness of the danger. She pelted it with more fire, enraging it.

The monster didn't slow. It made it three steps onto the bridge.

Three steps and no more.

The bridge gave way at her command, and the monster screamed its rage as it plummeted, tearing great chunks out of the ravine walls with its claws in an attempt to arrest its fall.

Sarah Jennifer raised her arms and commanded every loose stone above her to fall. The mountain responded by shedding its load.

The noise was incredible, the rushing, roaring landslide overwhelming Sarah Jennifer's hearing. Her eardrums burst and healed, then burst again, but still, she held fast as rocks poured down on either side of her, crushing the monster beneath their massive weight.

Her hearing returned as the landslide tapered off. The monster's death cries echoed up from below, shaking more scree loose.

Sarah Jennifer responded by tearing free the deep-rooted rocks that hadn't fallen in the first landslide and sending them hurtling down into the ravine to ensure she'd done the job right.

She collapsed to her knees as the monster's cries faded, utterly exhausted.

This was what it felt like to do *real* battle magic? She was drained yet wired, her mind and body caught between needing to sleep immediately and feeling like she'd drunk enough coffee to power the entire Defense Force for a month.

She forced herself to stand. She had to get back across the ravine, and that meant using magic again.

The thought sent a shiver down her spine. She wasn't sure she had it in her. Her knees had been replaced by jelly, and her vision swam with black spots.

She looked across the void, seeing a small crowd had gathered, including Olaf, Esme, Ezekiel, and Ezekiel's new friends.

They were all staring at her in wonder.

Sarah Jennifer waved weakly, then her knees gave way, and she slumped to the ground as unconsciousness stole over her.

# CHAPTER SIXTEEN

While Sarah Jennifer was taking her unscheduled nap, Theor was putting everything he knew about battle to the test. His radio was jammed to his ear as he yelled instructions from his birds-eye view of the battlefield, directing the flow of the soldiers under his command.

Theor had risen to the rank of sergeant over the years and was no stranger to the monotony of logistics. Prior to joining the pack, he had always believed his strength lay in his sword arm. However, as in this instance, leadership meant putting into practice everything he'd learned about what it meant to fight using his mind.

The Finnish mages had joined him at his request and were working one to three with the warrior units along the eastern line as the Mad swarmed their defenses.

He heard the news that Sarah Jennifer was being brought back to the mountain and suppressed it, knowing full well what the news that their commander had been taken out would do for morale. He trusted that whatever had happened, she would recover given time. The major wasn't indestructible, but Death himself would have a hard time arguing with her if she wasn't ready to tap out—and she never was.

Theor concentrated on maintaining the barrier between the Mad and the mountain. He began to see a pattern in their movements, as though they weren't heading for the mountain itself but the strange tear in reality beyond.

That gave him an idea.

His only job was to protect the mountain and what lay within. He'd heard about the alien creature that had come from the rift and how it had been unable to discriminate between the living and the walking dead.

He lifted his radio and dialed in the open channel. "All commanders, listen up. The Mad are not trying to get to the mountain. I repeat, the Mad are not trying to get to the mountain. They are heading for the rift."

"What are your orders?" was the reply from multiple radios at once.

Theor considered before answering. If he was wrong, he was leaving the field wide open. However, he was almost a hundred percent sure he wasn't wrong. "Retrograde to defense point B for your unit," he told them. "Protect the towns, make sure they can't get to the mountain. Otherwise, let them pass. All magic users, do what you can to funnel them to the end of the line."

Inside the mountain, Mary-Anne awoke.

She opened her eyes as the Pod-doc lid was raised. She

heard multiple voices speaking and saw Caitlin and Kain peering in at her.

"Can't a girl wake up in peace?" she grumbled, smiling nevertheless. Looking around the room, she saw that the radio on the bedside cabinet was the source of the many voices.

Caitlin threw her arms around her, distracting her from the radio.

"Ma, you're...*you*."

Mary-Anne flashed her fangs, feeling better than she had in a long time. "You bet your skinny ass I am." She turned her attention to Kain. "No hug from the wolf?"

Kain laughed and allowed himself to be drawn into the huddle. "Good to have you back, Ma."

Mary-Anne looked around the room, smelling more Weres and that odd tang she now associated with magic.

Sarah Jennifer was lying on a cot with an IV in her arm, her respiration deep and even. "What happened to Major Grumpy-pants?"

That earned her a growl from the Weres standing guard at the door.

"You might want to take that back," Ezekiel warned. "The pack doesn't take insults to their Alpha lightly."

Mary-Anne held her hands up and smiled. "My bad. I didn't mean any disrespect. I'm grateful for her help. Is she okay?"

"She's sleeping off Etheric drain," Ezekiel explained.

Mary-Anne frowned. "I thought she was a Were?"

"She's not just a Were. She has magic," Caitlin told Mary-Anne.

"You should have seen it," Kain cut in, his voice awed.

"She called pretty much an entire mountain down on the head of the beast that came through the rift."

Mary-Anne shook her head, confused. "Rift? Beast?"

Ezekiel spoke up. "They are called Skrima. They come from another world, and they are being sent to conquer us."

Caitlin whirled to face Ezekiel. "*They?* We only saw one."

Ezekiel's face was ashen and drawn. "While you were fighting the Mad, I looked beyond the rift. I wanted to see what kind of world Laughter came from. All I saw was legions of Skrima, all waiting to break through to this side."

Kain covered his face with his hands. "I don't believe it. As if the Mad aren't enough to contend with. Now there's an army of alien monsters waiting to invade?"

Esme swept into the room, carrying a fresh bag for Sarah Jennifer's IV. "Don't lose hope. We have a short window to take care of the Madness. Ezekiel and Lilith can hold the rift for a short time with your help. As soon as I have Sarah Jennifer patched up, she and I will release the cure, as you seem bent on calling it."

"How?" Caitlin asked as Esme connected the bag to the line feeding into Sarah Jennifer's vein. "What *is* the cure?"

Esme shook her head. "All in good time."

Kain was quiet, his eyes fixed on Sarah Jennifer. Jaxon had claimed the space at the foot of her cot, his ears pricked. He looked relaxed, but Caitlin knew her canine companion. The German Shepherd was in guard mode.

Caitlin threw her hands up. "Fine. What can we do to help?"

Esme thought for a moment. "Wait a minute." She

picked up the radio. "Home Base to Base Camp. Come in, Theor."

"What is it, Esme?" the reply came.

"Do you need support? I have a Pricolici, a vampire, and a sword going spare here."

Caitlin raised an eyebrow at being reduced to her weapons capability.

"The plan has changed," Theor told her. "The Mad are not coming for Lilith's mountain. They are being drawn to the rift. We're diverting them from the towns and villages. We're going to herd them toward the rift and pen them in along the valley."

That was news to Esme. "Seems like you should have reported that, Sergeant."

"The major wasn't answering her radio, then I heard she was being brought in. Tell me she's not…"

"No, she's alive," Esme told him. "Just out for the count for the minute. Okay, I'm going to send these three to the rift."

"What about Ezekiel?" Theor inquired. "Is he in the fight?"

Esme glanced at Ezekiel. "No. He's staying here to protect Lilith. Keep diverting everyone you can to the rift. The real danger is coming from beyond Earth."

"The Urai reported a gigantic beast," Theor returned. "I don't want to dismiss their claims, but—"

"Don't dismiss them," Esme told him. "There are aliens beyond the rift. Skrima. And a Kurtherian enemy who intends to use them to conquer us. I need you on your game. As soon as Sarah Jennifer wakes up, we have to get up to the BYPS to begin the saturation. That will take care of the Mad. Then we'll just have the Skrima to deal with."

"*Just?*" Ezekiel muttered. "You didn't see them."

"Understood," Theor assured her. "I'm pulling the line in around the Mad as they pass. We'll surround the rift. Is Olaf there? I could use him."

Olaf already had his clothing and sword bundled. "I'm heading back to the rift now that I know the major is going to be okay. The Urai are out there with no support."

"I don't think Laughter can send all the Skrima through at once," Ezekiel told them. "I hurt her badly when I turned her attack back on her."

"You still there?" Theor sent.

"Still here," Esme assured him. "Olaf will get the troops at the rift organized."

Theor's laugh came through loud and clear. "Yeah? I think Mika will have something to say about that."

"Mika can say what she likes," Olaf interjected. "We have a chain of command for a reason, and until Sarah Jennifer wakes up, that's me and you, buddy."

He turned to Caitlin, Mary-Anne, and Kain. "I hope you three are in a fighting mood."

Kain grinned. "Wait until you get to know these two. You'll regret hoping."

Caitlin punched Kain in the arm, then strode to the door. "Asshole. See if I save you from the next Mad that decides you look like a snack."

Kain threw up his hands. "What did I say? Kitty-Cat just has a combative attitude. Besides, I *am* a snack."

Caitlin stuck her tongue out at him. "You're a bighead, is what. Come on, Jax."

"Nice friends you made," Esme commented to Ezekiel as they left with Olaf, bickering happily, with Jaxon prancing around their feet.

Ezekiel smiled. "Yeah."

Esme's eyes twinkled with empathy and sadness. "You had to end Helena's life, didn't you." It wasn't a question.

Ezekiel nodded miserably. "I would have been on my own when Helena succumbed to the Madness if not for them. I...I don't know if I would have had the strength to give her the end she wanted if I hadn't needed to keep them safe."

Sarah Jennifer murmured, returning to consciousness.

"Leave it for now," Esme told him. "I'm here if you want to talk after this is over, but right now, we have to focus on what needs doing."

Ezekiel moved to stand at the foot of Sarah Jennifer's cot. He smiled when she opened her eyes, all the angst he'd let build up vanishing, replaced by an overwhelming gladness. He braced himself for a verbal dressing down as the muzziness in her eyes cleared.

Sarah Jennifer groaned, her hand going to her forehead. She felt the IV in her arm and pulled it out. "What happened?"

Esme chuckled and handed her a glass of water. "You sucked up fair half the Etheric to deal with that ugly brute. You have a hangover, I'm guessing."

Sarah Jennifer sipped the water gratefully, and when she was satisfied she was going to keep it down, she drained the glass. "I don't think I've ever felt so hungry in my life."

"If you can walk, we'll go to the mess and grab a bite before we leave." Esme offered her an arm.

Sarah Jennifer sat back against the wall. "Give me a minute. My head is still swimming." She looked past Esme to where Ezekiel was standing quietly. "Welcome back."

Ezekiel was taken aback. "What, no verbal flaying?"

Sarah Jennifer shook her head and regretted it instantly when her eyes rattled almost audibly in her skull. "No lecture. We'll have time to talk out the past, but right now, I need to know what's going on out there."

"Told you," Esme cut in. "More important things than ego right now, my lad."

Sarah Jennifer steeled herself and inched to the edge of the cot. "Food. Briefing. Coffee. Lots and lots of coffee."

Twenty minutes later, she was sitting in the mess with a plate piled with a little bit of everything they had in the food stores. Esme and Ezekiel sat down opposite her, and Lilith joined them via the speaker.

Sarah Jennifer speared a pork chop and took a huge bite, chewing gingerly to avoid setting off the percussion section that had taken up residence in her skull.

"You eat, I'll talk," Esme told her.

"Mmf, shounds good to me," Sarah Jennifer replied between bites.

Esme chuckled. "After you left for the rift, Ezekiel took care of Lilith's predicament." She turned to him. "Maybe you should tell this part."

Ezekiel nodded. "Okay. Laughter is on another planet. She was using some kind of Kurtherian technology to connect mentally to Lilith. She attacked me when I interceded, but I was able to turn that around and get a good look at where she was."

Sarah Jennifer frowned. "Which is?"

"In a Pod-doc. Or she was. I broke it, but she got out before I could kill her for what she did to Lilith." Ezekiel scowled, his anger rising again. "While you were taking care of the Skrim she sent through, I got a look beyond the rift. She has an untold number of those things. She's planning to send them through to destroy us."

Sarah Jennifer dropped her chop. "We need to close that rift."

"I don't know how," Ezekiel admitted.

Esme shook her head in response to Sarah Jennifer's questioning stare. "No can do, Duckie. It's beyond me how she opened it in the first place."

Sarah Jennifer sighed. "Lilith? Anything to add?"

"I could make an educated guess as to how a rift is generated," the Kurtherian answered. "But I can't tell you how to close it. That knowledge was forbidden to all but the rulers of the clans. I can't understand how Laughter-Brings-Meaning-To-Life acquired it. She was a lowly geneticist like me."

Sarah Jennifer thought for a moment. "Is there anything we can do to limit her access through the rift?"

"I'll work on it," Lilith told her.

"I'll help," Ezekiel added.

Esme got to her feet. "If you're done fueling up, we need to get up to the BYPS and get started with the saturation."

Sarah Jennifer nodded. "I'll take the rest of this to go. Damn that Kurtherian. How did she get past the BYPS?"

"It's made to protect us from outside threats," Esme

reminded her. "Nothing could have prepared us for an attack from the Etheric."

Sarah Jennifer picked up her plate and got to her feet. "Then all we can do is get back on track with the plan. I just hope we can get the saturation taken care of and get back here before Laughter makes her move."

"Call Enora," Esme told her. "I'll head below and get the pallets brought up to the plateau."

Sarah Jennifer watched as the last of the antigrav pallets they had used to bring up the barrels loaded itself onto the airship. The preservative the nanocytes were suspended in would evaporate on contact with the atmosphere, but first they had to reconfigure the BYPS.

Enora was in high spirits as they took off from the mountain. "All complications aside, it is a joyous day," she enthused. "The Madness will soon be a thing of the past."

"How are the simulations looking?" Sarah Jennifer asked as she took her seat.

"Prevailing winds are favorable," Enora confirmed, pulling up a real-time projection of the planet on the viewscreen. The global wind currents were shown with various colored arrows. "There are, as we were expecting, places where we will need to have the climate control modules intercede to ensure complete coverage. However, my projections have identified those areas. There will be no problems manipulating the weather systems to achieve our goals."

"Your program should have finished uploading by now,"

Esme told the AI. "We didn't have time to check on it thanks to Laughter, but it'll be no effort to send it out to the modules once we're back inside the primary satellite."

"The projection goes past ten days?" Sarah Jennifer inquired, recalling the brief had stated that as the outer limit of predictions.

Enora smiled. "Yes. Since we are modifying and controlling the systems, chaos theory is not a factor. We should see a reaction in the Madness-inflicted population within hours, and the saturation will be complete within six months as projected."

Sarah Jennifer nodded. "Good enough. What's our ETA at the BYPS?"

"Three minutes," Enora answered.

"Do we have any messages from Mars to deal with before we are cut off?" Sarah Jennifer asked as Esme entered the cockpit.

"No messages currently," Enora confirmed. "Etheric comms are active, with the BYPSs around both planets maintaining a stable connection. We won't be completely cut off."

Esme slid into the co-pilot's seat. "I have the nanocytes hooked up, ready to be dispersed. We're good to go."

Sarah Jennifer was eager to get it over and done with so they could get back to the ongoing crisis in Arkhangelsk. "Then I guess we should get this show on the road."

The witch had a grin plastered on her face. "This is going to be pretty spectacular to see."

They arrived at the primary satellite and went through the process of verifying their authority to access the network. Esme checked that the program for the climate control modules was ready and sent it out, then there was a few moments' wait while she uploaded her modifications to the operating system.

Sarah Jennifer used the time to compose a short report for Bethany Anne. She knew it would be some time before it reached the Queen since the *Baba Yaga* was still far beyond the Federation, hunting down Kurtherians.

They returned to the *Enora*. Sarah Jennifer wasn't alone in feeling the urge to complete their task and get back to New Romanov. The thought of Laughter recovering from the nasty shock Ezekiel had given her and sending the Skrima through the rift was at the forefront of their minds.

Enora was waiting with the interface to the BYPS onscreen when they got back to the cockpit. "I have confirmation from the EI that the modifications will work as you intended, Esme. The system is waiting for your authorization to enact the changes, Major."

Sarah Jennifer swallowed hard, reminding herself that Bethany Anne trusted her to save humanity. She had no doubt that her intentions were good, and time was of the essence. However, there was something preventing her from activating the BYPS.

She made her decision. "Hold off. I need to speak to the Colonel. Call Keeg Station, Enora. I want to see my grandparents."

"Activating the IICS," Enora confirmed.

There was a short wait while the call was rerouted to the All Guns Blazing Terry Henry had the franchise for.

He answered from his office. "Wildflower! What a pleasant surprise. I wasn't expecting to hear from you until the end of the month." He twisted his head to check the calendar on the wall behind him. "No, I'm not losing track of time."

Sarah Jennifer laughed, immediately put at ease by his theatrics. "I know you didn't lose track of time. It's good to see you're getting some time to spend in your bar."

Terry Henry grinned. "That's what retirement is for. But you didn't call to chat, I'm guessing?"

Sarah Jennifer shook her head. "No. We're about to release the fix for the Madness."

"About time!" Char's voice came from off-camera. She ducked into view, her smile a welcome sight as she leaned over the back of TH's chair and wrapped her arms around his shoulders.

Sarah Jennifer's tension melted at the sight of the two of them together. "It's taken a long time and an incredible effort. My team—"

"She means me," Esme cut in. "I'm the team."

Sarah Jennifer rolled her eyes. "Okay, *Esme* has come up with a modification to the BYPS that will disperse replacement nanocytes across the Earth. The Madness is going to be eradicated within six months, but we're going to be cut off for some of that time. I guess I wanted to see your faces before that happened and make sure you weren't worried when I didn't check in."

"Does your sister know about this?" Char asked.

Sarah Jennifer nodded. "I've had Etheric comms made for everyone with family off-world since Ted isn't available to send additional units. It fell to me—you know, the responsible one."

Char nodded slowly. "Thanks to you, at least we know

she's alive. Ted! He hasn't changed in hundreds of years. Only our understanding of him has."

Terry Henry leaned into the camera. "Eat your vegetables!"

Sarah Jennifer laughed. "Grandpa!"

TH wagged his finger at her. "Granddaughter, daughters, and their mothers. I'd never get a word in edgewise on these all-too-brief calls. I'm outnumbered, even with Dokken on my side."

"It was always that way, and you have nothing to complain about," Sarah Jennifer chastised fondly. "How's retirement treating you two?"

"Same," TH replied, a devilish look appearing on his face just before Char jumped when his hand went somewhere it shouldn't have. "Busier than a one-legged man in an ass-kicking contest."

Sarah Jennifer shook her head. "A life well-lived. I want to be you when I grow up."

"You already are," Char told her. "We're proud of you, dear. Cory is away again. We need to make sure she has a comm unit with her. You should talk to your mother more."

"Grandma!" They went through the motions of this every month, and Sarah Jennifer didn't mind one bit. Family was what kept her grounded during the harsh times. "I love you both. I want you to know that, whatever happens."

TH narrowed his eyes. "What haven't you told us?"

Sarah Jennifer had hoped she wouldn't have to get into this. She gave them a quick rundown of the events at New Romanov. "We've got it handled, and I've reported to

Bethany Anne. No Kurtherian will get their greedy hands on Earth while I'm around to stop it from happening, I swear it."

Char turned to Terry Henry with her best shocked face before looking into the camera with a beatific smile. "I'd say I feel sorry for the Kurtherian, but we've had our own dealings with Laughter and the Skrima. Kick her ass, honey. We'll be cheering you on from here."

Sarah Jennifer smiled. "Give my best to my mom, and hopefully, we'll get to see her soon."

They signed off, but Sarah Jennifer didn't look away from the darkened screen until Enora switched it back to the inert BYPS interface.

"You feel better?" Esme asked.

Feeling reassured, Sarah Jennifer took a deep breath. "Yes. Here we go. All or nothing. Enora, connect me to the BYPS."

The BYPS' EI asked for her authorization.

Sarah Jennifer gave the code, then waited for the system to give Enora access. "Take us out of range and initiate the modified output parameters, Enora."

## CHAPTER SEVENTEEN

The laser grid blazed into existence, washing out the viewscreen with red light. An alarm went off, quickly subdued by Enora.

"I'm sorry," the AI explained. "I had to wait for the activation to discern what changes to my shielding frequency were necessary."

"Are we good?" Sarah Jennifer asked.

"All systems are optimal," Enora confirmed. "We may begin the dispersal procedure when you are ready."

"That's all I wanted to hear," Esme announced, getting up from her seat. "If you need me, you don't. I'll be in the drop bay making sure nothing goes wrong. We don't have time to waste."

Sarah Jennifer nodded. "Call when we're good to go." She pulled up the route data for the dispersal as Esme made herself scarce. She planned to take care of New Romanov and the surrounding area first.

"Enora, take us to Siberia and patch me into Theor's radio. I want to hear what's going on down there."

She had to trust that the nanocytes would take effect and quell the Mad before the situation there became untenable for the warriors, leaving the rift unguarded.

The next few hours were spent circumnavigating the globe while releasing billions of nanocytes into the atmosphere. The procedure almost mirrored the one undertaken by Bethany Anne's people in WWDE+150. The main difference was the precision with which they released the precious load, due to their limited resources.

She listened in on the effort to steer the Mad away from the living as the airship sliced through the troposphere. Her heart sank as the reports coming to Theor became steadily worse.

The number of deaths ratcheted up as the battle got underway, the weight of every loss settling on her conscience. Her imagination needed no assistance to build a mental picture of their overwhelming failure to hold the Mad back.

Still, she didn't deviate from her duty, repeating to herself that they would recover those lost to the Madness once the patches went out until it became a mantra whose words had no meaning.

The only mercy was that the rift remained inactive.


**Arkhangelsk, Rift Valley**

The Urai had been joined by companies of warriors from many other towns and villages, as well as the Defense Force troops coming in from America. Theor and Olaf had sent out the order for the united forces to herd the Mad into the valley, where the magic users had raised a rock-and-earth maze designed to contain them once inside the two-kilometer-wide dip in the land.

Over thirty thousand men and women were spread across the plain, arrayed in phalanxes ten deep. They were split so there were five ranks standing back to back in each, forming gauntlets into the valley for the Defense Force to drive the Mad along.

The entire valley reverberated with the screams of the trapped Mad, angry, echoing, melancholy hunger in their voices. The desperate wails rose above the beating of swords on shields from the warriors standing strong.

The rift glittered darkly overhead, the oppressive energy it spilled over the assembled warriors stealing their optimism. They worked with their mouths stretched in grim, silent lines beneath their leather masks, the usual banter that passed between them abandoned as they fought to contain the surging hordes.

Kain was unaffected by the cheerless demeanor of his fellow fighters, buoyed by his discovery that the pack had been there this whole time. Not just the pack, but a whole layer to the UnknownWorld he'd had no clue existed.

The existence of so many Weres had come as a welcome shock to Kain. He had believed his kind was doomed to die out, forced to choose between forms. Their presence and the knowledge that there were many more Weres spread around the world had given him hope for the future.

He loped through the forest, feeling whole for the first time in a long time. Caitlin and Mary-Anne were his family by choice, but nothing could ever replace the bond Weres had with each other. Thousands of miles from the place he had been born and raised, the scent of pack filled his nose, and he felt like he'd come home.

While the majority of the Weres roaming the forest were in their wolf form, he appeared to be the only one with the ability to shift to the ultimate form. Assured by Olaf that he was no longer in danger of getting stuck in Were form, he'd unleashed his Pricolici nature, exulting in the freedom as he tore through the trees with Mary-Anne, the two of them working with the Defense Force to drive the Mad toward the warriors staged on the plain between the forest's edge and the valley's mouth.

The comm buds they'd been given constantly fed them information about incoming groups of Mad. The Mad bore down on the rift valley from the east and west, swarming the forest around its mouth.

Olaf's voice rang in his ear. "Two hundred-plus approaching from Sector Six. Team Canada, respond."

"On it," Kain replied, switching direction to head for the already-trampled undergrowth the Mad were coming out of. "We need a better callsign than Team-freaking-Canada."

"Less talking, more scaring the shit out of the Mad." Mary-Anne blurred ahead, leaving him in her wake.

Kain howled as he pounded through the frozen under-growth, adrenaline coursing through his body. He had never been in a fight like this. Hell, he hadn't seen this many people, Mad or not, in decades.

A chorus of wolf howls answered his call.

The Mad were driven into a frenzy by the sounds, their

primal instincts telling them to avoid the apex predators at all costs.

On the shield wall, Caitlin was used to the disparity in their abilities and was more than making up for it with her expertise and natural leadership. She had ascertained which direction Kain and Mary-Anne were driving the Mad from and directed the warriors assembled along her section where to form the gauntlet.

Her eyes narrowed as she tracked the disturbance in the forest. "Incoming! Weapons up!" She pointed at the place the Mad were going to break through the tree line and the warriors under her command moved as one, their shields locked and their swords, spears, pikes, and halberds poised and ready to repel the Mad.

Caitlin gripped her borrowed shield, her muscles straining with the denied urge to fight. She felt the same urge from the warriors to her left and right. "HOLD!"

The trees shook as the Mad closed in, driven into a fearful frenzy by Kain and Mary-Anne. The warriors stood fast despite their instinct to flee as the waves of fear emitted by Mary-Anne and Kain announced their imminent arrival.

Every man and woman there had faced their share of Mad over the years and were somewhat desensitized to the horror they brought. Compared to a vampire in full battle-mode, honest-to-Matriarch werewolves, and the scary-as-shit Pricolici, the Mad seemed no more dangerous than rabid animals.

The Mad charged out of the tree line and tore across the open space, instinct drawing them toward the prospect of fresh flesh.

Caitlin let rip, her war cry rising with the other warriors' as they closed in.

Mary-Anne's voice came over the comm. "There are a fuck-ton more than two hundred, Olaf! The Mad we passed over on the way are here. Get ready for them. We're coming in!"

Hundreds of wolves streamed out of the forest, overwhelmed by the sheer number of Mad pursuing them.

Somewhere to Caitlin's right, a guttural scream cut above the battle cries.

Her heart pounded when she realized that someone on the wall had gone Mad.

Olaf and Theor paced their vantage point on the ridge. The high ground gave them a view of the battle. It also prevented them from acting immediately when the Madness rippled out through the shield wall.

"What do we do?" Olaf moaned.

Theor had his radio jammed to his ear. "All Weres, we have an outbreak in the sixth phalanx. Isolate the Mad and protect the uninfected." He turned to Olaf. "We have to hope the nanocytes act soon."

The *Enora* had passed over a while ago, trailing what looked like green smoke behind her. The mist hovering over the plain and the valley floor had taken on a tint of green, signifying the beginning of the waiting game.

It wasn't enough for Olaf. "I have to get down there. I'm immune to the Madness; the warriors are not. *Mika!* I could not bear it if she was lost."

"Go, save your woman," Theor told him, understanding that the call to the werebear's heart overrode everything else. "I will remain here."

Olaf clasped Theor's arm. "Don't let her hear you call her my woman. She has other ideas. Still, I must go to her."

He bounded down the mountainside, shedding his clothes as he ran. He shifted in the next instant, thundering toward the chaos on four paws.

---

Mika swore bitterly as the shield wall disintegrated around her. The Madness rippled through her people, turning men and women she'd known her whole life into mindless, meat-hungry killers.

The no-kill order meant nothing in the face of the ravening beasts that had replaced her kin. She screamed her rage as she hacked and sliced her way to those who had not turned, ordering them into a tight defensive circle. Back to back, they fought as one, grief and anger driving them to survive no matter the cost. She used her shield as a weapon, the sharpened edge as good as a blade when she rammed it into the faces of her attackers.

She stepped to the left and swung her sword as the Mad bearing her childhood friend Yani's face lunged at her. Davina, Karl, Marius, Frederika, Van Dyk, Janus, Leif—they all fell to her blade.

It wasn't enough.

Her circle grew increasingly smaller as the living fell or turned, leaving Mika alone in the center of a sea of Mad. She discarded her shield and hefted her sword two-handed, prepared to meet her end on her feet like a true warrior. "Come on, then!" she screamed. "I'll see you at the gates of Hell!"

They took her invitation, swarming her. Mika lost her sword, and she felt their teeth all over her leather-and-mail-clad body. She kicked and punched, determined to fight to her last breath.

Somehow, she broke free. She grabbed two discarded swords as she rolled to her feet and resumed the fight, cleaving the head from one Mad and the arm from another.

A chilling roar cut through the growls of those attacking her. Mika didn't pause as Olaf came barreling through, knocking the Mad aside with swipes of his mighty paws.

He slid to a stop just long enough for Mika to haul herself onto his back.

She sheathed one of her swords and clung to his fur with her free hand as he leapt over the crush, stabbing any Mad who got close enough to them with the sword she'd kept.

Olaf made like a juggernaut, his determination to get Mika to safety his only concern. The battle was lost; there was no way the majority were getting out of there. Their only hope was for the nanocytes blanketing the valley to take effect.

Mika spotted a group of warriors penned in by the rockface. "Olaf, over there! We have to help them!"

He ignored her and kept running for a few paces. Mika released her grip on his fur and slapped him upside the head. "Hey, asshole, I'm not important! Move, or I go by myself!"

Resigned to her determination to get them both killed, Olaf altered the trajectory of his run to take them to the warriors in need.

Mika slipped off his back as they arrived, drawing her second sword in the same fluid movement. Her blades spun in deadly arcs as she cut her way through to the warriors while Olaf tossed Mad aside like rag dolls.

The warriors renewed their fight, heartened by the unexpected intervention.

"This way!" Mika yelled, waving her right blade to indicate a gap in the horde. The reason for the gap became apparent when they saw Mary-Anne, Caitlin, Kain, and a few dozen Weres fighting their way through.

Olaf roared, calling Kain and Mary-Anne to him.

The Mad parted, flowing to the sides to avoid the vampire. Behind her came the ragged remains of the fighting forces, surrounded by Weres, with Kain protecting their rear.

Mary-Anne's eyes blazed red, her fangs fully extended and her nails lengthened into bloody claws. "Need some help?"

"Not a minute too soon," Mika told her. "Think you can clear our way to the mountain?"

Mary-Anne grinned. "My pleasure." She turned to Olaf. "Keep my human safe, will you?"

Caitlin bumped her with a shoulder as she moved past her to stand by Mika. "You are my vampire, and don't forget it."

"Nooo talkinnngg!" Kain bitched, his speech altered in Pricolici form. "Rrrrunnn!"

The warriors fought bravely, knowing they could go Mad at any moment, while the UnknownWorlders did everything they could to force a path through the carnage.

The Mad kept up the pressure, contracting and expanding around them as they pushed toward the mountain, gathering the survivors as they went. There was no way of discerning whose blood they were wading through. Many of the people they came across refused to join them, telling the group they had been bitten.

They had no choice but to keep moving.

Soon, they ceased to find anyone still fighting. All that remained were Mad blocking their way. They swarmed the remainder of the warriors with hunger in their dull red eyes.

Olaf ground to a halt as the others took their stand.

Caitlin bared her teeth. "We were so close! This isn't *fair!*"

She wasn't wrong. They were only a few hundred feet from the safety of the mountainside, where the magic users could protect them.

"Here we go again," Mika growled. She wrapped an arm around Olaf's neck. "If you weren't so damned furry right now, I'd kiss you goodbye. It's been a good run. You aren't the asshole I thought you were, Bear Man."

Kain and Mary-Anne flanked Caitlin as hope faded.

The remaining Weres formed a circle around the group, prepared to die protecting the humans.

Without warning, the ground ahead of them imploded, spraying dirt and body parts in all directions.

Another kinetic hit, and another, carving a path through the Mad.

Olaf looked up, seeing the *Enora* swoop overhead.

"Air support!" Mary-Anne whooped with joy. "Quick! Go!"

They charged into the space left by the bombardment, putting everything they had into racing for safety. The Mad had recovered and resumed their pursuit.

The Weres continued to put the lives of the unenhanced above their own. Many of the wolves were pulled into the horde alongside the humans.

Olaf and Kain fell back, rescuing everyone they could reach while Mary-Anne, Mika, and Caitlin cut down the Mad who gained on them.

The desperate scramble for survival continued as they hit the slope.

However, they were in range of the magic users now.

Lightning and fire razed the ground around them as they climbed to the unnatural cliff the rock mages had pulled out of the mountainside.

The Mad were driven back by a hail of rock shards, giving the group the breathing space they needed to make the final ascent.

The rock wall parted to allow them through and the warriors streamed through without slowing, followed by the UnknownWorlders.

Last through was Olaf. He was limping and bleeding from a multitude of bites. Kain was in a similar state, but unlike Olaf, he hadn't had the benefit of Pod-doc treatment.

As the others collapsed on the plateau behind the wall,

he felt the Madness rising within. He turned and ran for the rapidly-closing gap in the wall, slipping through just before the rock clapped shut.

Caitlin was on her feet in an instant. She ran for the wall and began hitting it with her already bloodied fists. "Kain! *NO!*" She beat on the rock, screaming, "Let me out there! Let me OUT!"

# CHAPTER EIGHTEEN

Sarah Jennifer let up on the kinetics as her people made it through the wall. "Bring us around, Enora."

"Major, Ezekiel's Were friend is not inside with the others," Enora informed her.

Sarah Jennifer had seen Kain limp in at Olaf's side. "Who? You mean Kain?"

"Yes," Enora clarified. "He went back out before the wall was closed."

"Give me a visual," Sarah Jennifer instructed.

Enora focused the external camera on the Pricolici tearing through the Mad massing at the wall. Sarah Jennifer zoomed in on him and saw his eyes flash red. "*Shit. He's Mad.*" She reached for the internal comm. "Esme, can we send out the patches yet? One of our own is trapped on the wrong side of the wall, and he's been infected."

She didn't question the surge of protective emotion that drove her urge to save him. Kain might not have formally agreed to join the pack, but that meant nothing to her.

All Weres on Earth were hers to protect, hers to rule.

He belonged to her.

"Should be," Esme's reply came.

"Then deploy them," Sarah Jennifer commanded, her voice dropping to a growl. She rose from her chair and headed for the armory. "Enora, take us in. I'm going down there to pull him out."

"Major, he is Mad," Enora cautioned.

"And we have a Pod-doc in the mountain," Sarah Jennifer shot back. "Call Ezekiel and tell him to get it ready for him."

She paused in the armory to grab the Jean Dukes Specials Bethany Anne had sent her. This would be the first time she'd used them off the practice range. She dialed them to five, unsure whether she'd be able to handle the recoil on the higher settings and unwilling to find out. The grips warmed to her touch as if they were absorbing the heat of her rage.

She ran for the drop bay, calling for Enora to open the doors.

Esme was waiting with a G-rig and a knowing smile. She held it out as Sarah Jennifer burst through the door. "Go get your man," was all she said.

Sarah Jennifer shrugged into the harness without a word and cinched the straps tight as she strode to the open drop doors.

She stepped through, activating the gravity rig as she plummeted toward the Earth. The wind whipped, enveloping her as she hurtled toward the ground. She barely felt the rush, her body already flooded with adrenaline.

Her usual cool was nowhere to be found. She was

beyond angry. Beyond any emotions she could name. Being airborne while her people fought and died had her wound up to the point of exploding. Kain's attempt to sacrifice himself pushed her past the point of restraint.

She spotted Kain and altered her freefall to take her to his position. The G-rig arrested her descent smoothly, preventing her from smashing into the side of the mountain.

Sarah Jennifer was almost there. She hit the release on the G-rig, dropping the final ten feet. She landed hard, transferring the shock that traveled up her legs into a forward roll.

Kain was too far gone to realize help had arrived. He was losing his hold on his form, his body shrinking as his ability to shift was corrupted by the Madness. Still, he retained enough of his mind to turn his urge to kill on the Mad and not the people watching from the top of the wall.

Sarah Jennifer flowed to her feet, her fingers stroking the triggers. Her Jean Dukes Specials kicked back as she fired on the Mad swarming Kain, then opened her comm. "Those patches would come in handy right about now, Esme."

"Thirty seconds," Esme promised.

"Enora, find a landing space," Sarah Jennifer instructed. "This won't take long."

Thirty seconds was a long time when every living thing around her wanted to eat her. Sarah Jennifer was still loath to kill the Mad. She kept her aim low as she took them out, reasoning that they would heal from the injuries she caused them once their nanocytes began repairing their bodies instead of corrupting them.

At last, she caught a break. The Mad began to fall as the patch took effect.

Taking the heat off Kain drew his attention to her. He wasn't fully turned; he was half-Mad, half-driven by his Pricolici instinct to wreak complete and utter destruction on everything around him, which was still in the ascendancy.

"Easy, Kain," Sarah Jennifer called as his dull red eyes fixed on her.

He shook his head, fighting the drowsiness that stole over him as the patch took effect. Sarah Jennifer stared him down, willing him to fall asleep like the rest of the Mad. She didn't have any experience with Pricolici, but her instincts told her he wouldn't go down easily. She wished she had a tranquilizer in her Jean Dukes Specials to help him past his blockheadedness.

Kain growled low in his throat and took a step toward her, panting as saliva dripped from his open jaws.

Sarah Jennifer recognized the look. She stood her ground, her Jean Dukes raised. "Listen to my voice. I am your Alpha. I am safety. I am home. Stand down, Kain. Don't make me shoot you."

His head moved from side to side as he fought the instinct to hunt. He howled, a miserable sound full of pain and regret. His head dipped, his muscles tensing.

Sarah Jennifer read the intent in his posture before he leapt. She fired twice without hesitation. Her aim was true.

Kain was knocked back by the force of the rounds that hit him in his shoulder and hip. He roared in fury as agony ripped through him, stumbling as his body fought to return to full Pricolici form in defense.

Sarah Jennifer didn't wait to see if she'd done enough to stop him. Unaware she was drawing from the Etheric, her eyes blazed brilliant red as she covered the ground between them in a flash and coldcocked him, breaking every bone in her hand along with his jaw as she pounded him on the night-night button.

Kain collapsed instantly. His body shrank and his fur receded, leaving him naked and human in a pool of his own blood.

Sarah Jennifer bent and scooped him up, ignoring the pain radiating from her hand. "Enora, where are you?" she sent over the comm.

"On the ridge behind the wall," the AI replied.

"I'm on my way. Have the airship ready for takeoff." Kain was almost twice Sarah Jennifer's size. Without her enhanced strength, she wouldn't have been able to lift him. As it was, she held him in her arms, cradled like the world's largest baby and just as precious to her.

She was in no state of mind to question why this particular Were was so important to her when so many of her people lay dead or comatose on the plain. All she had was her instinct, and for once in her long life, she didn't suppress it.

She tightened her hold on Kain's body and ran for the wall.

Caitlin dashed out as the wall parted to give Sarah Jennifer access. "What did you do to him?" she demanded, her face streaked with dirt and angry tears.

"I saved his damned life," Sarah Jennifer retorted. "Now *move.*"

Mary-Anne eased Caitlin back as Sarah Jennifer shouldered her way through. Caitlin made to argue, but Mary-Anne shook her head. "They are Weres. They operate differently from the rest of us. She'll rip your throat out before she lets him go now that she's claimed him."

Caitlin's gaze shifted to Sarah Jennifer. "Claimed him?"

Mary-Anne's nose twitched. "Be glad you can't smell pheromones."

"Does Kain get a say in this?" Caitlin murmured.

"I don't think either of them does," Mary-Anne replied.

They followed Sarah Jennifer as she strode through the walking wounded with Kain in her arms, heading for the airship as those who were able to be of use began streaming out to sort the comatose Mad from the dead.

The rest of the day passed in a blur for Sarah Jennifer. She barely remembered getting Kain onboard the *Enora* or the short journey to Lilith's mountain with Caitlin and Mary-Anne accompanying them.

Exhaustion stole over her once Kain was inside the Pod-doc. She fell on the cot she'd woken up on what seemed like a year ago but was only yesterday.

---

When Sarah Jennifer awoke, Kain was on a cot across from her.

His eyes snapped to her as she struggled to a sitting position. Sarah Jennifer groaned as the bandage around her hand brought back the events that had led to her being back in the med bay.

"Hey, you're awake." Kain's voice was low and hoarse.

Sarah Jennifer flushed red, embarrassed by her actions

on the battlefield. She didn't even know this man and she'd risked her life to save him. Why? "And you're not Mad," she replied eventually.

Kain just stared at her.

Sarah Jennifer squirmed under his gaze. "Do I have a target on my head?"

Kain grinned. "No. It's just…"

"Just what?" she snapped a little more harshly than she intended.

"I remember you coming at me, eyes blazing, yelling like a goddamn banshee. You were magnificent." Kain's face reddened, and he looked away at last.

Sarah Jennifer closed her mouth. She didn't know what to do with the compliment. "You're pack. I'm the Alpha. That makes you my responsibility, Pricolici or not."

Not strictly the truth, but she wasn't about to admit she'd abandoned all sense at the thought of him in danger.

The door opened, saving her from her muddled thoughts. Esme walked in, followed by Ezekiel and Caitlin.

Caitlin went to Kain's bed and sat on the edge, her voice low as she spoke to him.

"What's going on out there?" Sarah Jennifer asked Esme, easing herself out of bed.

"Everything is going just fine," the witch told her. "Back in that bed, Duckie. You need rest."

Sarah Jennifer ignored the order. She looked around and saw her jacket—the one that had once belonged to TH—hanging on a hook on the wall. She limped over to get it, her knee giving her more grief than ever. "I need to be there. I can't hide in here while everyone else is working."

She slipped her jacket on and bent to rub her knee. "This isn't helping."

"You can't heal it?" Kain asked. "I thought you had magic."

Sarah Jennifer sighed. "Not the healing kind. I wish my mother was here. She could fix it for good."

"What's wrong with your knee?" Caitlin asked.

"It's a holdover from the days when I had more pride than sense," Sarah Jennifer answered ruefully. "Esme, can you…"

Esme's hands glowed with golden light as she laid them on Sarah Jennifer's knee. "One of these days, you're going to have to stop blocking yourself and do something about this."

Sarah Jennifer glanced at the others, her voice low as she spoke. "One of these days, yeah. Not today. I should put myself on Team Dumbass for what I did. No one life is worth more than the rest."

Esme clucked in that motherly way she had. "You did what your heart dictated. It's not an everyday occurrence for you."

Sarah Jennifer stole another glance at Kain, who was deep in conversation with Caitlin, and frowned. "My heart had nothing to do with it."

"If you say so, Duckie." Esme extended a hand toward the door. "If you're set on getting out there, Amelie had her people set up a field hospital in the valley. We've been moving the Mad there for the last ten hours."

"I slept ten hours?" Sarah Jennifer went ahead of Esme. "I want a rundown of everything I missed while I was out," she told the witch as they made their way to the upper levels.

"Not much to say," Esme told her. "The rift has been quiet. The radio has not. Whatever Ezekiel did to Laughter must have hurt her. She hasn't sent any more Skrima through. Everyone who wasn't infected has been moving the worst affected to the caverns the rock mages created after the battle."

"How many?" Sarah Jennifer asked.

"Too many to count," Esme admitted. "It's going to take a while to clear the valley. Mary-Anne hasn't taken a break. Good thing she's here since we're short on Weres until those who were injured are back in the game."

Sarah Jennifer was glad for the vampire's strength. "I'm up and about now. You and I can relieve her."

Esme shook her head. "I need to stay here and keep on top of the calls coming in from around the world. Izzy is doing her part, but she needs some help."

Sarah Jennifer nodded. "I need to get out there."

"Understood," Esme agreed.

"How are you doing, Lilith?" Sarah Jennifer asked as they entered the main cavern.

"I am recovering," the Kurtherian replied.

Sarah Jennifer glanced at the makeshift bed Ezekiel was sleeping on. "Kid tired himself out, huh?"

"He has been feeding me energy to replenish my stores," Lilith informed her.

"Laughter burned through her reserves," Esme explained.

Sarah Jennifer nodded in understanding.

Ezekiel stirred as they walked by. He peered at Sarah Jennifer groggily. "Wait. Don't go just yet."

Sarah Jennifer paused. "Want to walk over to the valley with me?"

He scrambled to his feet. "Okay."

"I'll have food and beds ready for those coming in," Esme told them. "I want to keep an eye on that Were of yours anyway."

Sarah Jennifer ignored the comment about Kain. "Call if there's any change with Lilith, and we'll come straight back."

The two of them left the mountain, emerging into the chilly fog that shrouded the mountain.

Ezekiel was quiet as they left the road.

Sarah Jennifer had a thousand things she wanted to say, but every one of them was going to reopen the wounds they'd caused one another. Eventually, she settled on, "How did you end up in Indiana?"

"Almost by accident," Ezekiel told her, seizing the opening. "We were in Chicago when Helena was infected. She wanted to get as far away from people as we could after that. We found the house while we were heading away from the cities."

Sarah Jennifer put a hand on his shoulder. "You did the honorable thing."

Ezekiel swallowed the lump in his throat. "Yeah, well, it was about time. I'm so sorry, Sarah Jennifer. I shouldn't have run away like that."

Sarah Jennifer's eyes stung with emotion. "I should have been there for you. You were grieving and angry. I should have shared my experiences with those things instead of letting you stew on them."

Ezekiel flung his arms around her, pulling them both to a stop. "I wish I could say we won't be separated again, but I know the time is coming. Lilith told me about Mars. I'm not going with you when you leave."

Sarah Jennifer returned his embrace, holding him tightly. "I know, kiddo. I know. You are needed here. You have to teach people how to access their magic."

They let go. Ezekiel sniffled as they continued walking. "What's the deal with you and Kain?" he asked tentatively.

"No deal," Sarah Jennifer told him.

"You seemed to be pretty upset he was hurt," Ezekiel commented.

"I was the one who hurt him," Sarah Jennifer pointed out.

"Yeah, to save him." Ezekiel smiled. "Do you like him?"

"I don't know him," Sarah Jennifer told him. "What's with the interrogation?"

Ezekiel shrugged. "I dunno. He's a good guy. You could do worse."

"I don't intend to find out," Sarah Jennifer stated. "I had one husband. It didn't work out so well. I'd rather be alone."

"You were *married*?" Ezekiel couldn't hide his shock. "You never told me that."

"There's a lot I never told you," Sarah Jennifer replied. The silence stretched out between them. "Jeremiah. He worked on my ranch."

"You had a ranch?"

Sarah Jennifer nodded. "After I walked out on the FDG and my family. I settled."

"He was a Were?" Ezekiel asked.

Sarah Jennifer shook her head. "He was unenhanced."

Ezekiel didn't need to be a genius to figure the rest. "I'm sorry. That must have hurt a lot."

"So much that I'm not inclined to go through it again," she admitted.

"Kain is a Were. A Pricolici. He's not fragile." Ezekiel picked up his pace to keep up with her.

"No, no, and no again," Sarah Jennifer told him. "He is welcome in the pack, but I'm not about to welcome him into my bed."

"Or your heart?"

"That either," she agreed.

They met up with the group of people coming from New Romanov as they reached the place their path intersected with the path the Mad had trampled into the valley.

Irina and Curtis were at the head of the group. Ezekiel was overjoyed to see his childhood friend again. The two of them peeled off from the group to talk.

Irina nodded at Sarah Jennifer in her usual brusque manner. "Major."

Sarah Jennifer smiled. "How are you, Irina?"

The woman snorted. "I'd be a lot better if this operation was being managed by your people. Those mages are a bit lah-di-dah by my thinking. Running around talking to the plants and the air, indeed. The Matriarch's blessings are wasted on them, in my opinion. They'd do better focusing on developing real magic like Esme and David."

Sarah Jennifer knew better than to expect praise from

the irascible Irina. "David isn't here at the moment, and communing with nature is a vital branch of magic. How else do you think the Protectorate produces all the grain they ship?"

"Pah!" Irina exclaimed. "They're no use here. Some of them would struggle to pour water out of a boot with instructions on the heel."

Sarah Jennifer decided she'd had enough Irina time. "I'm going to go ahead and check in with Olaf. Try not to annoy our allies."

She walked off before Irina could reply.

# CHAPTER NINETEEN

Caitlin waited until Sarah Jennifer and Esme had gone before rounding on Kain. "Okay, spill. What is it with you and her?"

Kain grinned. "Wish I knew, Kitty-Cat. She's something though, right?"

Caitlin narrowed her eyes. "Mary-Anne said something about her claiming you. What kind of bullshit is that?"

Kain shrugged. "It's like that for Weres sometimes. When you meet The One, you know it."

"HA!" Caitlin slid off the bed. "She doesn't seem to like you very much now that the heat of battle has died down."

Kain shuffled to the edge of the cot and swung his legs off the side. "How would you feel if you met someone for the first time and felt…"

"Felt what?"

Kain didn't know how to answer. "A connection," he admitted after a long pause. Caitlin was his family. They had no secrets. "Like I was made for her, Kitty-Cat. Like everything I was before now was just the prelude to who I'm meant to be."

Caitlin stood aside while he got to his feet, her expression drawn with concern. *"Damn.* That's…intense."

Kain dressed in silence. Intense didn't begin to cover how he felt.

He had known love only once before in his long life, and it hadn't ended well. He hadn't discovered his ability to shift to the ultimate form until long after he'd abandoned his pack. Being the runt of said pack, he hadn't had the standing or the strength to keep Isabel.

Since her betrayal, he'd kept a barrier around his heart that no female had been permitted to scale, lest his vulnerability was met with rejection again. He loved women but left without giving any more than his body. That way, he didn't get his heart broken.

However, as much as he'd like to lay the blame for his feelings squarely on his Were side, this went beyond the instinct to submit to her as his Alpha. An ocean of need had been stirred up inside him. He could drown in Sarah Jennifer and die happy. He didn't know her at all, but his soul recognized hers as the other half of his.

It scared the living shit out of him.

"What are you going to do?" Caitlin asked.

Kain headed for the door. "What I always do. Put one foot in front of the other and let life take care of itself."

Caitlin followed him, her brows knit in annoyance. "What does that even mean?"

"It means, Kitty-Cat," Kain headed for the door, resolving to keep his distance from Sarah Jennifer Walton, "that there's work to be done. People who need our help. We came to find the cure for the Madness, and we found it. Now we're going to do everything we can to make sure people get to move on from what they've been through."

---

Sarah Jennifer found Olaf on the battlefield. The werebear was loading the sleeping Mad onto antigrav pallets normally used for hauling heavy equipment.

He lifted a hand in greeting as Sarah Jennifer walked toward him.

"Time for you to get some rest," Sarah Jennifer told him.

Olaf grunted. "Not while there are people here who need me."

Sarah Jennifer saw the exhaustion in his eyes and put a hand on his arm. "Olaf. You need to rest. Laughter won't be put off by Ezekiel's reprimand forever."

Amelie spotted them and came over, pushing her tangled curls out of the way to reveal her grime-streaked face. "Welcome back to the land of the living."

Sarah Jennifer embraced her. "I'm here to relieve you and Olaf." She looked around for the vampire. "And Mary-Anne. Where is she?"

Amelie pointed at the valley floor. "Out there...somewhere. None of us have stopped since the Mad fell into their sleep."

Sarah Jennifer saw the tiredness in her old friend's eyes. "Go. Take your people and get some chow and some rack time. Esme is at the mountain. She'll see you taken care of."

Amelie didn't argue. "Honestly, that old woman was

enough to drive us out of here even if we hadn't been working ourselves to the bone. What's her deal?"

Sarah Jennifer winced. "Irina? She's good people. Just… opinionated, and not afraid to express herself."

Amelie snorted. "Well, unless I can beat some respect into her, I think I should be wherever she isn't."

Sarah Jennifer laughed. They'd all been there with the Widow Shutov. "Fair enough. I'll see you later."

As they left, Sarah Jennifer felt the hair on the back of her neck rise. She turned and saw Kain and Caitlin walking out of the forest.

She turned away and resumed stacking comatose people on the antigrav pallet, not wanting to deal with the swirl of emotions that overtook her when she looked at Kain. He was a stranger, and she wasn't the kind of woman to lust after someone she'd just met. There was a reason she'd been alone since she'd left Jeremiah. Her heart was not open to being scourged again.

Pallet loaded, she took the controller and guided it toward the mountain. Everyone with any medical training or healing ability was bustling around the field hospital there, working to take care of the incoming.

She bumped into Theor as she left the cavern. He was coming in with Mary-Anne, both of them guiding antigrav pallets loaded with sleeping, healing Mad.

Sarah Jennifer pointed at the pair of them. "Why are you two still here? You were supposed to head back to Lilith's mountain with Olaf and Amelie and her people."

Mary-Anne flashed a grin. "I don't tire like the rest of you. Especially since I got out of the Pod-doc and found I don't need blood anymore."

Sarah Jennifer allowed that. Theor, however, was a different matter.

The Icelandic Were shriveled under her scrutiny as the vampire left to resume her work. He held up his hands before she said a word. "Sorry, Major. I can't step back while there's so much to be done."

"There are a few thousand of us working to make sure it gets done," Sarah Jennifer stated. "If I don't hear you're back at the mountain within half an hour, I'm not going to be responsible for my loss of temper. Do you hear me?"

Theor grinned. "I don't know, Major. I've always wanted to hear you curse."

"I'll give you a curse!" Sarah Jennifer's voice rose an octave as she clipped him fondly on the back of the head. "You'll be on shit duty for the next six months if I have to repeat myself, Sergeant! My responsibility is to..." She trailed off as Kain walked up the path with a slight bundle cradled in his arms.

She saw right away that he was carrying a child. Her heart skipped a beat, sorrow overtaking her irritation.

"Hey, this way," she called softly.

His eyes lifted to meet hers. "I found her in the valley," he murmured, his voice torn with emotion. He pulled back the blanket covering the little girl, whose body was mottled with bruises where it wasn't ravaged with bites. "She's so small. I didn't know if anyone here could..."

Sarah Jennifer held out her arms to take the child. "If there's anything that can be done for her, the people to do it are here."

Kain handed the little girl over gently. "I'd better go.

Caitlin and Ma are out there. Let me know how it goes for her?"

Sarah Jennifer nodded. "I will."

Theor had remained quiet during the whole exchange. "Who is he?" he asked after Kain had departed.

Sarah Jennifer didn't hear him the first time, her attention on Kain. She shook her head. "Friend of Ezekiel's," she told him when he repeated the question. "Why are you still here, Theor?"

She turned on her heel and strode back into the cavern, leaving Theor standing there with his mouth hanging open.

---

Three weeks passed, and the majority of the Mad were on the way to recovery. After the valley had been cleared, Sarah Jennifer and Esme had gone on a whirlwind tour of the major centers of population around the world to ensure the local governments had everything in hand.

She'd avoided Kain, focusing on duty like she always did when she didn't want to deal with the personal aspects of her life.

However, now she was back in New Romanov, and there was no getting away from facing him. Esme had gone straight to Lilith's mountain. Sarah Jennifer had to go into New Romanov to check on the people who had been moved there after recovering.

She wished the BYPS could be deactivated so she could run to Mars.

No such luck.

While the human and animal populations had all gotten their patches, the Earth needed more time for the new nanocytes to saturate the ground and ensure that every trace of the Madness-corrupted nanocytes had been wiped out.

She walked through New Romanov after taking care of her duty, the hair on her neck tingling with an anticipation she didn't want to feel. It wasn't that Kain was unattractive. In fact, the opposite was true. What she didn't like was the sensation of missing him when they hadn't spent more than a few hours in each other's company since they met.

She didn't want to be pushed by her nature into a relationship she hadn't chosen for herself. Her dislike of the situation was so great, she'd considered putting herself in the Pod-doc to remove whatever it was that had her thoughts turning to him every time she laid her head down to sleep.

Esme had just laughed at her when she'd brought it up, telling her to take the stick out of her ass and consider that it wasn't her wolf that was making her feel so strongly but the fact that a human being wasn't meant to be alone their whole life.

Ezekiel was outside the tavern. His face split in a wide smile when he saw her walking up the street. "Sarah Jennifer, you're back!"

Sarah Jennifer couldn't resist his smile, still boyish despite him being in his thirties. "You guys are living it up, I see." She nodded at the tavern door, which was ajar and spilling warm light into the night, along with music and laughter.

Ezekiel waved her in. "We're celebrating. The ale is good. Everyone is happy."

Sarah Jennifer grinned. "And you're out here?"

"I needed a little air," Ezekiel explained with a blush. "Like I said, the ale is good."

Sarah Jennifer decided she wouldn't mind a few drinks herself. "I'll believe it when I've tasted it." She reached out and ruffled Ezekiel's hair. "Come on, Kiddo."

The first thing that hit her when they stepped through the door was the smell of logs on the fire mixed with the sawdust on the floor, the earthy scents blending naturally with the tang of what her nose told her was good barley beer. The tavern was packed almost to capacity with townsfolk and Weres, and the band on the stage was playing their hearts out.

Sarah Jennifer scanned the room and relaxed, her senses telling her there was no danger present.

Ezekiel tugged her sleeve. "We're sitting over here," he told her, nodding at a table near the back where Olaf, Theor, Amelie, Curtis, Caitlin, Mary-Anne, and Kain were engrossed in some tale Mika was telling.

The werebear and the Urai warrior were sitting close and touching often. Sarah Jennifer smiled, glad to see Boris' son had persuaded Mika to look at him as more than a protector of the people.

Kain's eyes flicked to her as she approached the table. He dipped his head, then returned his attention to the story.

Sarah Jennifer slid onto a bench beside Theor and accepted the tankard Curtis slid across the table without interrupting Mika's flow.

Mika's hands danced as she talked, her pale eyes flashing with mirth. "This asshole thought he was the second coming or some shit. He faces Olaf down, expecting him to back off, and long, tall, and hairy here drops his britches and lets it all hang out for a few seconds before shifting!"

Everyone laughed, having all seen Olaf's ass at one time or another.

"Hey!" the werebear protested through his laughter. "I'm not about to ruin a good pair of trousers just because some asshole feels like he can walk into town and demand tribute just because he's high on the weed."

Kain raised his tankard. "I feel *that*."

Mika put her hand on Olaf's. "I wasn't complaining."

Olaf pouted. "Of course not. You got a kick out of seeing my junk swinging free."

Mika's face colored pink. "Well…"

Ezekiel booed. "Get a room, you two! You're making me feel terminally single here."

Curtis threw an elbow into Ezekiel's ribs. "Doesn't have to be that way. Heidi was giving you the eye earlier."

"Really?" Ezekiel cocked his head, his gaze sliding to the pretty barmaid, who blew him a kiss.

Mary-Anne cut in, "If you're feeling lonely, I know somewhere you can bury your…*OW!*"

Caitlin pulled her foot back and gave her a satisfied smile. "Serves you right," she murmured as she brought her tankard to her mouth.

Mary-Anne scowled, humor sparkling in her eyes. "See if I wing-woman for you again."

Sarah Jennifer sipped her beer, soaking up the conversation.

Theor leaned in to be heard above the raucous banter flying thick and fast around the tables. "You're quiet tonight."

Sarah Jennifer chuckled. "That's different from any other time how?"

"Quieter than usual," Theor modified. "Everything all right?"

Sarah Jennifer nodded. "Glad to be here. Glad for a few hours' peace and a break from being in charge." She refilled her tankard from one of the jugs in the middle of the table. "Beer is good. Company is good. I'm good."

Theor smiled. "If the boss is happy, so am I." He got to his feet to take his turn at spinning a tale for the group, leaving Sarah Jennifer to her thoughts.

The warriors around the tables slowly quieted as the band switched from lively folk music to a melancholy tune.

Amelie took up the tune, her voice rising true above the conversation in the room. *"The harvest of the sea comes to me; the ocean is my sister. I sail her with pride, and my men are blessed by her generosity. I am capricious like her, our natures are one. Anger us at your peril, we will strip you to the bone."*

She got to her feet and climbed onto the table as the assembled company stamped their feet in time to the music.

*"My sister, she is wild. Her depths are hidden. Beware the unwary, for she is quick to reveal them. When the call to battle comes, the wind fills my sails. A brave man it is who dares to take on the waves."*

Sarah Jennifer glanced at Kain while his attention was

on the trade mistress. His face was flushed from the warmth of the room and the flowing alcohol, adding to his rugged good looks.

Maybe it was the large quantity of beer she'd consumed, but...she wasn't feeling the same frustration with her attraction to him that she'd been wallowing in for the last few weeks.

He sensed her scrutiny and looked her way. He winked before returning his attention to the song.

Sarah Jennifer blushed.

Kain drained his drink and slammed the tankard down before leaping up onto the table next to Amelie.

The trade mistress bowed and stepped down as the Were added his verse to the song.

*"I have never sailed the sea. But the land speaks to me. Long have I run under the moon. Alone in the pack, family I found. Women come and go, and I never stick around."*

That got a bawdy cheer. "Player!" Sarah Jennifer catcalled, reading between the lines.

Kain flashed her a grin and continued without missing a beat. *"With the moon in the sky, beauty catching my eye, who knows where the night will go?"*

*Not anywhere I'm planning to lead,* Sarah Jennifer thought.

Kain hopped down from the table, making way for the burly warrior who stepped up a few tables over.

Sarah Jennifer scrutinized Kain as the unfamiliar warrior began an unsubtle ode to his sword. Now she understood why Kain had given her as wide a berth as she'd given him.

Puppy was afraid to lose his heart as much as she was.

The singing went on into the small of the night as the ale continued to flow.

At some point, Olaf and Mika slipped away. Ezekiel vanished around the same time Heidi's shift ended. One by one the party departed, eventually leaving Sarah Jennifer and Kain alone at the table.

Heidi's replacement brought a fresh jug of ale, taking her time to clear the empties away in the hope of being the one to catch Kain's eye.

The Were only had eyes for Sarah Jennifer.

He pushed the jug toward her. Sarah Jennifer picked it up and refilled her tankard without a word.

Kain watched her for a long moment before speaking. "Are we going to ignore whatever this is between us?"

Sarah Jennifer took a deep drink before replying. "Suits me. I'm not looking to get involved."

"Me either," he told her. "But you can't tell me there isn't something there."

Sarah Jennifer lifted a shoulder. "Didn't say there wasn't."

Kain's eyebrows met in thought. "What *are* you saying?"

Sarah Jennifer leaned over the table to fill Kain's tankard. "I'm saying nothing. Drink up, Player. This night is almost over, and duty will be calling all too soon."

"Fuck duty." Kain laughed at her scowl. "Fine. Have it that way."

Sarah Jennifer smiled. "Are you looking to join the pack?"

Kain's smile faded. "Unlikely. I had a pack. The politics of fuckheads fighting for supremacy wasn't my scene."

"I don't appreciate poor language," Sarah Jennifer told

him. "However, knowing what pack life can be like without a worthy Alpha, I'm inclined to let it slide without discipline just this once."

Kain's grin returned. "Sweetheart, I say fuck a *lot*. If you want me to stick around, you're gonna have to get used to it."

Sarah Jennifer met his stare. "If you want to stick around, you'll be joining the pack, and your ass will be mine to command."

Kain raised an eyebrow, a sly grin appearing on his face. "Thought you didn't want my ass?"

Sarah Jennifer raised her tankard. "Touché, Player."

Kain bumped his tankard against hers. "Anytime, Princess."

A commotion outside the tavern forestalled her reply. Their heads snapped to the door as Curtis burst in, sweating and panting heavily. "Major! You're needed at the rift!"

CHAPTER TWENTY

Esme wished she had the juice to translocate. She'd left the mountain when she sensed the surge in energy from the rift and was running as fast as her legs could carry her toward the valley, her radio dangling from her belt to keep her hands free.

Her worst fears were realized when she reached the valley.

The Skrima were here.

Six of them had made it through so far.

Esme grabbed her radio and thumbed the button. "Enora, where are you?"

A kinetic impacted the valley floor, taking out two of the Skrima in a spray of dirt, ichor, and body parts.

"You're going to need more than kinetics!" Esme yelled into the radio. "Fire your Etheric cannons on that rift and make sure no more of those ugly bastards get across to our side!"

"On it," the AI replied.

Twin beams of energy lanced the darkness as the

ND ROBERTS & MICHAEL ANDERLE

airship came about, and Enora let rip on the rift with her Etheric cannons.

Esme heard screams from beyond the rift and sighed in relief. Enora would hold the rest back. She could deal with those that had already crossed the tear in reality.

She pulled on the Etheric and called fire from the air, encircling the valley. It wasn't enough to contain all of them.

One Skrim vaulted the ring of fire and crashed into the forest, heading away from New Romanov.

Esme had no choice but to focus on the remaining three. She dodged their attempts to crush her under their feet, darting between their legs as she called on the land to trap them.

Thick roots burst from the ground and twisted around the lower limbs of one of the Skrima. It fell with a roar, writhing to free itself as the roots wrapped its body and *squeezed*.

Esme had more skill than available energy. She needed Ezekiel and Sarah Jennifer. She called with her mind for them both as she continued to fight. The move cost her.

One of the Skrima kicked her, sending her flying across the valley. A handy tree halted her progress, dislocating her shoulder in the process.

Esme screamed to release the pain as she dragged herself to her feet. She slammed the shoulder into the tree trunk to realign her joint and ignited her magic as the Skrima came for her. "Ye're not getting past me so easily," she yelled, releasing a torrent of white-hot flames.

The Skrim she hit screamed as it was burned alive. Esme sagged against the tree trunk, drained. "Two down, just the biggest, baddest one to go. Enora, where's my backup?"

"I'm reading the major two minutes west of your location," the AI replied.

Two minutes was a lifetime. Esme picked up her courage and charged, screaming, *"FUCK IT!"* as she pushed the flames ahead of her.

At ten feet tall, the final Skrim was impervious to her attacks. It shrugged off the flames and tossed its horned head as it shrieked at her.

Esme felt her magic running low. Her draw on the Etheric was a trickle, her well almost empty.

She sensed Sarah Jennifer was almost at the valley and redoubled her efforts to keep the remaining Skrim occupied until her backup arrived.

At last, her magic failed. Esme ran for cover, screaming, *"ENORA!"*

Two blinding bolts of energy knocked the Skrim back before it could crush Esme.

A keening screech came from the rift as another two Skrima forced their way through, now that Enora wasn't there to hold them back. The AI's voice came over the radio, "Do I take care of the Skrima that are here, or prevent more from coming through?"

Before Esme could reply, Sarah Jennifer and Kain came crashing out of the tree line, Kain in his Pricolici form.

He didn't slow, gouging the smallest Skrim with his claws and teeth as he tackled it to the ground.

Olaf and Mika were the next to arrive. The warrior woman and the werebear flew out of the forest, Olaf roaring with fury.

Next came Ezekiel, followed by Caitlin.

Sarah Jennifer took charge. "Ezekiel, Esme, do what you can to seal that rift," Sarah Jennifer commanded as she called ice from the clouds above. Her eyes glowed red as the weather responded to her command. "The rest of you, drive those Skrima toward the mountain."

It began to rain hard. The temperature dropped, and the rain turned to hail as Sarah Jennifer reached deep inside and pulled on her connection to the Etheric.

She didn't *want* weather.

She wanted the ground to open up and swallow the Skrima whole.

As if it understood, the ground began to shake.

*"GET CLEAR!"* Sarah Jennifer screamed as a yawning chasm opened in the valley floor.

The Skrima vanished into the earth, their angry screeches shaking rocks loose from the mountainside. Olaf, Mika, Caitlin, and Kain dodged the rolling boulders as they ran for the safety of the mountainside. The Skrima were swallowed whole.

Beneath the rift, Ezekiel and Esme held hands and channeled their magic into the darkly malevolent tear. Sarah Jennifer ran to them, clasping Esme's free hand to add her energy to the effort to close the rift.

Esme's jaw was clenched, golden light surrounding her body as she pulled in the gifted energy.

"We can't close it!" Ezekiel screamed, sweat streaming down his face.

Evil laughter rang out, amplified by the Etheric energy pouring out of the rift.

*"YOU'LL NEVER DEFEAT ME!"* Laughter screamed, her voice filled with pride.

"We'll just see about that." Esme grunted, dropping her head as she pulled energy through Sarah Jennifer and Ezekiel and forced it to repair the tear in reality.

Sarah Jennifer felt herself being drained as the crack in the sky began to shrink.

Ezekiel dropped to his knees, maintaining his grip on Esme's hand as the energy she was pulling through him burned him up from the inside. "It's too much! Esme, you have to stop!"

Esme continued to fight through the pain. She sensed Laughter attempting to rip the rift wide open and countered with every ounce of her hardheaded determination to prevent the Kurtherian from getting her own way.

She pushed aside the pain of more Etheric energy than her body could handle running through her.

Sarah Jennifer collapsed to her knees at the same moment Ezekiel lost consciousness.

Esme released them and opened herself fully to the Etheric, consequences be damned. She became a conduit, the only hope they had to repel the evil on the other side. She rose into the air as the energy took her over.

Sarah Jennifer was still on her knees, her stomach heaving and her body wracked with burning pain. She missed Esme's ascent toward the rift, too late to do anything but watch as the witch's body was lost in a nimbus of golden light.

Laughter's taunting continued. *"SILLY HUMAN. WHAT DO YOU THINK YOU CAN DO AGAINST ME?"*

Esme's voice shook the valley. *"I CAN DO* THIS, *ABOMINATION."*

Her golden light exploded outward, pushing back the dark energy spilling from the rift.

Laughter screamed in pain, the sound lost among wild screams as Esme's light penetrated the rift and drove back every Skrim waiting on the other side.

Sarah Jennifer could only watch in stunned silence. Esme's voice spoke into her mind, *Don't let this hold you back, Duckie. I'm always with you.*

The rift receded, shrinking to a thin line as Esme fell to the ground and lay still.

"*NO!*" Sarah Jennifer screamed. She tried to stand, but her knee failed and she pitched forward, skinning her hands and face on the exposed ground.

She forced herself to crawl, her body refusing to allow her to do more than drag herself to where her best friend in the whole world lay in a broken heap on the blackened grass.

Her nails broke as she tore into the burned earth in her desperation to reach Esme. She threw up again, not caring that she was on the verge of passing out. She wiped her mouth and forced herself to keep moving, pulling herself hand over hand, her knees scraped by rocks.

After an effort that was beyond superhuman, she reached Esme and pulled her limp body into her lap.

The witch's eyes were blank.

Sobbing, Sarah Jennifer pried Esme's mouth open and attempted to breathe life back into her.

It was all for nothing.

Esme was gone.

Sarah Jennifer tipped her head back and screamed as grief consumed her.

Kain's heart was torn in two by the sound. He shifted, his instincts taking over. Caitlin's hand on his arm unfelt, he tore across the valley—and found he had no enemy to fight.

He found Sarah Jennifer cradling Esme's lifeless body, begging her to come back, to open her eyes and tell her she was just spent. Ezekiel was still unconscious. The rift was barely there. Kain hesitated. He could not fight death for her.

His body returned to its human form, and he slowly approached the keening, red-eyed woman his heart belonged to. He sank to his knees beside her and put an arm around her shoulders, saying nothing.

There was nothing to be said.

Ezekiel woke as Olaf, Mika, and Caitlin joined them, each finding a space near Sarah Jennifer and kneeling to form a protective circle around her. They surrounded her with love, which was all they could do. Ezekiel was unable to contain his shock and grief. He sobbed along with Sarah Jennifer, unashamed of his tears for the woman who had taught him how to access his magic.

Olaf shifted and voiced his emotions in great roars as Mika stood guard and let her tears fall in silent stoicism.

Even Caitlin, who hadn't known Esme well, was moved by her loss. She maintained a watch on the outskirts of the group, gazing at the rift with tears in her eyes.

Sarah Jennifer cried until she was sick again, then she cried some more.

Eventually, her tears refused to come. Her heart empty,

she struggled to get to her feet without letting go of Esme's body.

"Let me help," Kain offered in a low voice.

Sarah Jennifer clutched Esme tighter to her breast. She felt so slight, her light weight somehow disrespecting the huge personality she had projected in life. "*No.* She is mine to take care of."

Kain nodded. "Then let me help *you.*"

Sarah Jennifer looked long and hard at his extended arms before acquiescing to his support. Together, they began the long walk back to New Romanov, with the others forming an honor guard around them.

Kain held Sarah Jennifer up as she walked, lending his strength to her. She refused to let go of Esme's body as she leaned into him, and by the time they reached the foot of Lilith's mountain, he was almost carrying them both.

Ezekiel walked beside them, lost in his memories of everything Esme had done for him during the years he'd lived in Salem. Every kind word. Every time she'd accepted his failures and followed her inevitable pithy comment with the encouragement to keep reaching for his full potential.

He was going to miss her earthy sense of humor and her short temper.

Olaf and Mika went ahead as they climbed the path that led up the mountain.

When Sarah Jennifer stumbled into Lilith's cavern, she found that the werebear had cleared the main workbench and laid out a huge, thick fur to lay Esme's body on.

Lilith's voice was filled with sadness. "Olaf told me what happened. I felt the energy shift but had no idea."

Sarah Jennifer shrugged Kain's arm off and limped to the bench. She lifted Esme onto the fur and drew the sides over her body as though keeping her warm would make a difference. "She didn't die for nothing. Laughter can't send her army of monsters through the rift. She sacrificed herself to make sure of it."

She turned and slid to the floor, her back against the workbench. "Lilith, we need to make sure what Esme did sticks."

With that, she gave in to the exhaustion and pain wracking her body and closed her eyes.

Her dreams were fleeting, her perspective switching from the battle she'd just left to half-remembered conversations with Esme. One moment they were in the old cottage in Lynnwood drinking tea, and the next, Esme was burning in front of her, and she was helpless to do anything.

The pain of losing her all over again shocked Sarah Jennifer into wakefulness.

Her eyes snapped open. The cavern was dark, the lights dimmed.

Someone had wrapped her in a blanket. Despite the darkness, she knew she was not alone.

A gleam of yellow caught her attention.

There was Theor, standing guard over her from the doorway.

He inclined his head when he saw she was awake, saying nothing.

Sarah Jennifer slipped back into her fractured dreams, knowing she was safe.

The next morning, the people of New Romanov came to pay their respects. Sarah Jennifer accepted their condolences in a daze, disbelief clouding her responses.

Olaf had left the mountain during the night. Ezekiel was inconsolable. He stuck by Sarah Jennifer all through the day, saying little.

Everyone understood. Even Irina was gentle with them, sheathing her sharp tongue for once as she made sure Sarah Jennifer and Ezekiel ate the hot food she'd brought up from town.

Sarah Jennifer refused to leave Esme's side until the last of the townsfolk had departed. Then she went to tell Enora they would be leaving for Salem the next day.

When she returned to the mountain, Caitlin was waiting for her with the German Shepherd.

Jaxon padded over and pressed his head to Sarah Jennifer's leg, licking her hand.

"How are you holding up?" Caitlin asked.

Sarah Jennifer was numb. "I'm... I'll be okay. I have to make some calls. Arrangements need to be made."

Caitlin nodded and stood aside to let her pass. She touched Sarah Jennifer's arm lightly. "We're going to stay with you until you get back to your pack. You need friends right now."

Sarah Jennifer nodded. "Okay. Thank you."

Ezekiel was kneeling by Esme's body, his head bowed and his lips moving in silent pleas.

She tapped him on the shoulder. "Come on, kiddo. We need to let everyone know what went down here."

He looked up at her, his eyes red-rimmed with crying, and nodded slowly.

Sarah Jennifer led him to the comms room and took her seat at the radio. Her hand hovered over the transceiver.

"Where do I start?" she murmured, her heart constricting.

She called Salem.

# CHAPTER TWENTY-ONE

**Salem, MA**

Even the sky showed its grief on the day of Esme's funeral. Clouds tinged blood-red from the light of the BYPS grid released a steady, cold drizzle that matched the landscape of the mourners' hearts.

Sarah Jennifer walked through the rain at the head of the procession. The bier holding Esme's body was carried through the heart of the city by those closest to her.

The band came behind, playing a mournful tune that perfectly encapsulated the sadness of everyone present. They entered the cemetery, where chairs had been set out for dignitaries from around the world who had been flown in for the funeral.

Sarah Jennifer saw the pale glow in Amelie's eyes and understood that the rain was falling in response to her emotions.

The procession stopped at the mausoleum raised by Linda and the rock mages, and the bearers placed the bier on the raised plinth inside. Annie and Lenore broke away from the others as the pallbearers went to sit with the mourners.

Sarah Jennifer took Ezekiel's hand as the band ceased. "We'll get through this," she told him in a murmur. "You and me."

Ezekiel choked back his tears. "I still can't believe she's gone, Sarah Jennifer. I keep expecting her to wake up and yell at me."

Sarah Jennifer's heart hitched in her chest as she pulled him close. "Me too, kiddo. Me too."

Lenore gave her a nod, signaling it was time to begin. Sarah Jennifer released Ezekiel and walked in front of the mourners. She looked out across the sea of sad faces. "Esme was loved," she began, then paused as emotion stole her voice.

She swallowed hard and forced herself to keep talking. "Esme was loved, and she was loved because she *gave* love. There isn't anyone here whose life she didn't touch. I could talk about her contribution to the rebuilding of the world, but I won't. I could scream and rant and cry because she gave her life to prevent aliens from destroying everything we've fought to fix, but I won't. I want to tell you about my friend, the woman who was there for me when I was broken."

Sarah Jennifer squeezed her eyes closed to halt the fresh tears that formed there. "She was short-tempered and always had something to say when people were behaving like dumbasses. She always had time to talk, always offered comfort and tea when the magnitude of the task ahead got too much. She never once put up with my bullheaded stubbornness. She pushed me to be the best version of myself, to be the leader we needed to get us through the Madness. Well, the Madness is over, and Esme is gone, but I will never, ever forget the impact she had on my life. On everyone's lives. This whole world owes its future to her sacrifice."

She stepped down and went to sit with Ezekiel for the rest of the eulogies. One by one, people shared their stories about Esme. At some point, Ezekiel put his hand in hers and leaned his head on her shoulder, his tears flowing freely.

At last, it was his turn to speak.

He got up and walked to the front, head bowed, and faced the crowd. He said nothing for a long moment, listening to Lilith's voice in his mind.

His hands opened and clenched as he processed the Kurtherian's grief along with his own.

Then, he spoke.

"Esme was the first to say that the gifts we have are magic. She taught me how to apply what I learned from Lilith to the real world. I was a child when I was brought here. I was afraid, and I had lost my parents to the Madness. She was warmth. She was stability. She was the voice of reason whenever I was worked up about anything.

"We stood together on the battlefield, and she put everyone on the Earth ahead of herself. She... She died doing what she knew was right. She didn't back down. She didn't surrender even though she knew the price for holding back the Skrima. For holding back that bitch Laughter."

He looked down. "I failed her. I failed everyone every time I allowed fear to make my judgments for me. I avoided the responsibility I have always known was mine, and now Esme is dead."

Sarah Jennifer shook her head to deny his words, but Ezekiel knew what he had said was the truth. He lifted his chin, his tears still coming even through the resolution he felt hardening inside his soul. "I will never fail in my duty to humanity again. I will take the road fate has decided for me and bring magic to the world. Esme always supported my dream of teaching people how to access the gifts the Matriarch gave humanity. Until this moment, I have been selfish, whining like a child because what I wanted didn't fit with what the Defense Force was doing. No more. I will go back to Europe and begin the work I know is needed to take humanity into an age of magic."

He turned to face the darkened doorway, his next words for Esme alone. "I swear, I will not let your sacrifice be for nothing."

He faced Sarah Jennifer. "I'm not going to blame you for leaving anymore. You have given enough. It's my turn to take the mantle now. I'm ready."

He stepped down and walked out of the cemetery.

---

The departure from Salem was subdued, no one wanting to acknowledge that Esme's passing had marked the end of an era and it would soon be time for the Weres to leave Earth for good.

As the *Enora* set off under an unnaturally red sky, Sarah Jennifer wanted nothing more than to close herself off in her cabin and avoid discussing next steps with everyone aboard, but she knew she couldn't.

She walked into the crew lounge and nodded at Ezekiel, Olaf, Amelie, Reika, Brittvi, Linda, and Adrien before taking a seat at the head of the table that took up most of the space in the cabin.

Theor remained standing as Caitlin, Mary-Anne, and Kain squeezed in.

Sarah Jennifer waited for everyone to get comfortable before beginning the meeting. Esme would have made some comment that broke the ice, but that wasn't her style, and she felt the absence of her friend keenly. She suppressed her emotions and turned her head to look at Ezekiel. "What are your plans?"

Ezekiel had his hands folded on the table in front of him. "To do what I always said I would. I'm going to build schools where people can come to learn about their magic."

"Where?" Sarah Jennifer asked. "How, with what resources?"

"We can help," Linda put in. "We have the whole valley to build in. More space than we need, really."

The town of Bad Salzig had been lost to rising sea levels, and the people had relocated to what had formerly been the Rhine Gorge some four or five years previously, expanding the town the Defense Force had evacuated during the Madness.

Adrien looked like he was going to argue her offer.

"Problem, Adrien?" Sarah Jennifer asked.

"No," he replied after a long pause. "Not exactly."

Sarah Jennifer had little patience for the man. "If there

is a problem, air it now, before we divert resources for this project."

He lifted a shoulder. "I have to think of our people—"

"Linda's people," Sarah Jennifer corrected.

"Linda's people, then," he modified sourly. "How will they be affected by floods of new magic users descending on our home?"

"I should think they will be glad to be a center for the marvelous future ahead," Reika commented, giving him a suspicious look.

Linda put her hand over Adrien's. "I think what Adrien means is that we need to make sure we are prepared for a population surge."

Sarah Jennifer kept her counsel, knowing that had not been the slimeball's meaning.

Ezekiel seemed blind to Adrien's personality. He leaned forward. "What is needed is a city. We only need enough people with physical magic to raise it from the ground, and the rest will follow. Reika, I know you have the mage-power. Are you willing to help?"

The Thane considered his request. "I am, on the condition my people will be guaranteed places at this school of magic."

Linda stuck out her hand. "Done."

Reika shook the proffered hand. "Very well, Chancellor. I will prepare my people to travel on my return to Agatha's Mountain."

"I have to return to my post at New Romanov," Olaf told them, "but I will send any warriors who wish to broaden their horizons to this new city to provide protection for the people living there. The Rhine Valley is close to the former Danelands. There are still many who see conquest as a valid route to personal glory."

Amelie nodded. "Agreed. I will provide safe passage to those crossing the seas to reach this new city." She smiled at Ezekiel. "I also have a desire to pass on my knowledge."

Ezekiel nodded enthusiastically. "We will need teachers for all types of magic."

Sarah Jennifer listened to them all with half her mind on Mars. "Could be you'll get some magic users who want to move on from Salem once I've fully withdrawn the Defense Force. Failing that, there's always the option of searching out new forms of magic as they develop."

Caitlin cut in, "Is that what's going to happen? People are just going to wake up one day and find they can suddenly pull fire from thin air or move mountains?"

Sarah Jennifer chuckled. "Maybe not mountains. Not right away, at least."

"No one has explained to us how we got from vampires and Weres to magic in everyone," Kain stated in confusion. "I mean, I have a rough idea about nanocytes and Kurtherians using the planet like their own personal petri dish, but how does everything you've done translate for Ma and me? Is Caitlin going to get magic?"

"How long will the BYPS be up for?" Mary-Anne added. "Or more accurately, how long until you take the Weres away and leave people to fend for themselves?"

"One question at a time," Sarah Jennifer told them. "Caitlin is already enhanced. That's clear to me, even if you two can't see it. Not everyone with nanocytes was a vampire or a Were. There were always people like my grandfather who were a little stronger, a little faster and harder to hurt. I don't know how the saturation will affect Mary-Anne. I'm guessing since her nanocytes come from Michael, however indirectly, she will retain her vampiric abilities. Same for you, Kain. The Pod-doc fixed your nanocytes so they can't be affected by the Affliction. Even the Madness didn't take you completely when you were infected."

She paused. "I'm hoping that the three of you—and Jaxon—will decide to come with us when we leave."

Caitlin blanched. "I can't leave Earth. I have family I want to get back to."

"Where Caitlin goes, I go too," Mary-Anne declared.

Only Kain was silent.

Caitlin turned to look at him. "You're going to leave us, aren't you?"

Kain closed his eyes and sighed. "I don't know. I need time to decide what's right."

Mary-Anne put her arm around Caitlin. "Whatever you decide, we will understand."

Caitlin shrugged her off, her face reddening. "What? No, we won't! Kain, what about everything we've been through together? Doesn't that count for anything?"

Kain's gaze was on Sarah Jennifer. He tore his eyes away from her to look at Caitlin. "It counts for everything. I'm torn right now."

"The heart wants what it wants." Olaf smiled softly. "And the pack bond is not something a Were can cast off so easily. You are a wolf with two packs, it seems to me."

Kain nodded. "That about sums it up."

Sarah Jennifer didn't voice the dual discomfort and relief she felt at her deep-seated knowledge that Kain was going to choose to leave with her. She saw it in his eyes, and she knew he saw in hers what she was feeling.

"Let's just focus on what's in front of us right now," she told the group. "The BYPS will be up for another four months. Ezekiel's plan is solid, but it's going to take some work on everyone's part to make it a reality."

"We have the benefit of experience," Theor added. "I can get with Izzy and arrange for everyone who isn't needed elsewhere to be deployed to Germany."

Sarah Jennifer nodded. "That's a start. We'll need more than magic to raise this city. We can expedite the planning stage. You're right, we have the experience, and we're not going to face any of the problems the Mars team has had to overcome."

Linda clapped her hands, a wide smile lighting her features. "This will be fun! Hard work, but fun!" She glanced at Ezekiel. "A new city needs a name."

Ezekiel tilted his head. "What do you suggest?"

"There's only one name for the city, silly. You already know it." Linda beamed as Ezekiel's eyes misted over.

"*Arcadia.*"

### Germany, Rhine Gorge

Within four weeks, the sleepy gorge had become a hive of activity as the Defense Force, Reika's mages, and the warriors Olaf had sent arrived in fits and starts around the initial clearing of the city's foundations.

Even pre-WWDE, the area had been mostly given to agricultural use. After more than two hundred years of nature reclaiming the land, the forest had encroached on most of the territory outside the valley. However, the valley itself had housed people continuously, making it the perfect place to raise the shining city of Ezekiel's and Linda's childhood dreams.

Sarah Jennifer relished the opportunity to bury herself in physical labor while she worked through what life looked like without Esme.

She spent the majority of her time with Ezekiel, the two of them heading up training in the magical efforts involved in raising the city from the valley floor.

Bethany Anne's original plan had been to have the changes take effect over a number of generations. However, the calculations made by Esme, Lilith, and Enora had taken into account the likelihood of another corruption occurring before humanity evolved the abilities the Queen intended, and the BYPS could not remain activated indefinitely.

As a result of the modified enhancement process, which relied on the will and need of the individual, many of the residents of the old town were already developing the beginnings of magic. Ezekiel had split them into two groups. In the first, he'd placed anyone showing physical types of magic such as telekinesis and the manipulation of the elements, and in the other, he'd placed the people who styled themselves in the mold of the ancient Druids of Celtic and Germanic lore.

The first two hours of the day were spent in the open fields outside the city walls, teaching the people how to access and control their nascent abilities.

Linda joined them in the mornings, working with those whose skills leaned toward working with rock, while Sarah

Jennifer worked with the nature magic adepts who had expanded their connection to the land. Ezekiel darted between the groups, his acceptance of himself and his role giving him more control of his abilities than he'd ever had before.

Training ended with the midday meal, then everyone shifted their focus to the construction of Arcadia until the sun set. At the end of the day, everyone came together to eat and make plans for the next day under the red-rippling sky.

The arrival of the Defense Force brought engineers, who quickly got to work teaching the basics to the mechanically minded.

Slowly but surely, the city took shape as winter passed into early spring and the temperature began to rise. Grand buildings were raised in the citadel to provide centers of learning, commerce, and leadership. These presided over the residential quarters that spread out to the city walls, the houses of the inner-city boulevards separated by market squares and quaint rows of storefronts set aside for people who wished to start businesses of their own.

Farther out, there were larger houses planned for the next stage of expansion, when the need to stay close to the citadel was less of an issue for the citizens and people were able to focus on growing their families instead of working to survive.

Six weeks into the build, Sarah Jennifer was down in the belly of the magic school, working on the conundrum of how to provide a magical solution to the city's power requirements, when she heard a familiar voice filtering down from above.

"Make sure no one followed us," Adrien told someone. "I don't want this getting back to Major Busybody."

Sarah Jennifer realized she was hearing his voice from the air vent high on the wall above the table she was sitting at.

"We are alone," a feminine voice replied.

Sarah Jennifer's lip curled. What Linda saw in him, she couldn't figure out.

"Good," Adrien told the woman, whose soft reply was lost before it made it down the air duct to Sarah Jennifer. "Tell me what you found in the mountains."

Sarah Jennifer strained to hear, realizing her initial assessment of Adrien being a cheating sonofabitch was wrong and the woman must actually be a spy.

"They live in the mountains a few days' walk from here."

"And their abilities?" Adrien pressed, his sharp voice carrying clearly. "Do they pose any threat to us?"

"...made me see things that weren't there..."

Mind magic? Sarah Jennifer hadn't heard of anyone with that ability besides Esme.

The reminder stung her, and she missed what Adrien said next. Admonishing herself, she downed tools and climbed onto the table to press her ear to the air vent.

"They must be dealt with before Ezekiel finds out about them," Adrien snarled.

"Must they?" the mystery woman asked. "Or could this be the perfect opportunity to get him out of the city?"

There was a long pause, and Sarah Jennifer wondered if they had left whatever room they were hiding in. Then Adrien spoke again.

"That isn't the worst idea. Linda is much more... malleable without that twerp around to fill her head with ideas about justice and equality for all. Good work."

"Good work deserves a just reward," the woman purred. "What say you and I—"

Her suggestion was cut off by Adrien's voice. "Don't embarrass yourself. Linda is going to be my wife. Nothing will get in the way of that, not even one as...charming as you."

Sarah Jennifer had heard enough. She leapt lightly off the table and landed noiselessly on the naked stone.

The news of a community developing mind magic was huge. Adrien might well want to remove the threat he perceived from the mind mages, but it would be a cold day in Hell before she let him get his way.

# CHAPTER TWENTY-TWO

Ezekiel and Caitlin worked side by side to clear the plant life while Kain and Mary-Anne dug ditches for Arcadia's graywater runoff.

Caitlin was showing promise with nature magic. Tree roots pulled back at her direction, leaving a channel for the Were and the vampire to dig.

"How much farther do we have to go?" she asked.

Ezekiel released the boulder he was moving out of the loose earth, the bubble of magic dissipating as he lifted a hand to shade his eyes. "Maybe another half-mile?"

Caitlin smiled. "I could get used to magic taking the challenges out of projects like this." She sat back on the bank as Kain and Mary-Anne moved in with their shovels.

"Speak for yourself," Kain told her with a laugh. "Some of us like getting our hands dirty."

"Makes you feel all strong and manly, right?" Mary-Anne teased.

Kain grinned. "Damn straight. A Were's gotta work his energy out somehow."

ND ROBERTS & MICHAEL ANDERLE

Caitlin arched an eyebrow. "Well, you don't seem to be getting anywhere with the major."

"Hey!" Ezekiel scowled at her without malice. "Sarah Jennifer has been through a lot."

"That means she needs to keep rejecting my boy?" Caitlin inquired.

"No one is rejecting anyone," Kain cut in. "It's just not the right time for either of us."

"Oooh," Caitlin teased. "So you *have* been talking?"

Kain lifted a shoulder. "A gentleman doesn't tell."

Mary-Anne leaned on her shovel, her eyes dancing with mirth. "Good thing you're not a gentleman, then. Spill!"

"Not happening," Kain stated. He grinned as the ladies booed him. Caitlin was softening to the idea that he wouldn't be returning to Canada with them. He was almost ready to voice his decision.

Ezekiel put his fingers in his ears. "Good. I don't want to hear about Sarah Jennifer's love life, thank you all very much. She's been like a mother to me. It's weird."

Caitlin jumped up from the grassy bank and darted over to tickle Ezekiel. "Awww, Zeke doesn't want to hear that Sarah Jennifer could get up to all the things he likes to do with pretty barmaids."

Kain rolled his eyes. "Classy, Kitty-Cat."

Caitlin grinned. "I know you're not mistaking me for a lady, Pooch."

"Matriarch forbid the idea," he shot back with a deep laugh. "If you started getting airs and graces, we'd have to launch a mission to find out who replaced you with a doppelganger."

Caitlin lifted her chin. "Salt of the earth, that's me. If I ever stop saying it how it is, you damn well better send out a search party for the real me."

Ezekiel waved a hand, and the next section of the ditch opened under his direction. "Come on, guys. We don't want to be late to the *actual* party tonight."

"No, we don't," Mary-Anne agreed. "I heard a rumor the druids are coming in from the forest, and they *always* bring the fun."

"That's because they're not all uptight like the city folk," Caitlin reasoned. "Hopefully, they've been putting as much effort into their distillery as they have into persuading the trees to protect them. I'm sick of that piss-weak ale we've been drinking for the last few weeks."

Everyone agreed with that and they resumed the task at hand, each nursing fond thoughts of the gathering planned for that evening.

The day was warming up, and they were all working up a sweat.

Kain paused to wipe his forehead and caught sight of a golden streak heading straight for them. "Which Were is that?" he asked as the wolf got closer.

Ezekiel turned to look, his brow creasing. "That's Sarah Jennifer. I wonder why she's in such a hurry?"

They found out a few minutes later when she reached them.

She stayed in wolf form and spoke to Ezekiel mind to mind. *Brace yourself, kiddo. I just overheard Adrien talking. He proposed to Linda, and she accepted.*

Ezekiel frowned. *Is* that *what the party tonight is for?*

*Looks that way,* Sarah Jennifer told him. *There's more.*

*What?* Ezekiel asked.

*Adrien has been running spies. That's why I'm here in person. I don't know who is working for him yet, but I intend to find out before the party. The woman he was speaking to has just gotten back from a recon and reported finding mind-magic users in the mountains a few days' walk from here.*

*Mind magic?* Ezekiel's eyes widened. *I thought that ability was rare.*

*Rare enough,* Sarah Jennifer agreed. *But not so rare that it hasn't manifested in this community. Adrien is planning something. His spy suggested using the discovery to get you out of the city, for what reason they didn't say.*

"Probably so I don't persuade Linda to turn him down," Ezekiel muttered, drawing questioning looks from the others.

*I have to get back to the city before I'm missed,* Sarah Jennifer told him. *I'll see you all there later.*

*You mind if I share what's going on with Cait?* he asked.

Sarah Jennifer tilted her head and gave the gang a wolfish grin. *No, go ahead. We need everyone we trust on the same page.*

*I sure wish Olaf was here,* Ezekiel told her. *But we have his warriors guarding the gates.*

*That's my next stop,* Sarah Jennifer informed him. *I want to know who has been out of the city. See if I can figure who Adrien's spies are that way.*

Ezekiel nodded. *Good idea. Maybe putting some Weres on the gates wouldn't be a bad thing, either.*

*That's the plan.* Sarah Jennifer dipped her head. *I'll see you at the party.*

She streaked off across the fields again without another word.

"What was that?" Caitlin asked.

"Trouble," Ezekiel replied, his heart heavy.

Kain frowned. "When isn't there trouble? What kind?"

"We have to finish up here and get back to the city," Ezekiel told them. "Sarah Jennifer overheard Adrien talking to someone he has spying for him about some magic users a few days' walk from here."

"She couldn't tell us that over the radio?" Caitlin asked.

Ezekiel shook his head. "No. Not without risking Adrien's spies finding out she's onto him."

Kain's frown deepened. "Spies? Why would he need spies?"

Ezekiel's face was set in hard lines. "He has to know I'm the only obstacle to her marrying him."

"Ew, that guy gives me the creeps," Caitlin stated. "It's a little much, the way he's always hanging over her."

"She doesn't seem to mind," Mary-Anne commented. "You okay, Ezekiel?"

Ezekiel sighed. "I have no choice but to be okay. Linda is going to accept, I'm almost certain. He was her father's choice, and she's the kind of person to honor his wishes."

Kain observed the tightness in Ezekiel's shoulders. "You care about Linda a lot, don't you?"

Ezekiel nodded. "We were close when we were younger. Then her father died, and we drifted apart when she took over as chancellor."

"You ever tell her how you feel?" Mary-Anne asked.

Ezekiel shook his head. "She has her life. I have mine. We're different people now. I figured she was going to marry Adrien one day, but I guess I didn't want to consider it would actually happen."

Caitlin patted his shoulder in sympathy.

"We've all been there, buddy," Kain commiserated.

Mary-Anne nodded in agreement. "Mmhmm. That guy has the ick factor. I don't care how charming he is; he can't hide that greedy gleam in his eyes from me."

"What else did Sarah Jennifer say?" Kain asked, wishing he had the ability to speak mind to mind.

Ezekiel was quiet for a moment. He didn't dislike Adrien. They'd spent time talking about the future of Arcadia, and they had being orphans in common. "She didn't say much more than that. She's planning to let him think his plotting is working. She thinks he's going to pull something at the party tonight. She's gone to locate Magnus and find out who has come into the city in the last few days."

Caitlin's eyes glowed green as she called her magic. "Then we'd better get finished here."

Piet wandered through the citadel, his satchel weighing heavily on his shoulder. He could take it. Rearick were strong, thanks to the time they spent in the mines of their home.

He had arrived in Arcadia later than planned due to the hard time the guards on the city gate had given him when he hadn't wanted to show them the treasure he was carrying. Luckily, one of the Defense Force Weres had recognized him and told the armored guards to allow him access, no questions asked.

It seemed not everyone was forgetful of the part his

people had played in holding back the Mad from Bad Salzig and the surrounding towns.

Piet had other business on his mind now that the Madness was over. The rearick's leaders wanted gold to fund their mining efforts in exchange for the gems he was carrying.

A mage could draw power through the previously useless shinies, something that had been discovered recently. They had been tossing these gems on the slag pile with the rest of the detritus for years.

The news that Arcadia was set to be the new center for magic users made it the natural choice for the rearick to choose as the place to start. Now that magic had begun to appear, the leaders had renamed the clear gems "amphoralds" and sent Piet out with the directive to use that relationship to strike a deal. He had been chosen as the envoy because of his link to the chancellor. Truth be told, he was glad of the chance to see Linda again.

He found her house easily enough, but she wasn't home. There was a note stuck to her door. He tiptoed to read it.

"Lass is holdin' a party?" he murmured with a smile. "Sounds like the citadel is the place to be."

He hoisted his satchel and retraced his steps through the torchlit streets, happy to be among so many familiar faces. He had spent a lot of time in Bad Salzig and was well-remembered by the former citizens of the river town.

"Is that Piet?" a voice he recognized called.

The rearick flashed a wide grin when he saw who was calling him. "Stone me, is that young Ezekiel, all grown?"

Ezekiel bent to embrace the old warrior. "It's good to see you after so long, my friend. What brings you here?"

Piet looked past Ezekiel to the two women and a strapping male and decided to play his hand close until he was in front of the chancellor. "Business, mostly. Can't say it's not good to see you, though. You got any idea where I can find Linda?"

Ezekiel gave him a curious look. "She's at the Great Hall."

"What about my old friend the major?" Piet asked, noting that the man he didn't know reacted to his inquiry. "She'd be a sight for sore eyes as well."

Ezekiel laughed. "She's here. Come on, let's get you somewhere you can wash the travel off and get a cup of ale."

"I'm pretty parched, I'm not gonna lie," Piet returned with a laugh.

Ezekiel led the way, introducing Caitlin, Mary-Anne, and Kain as they crossed the cobbled street.

Piet's eyes widened. "A vampire? You're not gonna suck my blood now, are ya?"

Mary-Anne winked at him. "Not unless you ask nicely."

Piet laughed. "Well, all right, then."

They split up when they got to the hall. Ezekiel took Piet through winding, candlelit corridors and up two flights of stairs to Linda's office.

Linda was overjoyed to see the old rearick. "You came just in time! Tonight is my engagement party."

Piet turned to Ezekiel and grabbed his hand. "Congratulations. It's about time you made an honest woman out of her."

Ezekiel blushed, suppressing his reaction since he wasn't supposed to know about the proposal. "Not me. Adrien."

She showed them her ring. "Adrien asked me last night. A new city, a new life."

Ezekiel gave her a hug. "Congratulations, Linda. I hope you two have a great life together."

Piet didn't bother to hide his surprise. "Well, blow me down with a feather." He offered Linda a deep bow. "Then I guess all my congratulations go to you and your man."

"Piet's here on business, he says," Ezekiel told Linda, changing the subject.

Piet nodded. "It can wait until after your party, lass. I'll just need somewhere to store my bag until you're free to talk."

Linda smiled. "Go ahead. I have some time before I'm expected downstairs. What can I do for you?"

Piet grinned. "It's more what I can do for you. Or more accurately, what the rearick can do for the people of Arcadia."

He pulled one of the cloth-covered gems out of his bag and unwrapped it. "Needs a magic-user to show its true potential." He held the gem out to Ezekiel. "Pull a wee bit of magic through this. Just a smidge, mind. We don't want any accidents."

Ezekiel furrowed his brow in curiosity but did as the rearick directed.

Linda's mouth dropped open when the amphorald began to glow. "What's happening?"

Ezekiel was amazed. "It's storing the Etheric energy I'm pulling through it like a battery."

"Really?" Linda's eyes widened. "Piet, do your people have more of these…what do you call them?"

"Amphoralds, lass." Piet handed the stone to Linda. "There's plenty more where that came from. I've been sent to tell you we have an almost limitless supply for sale."

Linda couldn't tear her gaze away from the gem. "We could use these. What do your people want in return for them?"

"How are ye fixed for gold?" Piet asked.

The door opened before Linda could answer, and Adrien walked in. "Linda, dearest—" The amphorald caught his eye. "What have we here?"

"A solution to powering the city," Linda told him.

Adrien's eyes gleamed. "Yes, I can feel the energy within it. One gem isn't enough for our needs, though."

"You can have as many as you can buy," Piet informed him.

Adrien fixed the rearick with a shrewd look. "We can discuss this in more detail tomorrow." He moved to put his arm around Linda. "Tonight is for celebrating our engagement."

Ezekiel made himself smile. "It's good to have something to celebrate."

Linda's eyes sparkled. "Yes, and I need to get dressed, so out, all of you."

"The engineers are going to love this," Ezekiel enthused. "Piet, come with me. Sarah Jennifer needs to know about this wonder."

Sarah Jennifer sat at the bar, nursing a flagon of mead and her mixed feelings about tonight's gathering. The hall was packed with people coming in from their day's work, their voices raised in high spirits at the chance to get together.

Her investigation had yielded three names. Monica LeFevre was looking like the most likely owner of the second voice she'd overheard. The Danelander was nowhere to be seen in the crowded hall, but Sarah Jennifer didn't discount her making an appearance at some point. The other two people Olaf's warriors had identified were still out of the city and would be detained for questioning on their return.

Sarah Jennifer missed her pack. She hadn't informed them of Esme's death yet, not wanting to give them the bad news over an audio-only connection. There were plenty of Weres around, but they were no substitute for the twenty-five she called family. Still, she was among friends, and she was glad to see everyone taking a load off after the huge push to raise the residential quarters surrounding the citadel to make room for the people who had been drawn here by the news of a place where they could learn about the abilities appearing in the population.

A hand on her shoulder dragged her out of her thoughts.

"Major, this is a celebration," Dakota chastised with a smile. "You're bringing down the tone."

Sarah Jennifer laughed. "Sorry, Dakota. I guess my mind is on other things tonight."

The Were grinned. "I'd get it on that handsome guy friend of Ezekiel's if I was you. Dance a little!"

Sarah Jennifer wondered where Kain was. "You seen his group anywhere?"

Dakota hitched a thumb in the direction of the carvery pit. "I saw Caitlin's dog hanging around by the grill a little while ago. He's a character. You'd almost believe he understood what we were saying."

Sarah Jennifer chuckled. "Dogs are like that. Intelligent creatures who know exactly how to charm a bit of whatever you're eating from you."

"I haven't met one before Jaxon," Dakota admitted. "I sure hope they took some dogs to space. The Madness wiped most of them out here on Earth."

Sarah Jennifer smiled, remembering Clovis. "My family always had a dog. Maybe I should see about finding Jaxon a mate or three so we can get some puppies going."

"You thinking of pimping my dog out?" Caitlin asked, sliding onto the stool next to Sarah Jennifer. "Not a bad idea. I know a guy."

"You always know a guy, Kitty-Cat," Kain cut in as he took the next stool along from her.

"What's with all the dog talk?" Mary-Anne asked. "What we need are drinks. Ezekiel will be done with his friend soon, and I have a feeling he's going to want to drown his sorrows."

"Which friend would that be?" Sarah Jennifer inquired.

"Short guy, cute accent," Mary-Anne offered.

"He said he knew you," Caitlin added. "Piet?"

Sarah Jennifer's spirits lifted. "You're kidding? Piet is here?"

"Something about having business with the chancellor," Kain supplied, waving for the bartender's attention. "Did the druids make it yet? I've heard good things about their brewing."

Sarah Jennifer pointed at a group dressed in green. "There are the druids. I recommend you try the mead. Packs a punch."

Dakota snorted. "Just make sure you can walk back to wherever you're sleeping tonight."

"Are you and Harris staying in the citadel?" Sarah Jennifer asked.

Dakota shook her head. "No, we're in the camp with the rest of the Defense Force. No point getting comfortable when we're due to ship out soon."

Caitlin's smile faded at the reminder. She hopped down from the stool. "I see Jax is causing chaos." She took her drink with her.

"Dammit," Kain grumbled. "She's going to be in a mood all night now."

Mary-Anne shrugged. "She'll come around. She's going to miss you, is all."

"I haven't said I'm going to Mars for sure," Kain protested.

Mary-Anne put a hand on his shoulder and pressed her forehead to his. "Yeah, but we all know your decision is made." She straightened and glanced the way Caitlin had gone. "I'll make sure she doesn't start anything. You two kids have fun and don't do anything I wouldn't."

"That's a very short list," Kain called after her. "Bring some ribs back with you!"

"I'd better go find Harris," Dakota told them.

Sarah Jennifer saw that a table had opened up. "Let's move before I get pulled into something work-related."

"Suits me," Kain agreed.

They took their drinks over to the table. Kain was quiet for a long moment before speaking. "What's the deal with Mars? Why are you taking all the Weres and all the tech out there?"

"Ezekiel didn't tell you?" Sarah Jennifer raised an eyebrow when Kain shook his head.

"I don't know if you noticed Caitlin is a tad touchy about the subject?" he asked.

Sarah Jennifer understood. "Fair enough. Our time here is done. All my discussions with Bethany Anne and my grandparents led me to the conclusion that the only way for humanity to evolve is to remove the temptation to rely on technology instead of developing their magic."

Kain played with his glass. "That simple, huh?"

Sarah Jennifer sighed. "There's nothing simple about it."

Kain reached out to touch her hand. "Hey, I didn't mean anything by it."

She didn't pull her hand away. She sighed again, deeper this time. "Kain, can I be straight with you?"

"Always," he replied.

Sarah Jennifer met his eyes. "I want to be done with Earth. The sooner I'm off this planet and away from all the hurts I've taken here, the better."

He closed his fingers around hers. "Sounds like you want to run."

Now Sarah Jennifer did pull her hand away. "You don't know what you're talking about."

"I'm not judging," Kain told her. "I've done my fair share of running away from what hurt me."

"I'm not running away," she retorted. "I'm running to my family. My pack, our future. I…" She trailed off.

"What?" Kain tilted his head.

"I spent a chunk of my life trying to outrun my pain," she admitted. "I walked out on my birth family. I walked out on my husband. I walked across America for decades, never staying anywhere long enough to give anyone a chance. I took Ezekiel in as a kid and didn't tell him anything about myself that would have helped him to make better decisions when it came his time to deal with the pain of loss."

Kain listened without interrupting.

Sarah Jennifer clenched her hand into a fist. "I built the Defense Force and didn't give the Weres any more than a home and a pack to call their own. I've been a leader and a diplomat and a friend, and I'm still alone. Always alone. The only people I let into my heart, the only people with the power to break it are my pack—"

"And Esme," Kain finished.

She nodded, her eyes stinging. "And Esme. Damn it all, Esme! And she's gone. So I want to leave, too. At least on Mars, I won't see her every place I look."

Kain was quiet for a moment. "I'm coming with you. Even if you don't choose to take the connection we have any further, I'm going to be there for you. You are not alone, Sarah Jennifer Walton."

She looked at him, stunned by the certainty in his words. "Kain, we don't know each other. You don't owe me anything, whatever our wolf sides say."

Kain shrugged. "Never said I did. Whatever this is between us, it doesn't matter. I'm not following you to the stars in the hope you'll suddenly decide you want to be with me. It's bigger than that, so much bigger. You say you haven't given anything. Just in the short time I've been around you, I've seen that you've given everything. I haven't met a single Were, mage, or human who doesn't sing your praises. A home is all anyone wants. A pack is all any Were wants; I know *that* from experience. Your pack isn't anything like the pack I grew up in. They're more than good people, they're bonded so damn tightly they might as well be blood, and they've made me feel like I'm one of them. Do you know what it's like to come in from the cold after being an outcast for so long?"

Sarah Jennifer nodded, unable to voice her emotions.

He laughed, the sound devoid of humor. "Of course you do. I don't want to feel separate anymore, Sarah. These last weeks, I've been telling myself that I'm torn, but the reality is I don't want to hurt the ones I love by saying goodbye. I'm not making this decision lightly. Shit, Caitlin and Ma mean everything to me. *Everything*. But…I can't pass up the chance to be with my own kind, even if that means moving to another goddamn planet."

Sarah Jennifer felt something inside her break. She wished she had the capacity to love again. She wanted to let Kain in. His tough-guy, love 'em and leave 'em exterior hid a loyal heart. However, she doubted she could do anything but hurt him, and she would hate herself forever if she did that.

She settled for giving him the truth instead. "Kain… There's something else I haven't told anyone besides those closest to me. "

"And you want to tell me?" He didn't hide his curiosity.

She nodded. "You saw the damage one Kurtherian is capable of, and Laughter is not the top of the food chain."

Kain frowned. "She seemed to be plenty powerful from where I was standing."

Sarah Jennifer nodded. "Exactly. There's one worse than her. *Much* worse. Gödel has mastery of the Etheric on a level only the Queen and her closest people can counter. If the day ever comes that Gödel finds her way here, the pack will be the first line of defense."

Kain frowned. "The Matriarch wants you to protect Earth from space?"

Sarah Jennifer lifted a shoulder. "She didn't disagree with my reasoning, which from her is as good as permission."

Kain shook his head in disbelief. "It's crazy to think you are on speaking terms with the freaking Matriarch."

Sarah Jennifer smiled. "My family has been in her service for three generations."

"I read the *William Hawkins Histories*," Kain told her. "I know all about the FDG."

Sarah Jennifer tilted her head. "You like to read?"

"You picturing us spending cozy nights by the fireplace?" Kain shot back with a grin.

Sarah Jennifer opened her mouth and closed it again.

"Do they even have fireplaces on Mars?" Kain asked.

Sarah Jennifer nodded, appreciating the move away from painful subjects. "All the comforts of home without the asshats." She returned his grin. "What?"

Kain pointed at her, feigning shock. "You *cursed*."

Sarah Jennifer picked up her glass and sipped her drink. "It's not a curse if it's an apt description."

"'Asshat' is too mild a word for that fucker Adrien," Ezekiel's voice came from their left.

Sarah Jennifer turned her head and saw Piet was with Ezekiel. "Hey! I heard you were here. How's it hanging, mountain man?"

"Little to the left and just below my knee, thanks for askin'," Piet replied.

Kain lifted his glass to the rearick. "I knew I liked you. Join us."

"Don't mind if I do. I need a drink first." Piet wandered off, and Ezekiel slumped into the seat next to Sarah Jennifer.

"That bad, huh?" she asked.

Ezekiel nodded.

Piet returned with a full glass in one hand and a frosty pitcher in the other. Mary-Anne, Caitlin, and Jaxon were with him, Mary-Anne laden with a platter stacked high with various meats.

"Someone loves me," Mary-Anne stated. "They had chicken wings made with a good rub."

Piet snorted, wiggling his eyebrows suggestively. "A rub? Sounds like someone likes their food prep a bit too much."

"Ew!" Mary-Anne slapped him playfully. "That's not what a rub is!"

"Yeah," Caitlin agreed, sitting down next to Ezekiel. "Get your mind out of the gutter, Piet."

The rearick tilted his head. "Then what's a rub?"

"A spice blend for marinating," Caitlin explained. "*Not* whatever you were thinking."

Mary-Anne put the platter down in the center of the table. "Talk about taking brining to the next level."

"I don't think the chicken would appreciate being handled that way," Piet quipped.

Mary-Anne grinned when everyone groaned. "What? Blame the rearick, not me. That enough for everyone? I don't think we're welcome back at the grill for a while."

Caitlin fussed with Jaxon's ears. "*Someone* was making a nuisance of himself."

The dog whined, giving them all big puppy eyes.

"Aww, I'm not mad, Jax," Caitlin told him, snagging a sausage from the platter and tossing it for the German Shepherd to catch. She side-eyed Ezekiel. "'Sup, Zeke?"

"Lost love," Kain answered when Ezekiel just shrugged.

"You could always tell her," Mary-Anne suggested.

Ezekiel shook his head. "I'm not staying in Arcadia. It wouldn't be fair. I have to…I don't know, get over it and let her be happy."

"Here's your chance to put that into practice," Sarah Jennifer told him, indicating the grand staircase with a nod.

CHAPTER TWENTY-THREE

Linda looked stunning in a forest-green gown, with her hair swept up in a chignon. Adrien had also changed into evening wear, his slicked-back hair complimented by neat black and silver robes in the current fashion.

Ezekiel hated to admit it, but they made a good-looking couple.

He suppressed the pang of jealousy that spiked his heart when he saw how happy Linda looked.

She smiled at Adrien, and they descended the stairs arm in arm to rapturous applause. The druids at the base lifted their arms, and their eyes glowed as roses bloomed along the balustrades.

Adrien paused to pick one and offered it to Linda. "Nature's finest pales in comparison with your beauty," he announced loud enough to be heard by everyone watching.

"I think I'm going to puke," Caitlin murmured.

Linda took the rose and went up on tiptoe to give Adrien a chaste kiss. "You say the loveliest things." She turned to face the room. "Tonight is not only the celebration of mine and Adrien's love. It is also a chance for us all to take stock of what we have achieved in such a short time."

She held out the rose. "The Matriarch's blessings upon us all as we step into the future."

"Indeed," Adrien cut in. "Arcadia promises to be the center of a new and great civilization founded on magic. We will prosper and grow."

Ezekiel had heard enough. He nudged Piet. "Show Sarah Jennifer what you brought with you."

Piet grinned as he retrieved an inert amphorald from his pocket. "Pretty, huh? This baby can be used to power whatever your engineers can hook it up to."

Sarah Jennifer took the amphorald and examined it with interest. She felt it resonate with the ambient energy produced by the enhanced around the table. "It's an Etheric battery. Where did you get this, Piet?"

Piet told her about the stockpile and the abundant seams running beneath the mountains where the rearick lived and worked. "Whatever you did to turn back the Madness, it changed the amphoralds. I was hopin' to cut a fair deal with the chancellor, although it looks like I'm gonna be dealin' with her husband-to-be."

Sarah Jennifer glanced at Adrien as she handed the amphorald back. "Don't worry about Adrien. I'll make sure he's out of the way while you're negotiating with Linda."

Piet raised an eyebrow in curiosity. "Oh, yeah? How're you gonna manage that?"

Sarah Jennifer winked at him. "Wait and see, my old friend. All will be revealed soon enough."

"Soon enough" came sooner than Sarah Jennifer expected. The happy couple came over to their table as they were finishing their meal.

Sarah Jennifer almost forgave Adrien for being, well, Adrien, when she saw the joy Linda was feeling. She smiled and asked them to join her. "I want to raise a glass to your future."

Linda took the chair next to Sarah Jennifer and showed her the ring Adrien had given her. "It belonged to his grandmother. Isn't it just beautiful?"

Adrien slid into the chair vacated by Caitlin, who excused herself with a mutter about Jaxon needing to go outside. Mary-Anne went with her, throwing a glare at Adrien that only Ezekiel saw.

Ezekiel grinned at the vampire, appreciating her solidarity. He turned back to the table as Adrien switched the conversation from the wedding plans to the subject they'd been expecting.

"I'm sure I already told you about the scouts I sent out to spread the word about the magic school," he lied smoothly.

Sarah Jennifer met his easy smile with a cool gray stare. "I don't think you did. It must have slipped your mind."

Adrien chuckled. "Ah, well, I *have* been rather busy. One of my scouts returned today with news of a magical community living in the mountains the locals call the Heights."

"You mean, Selah's people?" Piet asked.

"You know them?" Sarah Jennifer grinned. "What am I talking about? Of course you know them. How far do they live from Craigston?"

Piet laughed. "It's a fair walk. They don't do too well bein' around people all the time, but they come into town to drink."

Linda frowned at Adrien. "Why didn't I hear anything about this?"

Adrien patted her hand. "I didn't want to distract you from your happiness today of all days, my love. However, seeing as our esteemed visitor," he turned his smile on Piet, "has given us the potential of a reprieve from our power conundrum, I thought it would be appropriate to bring it up."

Sarah Jennifer laced her fingers on the table. "I'm happy to take a group to the Heights and facilitate building a relationship. If these people are friendly, it makes sense to form an alliance. I think we should get the negotiation with the rearick out of the way first, though."

"I've always wanted to visit your home, Piet!" Linda clapped with delight. "We'll make arrangements first thing tomorrow."

A flash of concern flashed across Adrien's face. "Linda, darling, we can't leave the city at this critical time. We need to be here to arrange work on the power fix."

Sarah Jennifer smiled. For all Adrien's personality quirks, he was dedicated to the people and to Linda. "I have engineers here. They don't need to be supervised. In fact, giving them room to come up with a workable system using the amphoralds will be better. You don't want to get caught up in one of their debates, I promise you."

"I'm sure my ministers can keep everything else under control while we are away," the chancellor declared.

"Besides, I want to make sure every magic-user knows they are welcome here in Arcadia."

"Then it's settled. I'll requisition a Pod first thing in the morning." Sarah Jennifer raised her glass. "Now, I believe we were celebrating?"

There were plenty of sore heads the next morning. Sarah Jennifer couldn't hide her smile as those whose nanocytes didn't give them the gift of avoiding a hangover met her at the Defense Force camp outside the city walls.

Linda was first to arrive, accompanied by six stewards hauling three large chests of gold between them. Ezekiel was next, followed by Caitlin and Jaxon. Then Kain and Mary-Anne came out of the forest, the former looking like he'd had a hard night.

Sarah Jennifer waved them all into the Pod, promising coffee as soon as they were aboard. "I went over to the camp at sunup to pick up a vat of the good stuff, along with breakfast."

"There is not enough coffee in the world," Linda grumbled as she took her seat. "I spent all night coaxing that gold from the river."

"By yourself?" Sarah Jennifer asked.

Linda nodded. "My drunken self thought it was a good idea. This morning I feel like I dug it out using my head as the shovel."

Ezekiel was in a slightly better state, although not by much. "Remind me not to indulge in the druids' offerings so easily in future. Why are we doing this so early in the morning?" he mumbled as he made a beeline for the catering vat Sarah Jennifer had prepared.

"We haven't had the chance to check out the wider area for a few weeks," Sarah Jennifer told him. "Everyone will have time to pull themselves together before we get to Craigston."

Piet strode aboard with a chipper grin. "I don't know what you're all complaining about. It's good to have a light drink of an evening. That was a shindig an' a half, lass. I've gotta congratulate you on your hosting skills."

"You call that light?" Caitlin scoffed, her hand on Jaxon's back. "I saw you put away twice as much as the rest of us last night."

Piet threw her a wink. "We brew our drink a touch stronger in the Heights. Gotta cater to the people's needs, ya know. One thing's for sure; Arcadians know how to party."

Kain groaned as he slumped in his seat. "Coffee. Give me coffee."

Sarah Jennifer raised an eyebrow. "You've had a Pod-doc treatment. Your nanocytes should have taken care of the alcohol."

"It wasn't the alcohol," Kain admitted. "It was Alexander's mushroom wine."

Mary-Anne's laughter made everyone with a headache wince. "You should have been there. His half-shifted ass was tearing around the forest tripping balls until dawn."

Kain shot a glare her way. "Thanks, Ma. I'm sure everyone needed to know about that."

"I get the picture," Sarah Jennifer told the vampire with a smile. "Good of you to take it out of the city, Kain. Where's Adrien?"

Linda shrugged, covering her eyes to block out the light.

"I'm here, I'm here!" Adrien appeared at the Pod door, looking the worse for wear.

Sarah Jennifer shook her head in amusement at the sorry lot of them. "A fine party of diplomats you all make." She pulled the cover off the heated tray next to the vat of coffee. "Bacon in biscuits. Eat. Caffeinate. Pull yourselves together. Ezekiel, now would be a good time to practice your healing skills, starting with yourself. See if you can resemble something human before we get to the Heights."

"Why are you not feeling rough?" Ezekiel asked.

Sarah Jennifer grinned. "Can't wake up with a hangover if you didn't go to sleep."

"I think I hate you," Caitlin muttered over the rim of her coffee cup.

Sarah Jennifer just laughed as she headed for the Pod's controls. Unlike everyone else, she'd stuck to mead and moderated her consumption, knowing she'd end up in a maudlin state if she overindulged.

With a little help from Ezekiel, everyone was feeling more themselves by the time Sarah Jennifer was done with her aerial sweep of the neighboring valleys.

Ezekiel joined her up front as she brought the Pod in over the range of peaks the locals called the Heights.

"How are the walking wounded back there?" Sarah Jennifer inquired with a wry smile.

Ezekiel chuckled. "Just like you wanted, mostly human." His eyes widened in appreciation when the clouds parted, revealing pink-gold early morning light filtering between the snow-tipped peaks. "It's so beautiful up here."

"It really is," Sarah Jennifer agreed.

"What does Mars look like?" Ezekiel asked.

Sarah Jennifer didn't answer for a moment. "It's a different kind of beautiful. Last I was there, it was just starting to get green around the equator and on the plain where we're building the city." She smiled. "The buildings are pink."

Ezekiel laughed. "Really?"

She nodded. "Really. Jim did his research on traditional construction techniques, and the plaster on the buildings is made from the dirt we shifted when we leveled the land to build on."

"What else?" Ezekiel asked, leaning back in his seat and folding his hands behind his head.

"If you go a couple hundred kilometers outside the city, you can climb a volcano and watch the sun come up. Most of the day, the sky looks like butterscotch pudding, but at dawn, it's the bluest blue." Sarah Jennifer pointed out campfire smoke on one of the mountainsides. "There's someone there."

"Can we zoom in?" Ezekiel asked.

Sarah Jennifer adjusted the viewscreen setting, and they saw a tall black man sitting by the fire.

"I wonder if he is one of the mind mages?" Ezekiel pondered.

"Can you sense if he has magic from this far away?" Sarah Jennifer asked.

Ezekiel closed his eyes and touched the Etheric. "If he has magic, he's not using it right now."

The man looked up as the Pod passed over, his eyes glowing white.

Ezekiel's eyes flashed red. "Oh, wait. Yeah, that's Selah."

Selah extinguished his fire with a bucket of earth and set off down the mountain.

Sarah Jennifer returned the screen to its previous magnification. "Looks like he's headed for Craigston."

"He's going to gather his people and join us there," Ezekiel told her. "He wants to meet us."

Sarah Jennifer nodded. "Sounds good to me. I hope the rearick are as happy to see us."

---

They landed just outside the trading post at the foot of the mountain. Sarah Jennifer had Piet debark with her, not wanting the rearick to be alarmed by their unexpected arrival. Ezekiel came next, followed by Linda and Adrien, then Caitlin, Mary-Anne, and Kain. Jaxon padded out ahead of Caitlin, his ears pricked and his tail wagging.

"Most the cooperative leaders are here," Piet told Sarah Jennifer as an aside as he waved to the group of rearick who had gathered to meet the unexpected arrivals. "Ember, Tolliver, Ariel, Frederika, meet Major Sarah Jennifer Walton of the Defense Force, Ezekiel, and Chancellor Linda Schneider, the founders of Arcadia. This fella here is Adrien, the chancellor's husband-to-be, and these good people are Mary-Anne, Caitlin, and Kain."

"Pleasure to meet you all," Ember greeted, offering each of them his hand. "Welcome to Craigston."

"The pleasure is all mine," Linda answered when it was her turn. "I hope this is the first of many meetings and the beginning of a prosperous alliance between our two peoples."

"Let's go to the guildhall and show them some rearick hospitality while we hammer out a trade deal," Piet suggested.

"Excellent idea." Ariel smiled as she spoke. "Please, come this way."

They made their way up the winding mountain road into the town proper, where the market square was bustling with rearick going about their daily business.

Many of the people they saw were miners coming from their shifts.

"We're a mining people," Ember explained, seeing Caitlin's curious stare. "Going back generations, we've been carving out precious metals and gems from the Heights."

"Piet certainly surprised us with the amphoralds," Adrien commented.

Caitlin's gaze wandered over the crowd. "You mind if I go explore?" she asked. "You don't need me for the trade talk."

"Go ahead," Ember invited. "Visitors are welcome here. Make sure you stop in at Rachel's Bakery. Her pastries are to die for."

Caitlin grinned. "Sure, wouldn't miss it for the world. Coming, guys?" she asked Mary-Anne and Kain.

"You had me at 'bakery,'" Mary-Anne enthused. "I haven't tasted stollen for over a century."

"I'm gonna stay and listen in on the talks," Kain told them. "Have fun, ladies. Try not to buy the whole store."

Ezekiel had other things on his mind. "I'm expecting to meet a man called Selah," he told Ember.

The rearick smiled. "The mystic?" He tapped his temple. "Strange gifts that man has. Don't worry. He'll find you."

That proved to be true. When they reached the guild-hall, Selah was waiting on the steps with another man and a woman he introduced as Artemis and Margit.

Ezekiel remained with the mystics while the rest went inside the hall.

Sarah Jennifer fell back, leaving Linda to take the lead on the diplomatic discussion as they left the long corridor and entered the main meeting hall. She politely declined the offer to join the leaders at the table. "My role here is limited to providing transport for Linda and making sure she's safe."

Kain followed Sarah Jennifer's lead, taking a position at the door.

Tolliver and Ariel left to get refreshments while Linda and Adrien began the negotiations. For once Adrien didn't talk over her, and her effervescent personality soon put the rearick cooperatives' leaders at ease.

"She's a natural at this," Kain whispered to Sarah Jennifer.

"She was raised for the role," Sarah Jennifer told him in a quiet voice. "Her father was the chancellor of Bad Salzig until he was killed by a Mad. Linda took over before her eighteenth birthday."

Kain's forehead creased in sympathy. "Shit, that had to have been hard on her. Is that why she's so set on Adrien?"

Sarah Jennifer exchanged wry glances with him. "You don't like him either, huh?"

"Does anyone?" Kain replied in the same low voice. "I'm sure he means well, but, damn, the man is abrasive at times."

Sarah Jennifer had pondered the Adrien problem. Not that she considered him a problem despite not liking him very much. "Not everyone is pleasant to get along with. Linda is. She's not naïve, but she's quick to trust. Adrien's pessimism will balance that out, I hope. Ezekiel is not the kind to settle. I expect he'll be in and out of Arcadia over the years, but he has his own goals. Adrien will protect Linda. As abrasive as he is, he loves her."

Kain nodded. "Fair enough."

Ezekiel came in a couple of hours into the talks. He waved at Sarah Jennifer, indicating he wanted to speak to her privately.

She excused herself and left Kain to watch over Linda and Adrien. "What's up?" she asked Ezekiel.

"Selah and the others have agreed to come to Arcadia," he told her. "But first, I'm going to visit their home. It's a few hours' walk from the town."

Sarah Jennifer nodded. "I don't see us being done here anytime soon. See if you can find Caitlin and Mary-Anne. I don't like the idea of you wandering alone in the mountains with magic users we don't know."

"Selah is cool," Ezekiel assured her, "But I was going to go find them anyway. The mystics told me there were nomads in the area."

Sarah Jennifer frowned. "What kind of nomads?"

"Not the good kind," Ezekiel answered with a look of concern. "They call them the remnant here. A blood leech is a blood leech, as far as I'm concerned. I'll be careful."

Sarah Jennifer put her hand on his shoulder. "See that you are. Otherwise, have fun with your new friends. You're going to need allies if you're planning to wander the continent looking for more magic users."

# CHAPTER TWENTY-FOUR

The trade talk was done by sunset, and the group reconvened in the tavern, where rooms had been laid on for the group. Ezekiel returned with Caitlin, Mary-Anne, Selah, and Margit just as Yelena, the tavern owner, was wheeling out a whole roast hog complete with a roasted apple in its mouth.

The mystics were well-received by the tavern owner, as was the barrel of their special recipe liquor they rolled in with them.

"Ye're a good'un, Selah," Yelena announced. "One of these days, you're gonna hafta tell me how ye brew somethin' so strong that doesn't addle the brains of the drinker."

Selah tapped the side of his nose and winked. "If I did that, what would we have to trade besides our stories?"

The rearick drinking in the tavern called for one of Selah's stories, and the mystic obliged after Yelena handed him a huge tankard of his own beverage. The tankard looked small in the huge man's hand. He took a deep draught, and his eyes turned white. "Ezekiel, you want to go first? I was impressed with your progress today."

Ezekiel turned bright red. "I don't know if I can create anything as clearly as you."

Yelena slid a tankard Ezekiel's way. "Have at it, young'un. Worst ya can do is fuck it up."

Ezekiel got to his feet, looking nervous. "Okay, then."

His eyes glowed red, and everyone in the room was transported into his vision as he cast the mind magic. "I want to show you the future. A future where everyone has magic, and everyone lives in peace and harmony."

Sarah Jennifer gasped when she saw Arcadia, but not as it was now. The city stretched far beyond the valley, the endless spires and towers competing to touch the heavens. This was unlike Esme's version of mind magic, which created an external vision. She was *there*, walking the streets, surrounded by people laughing and enjoying life.

"There will be no more war," Ezekiel continued. "No more scarcity. Whatever we need, we will be able to create it for ourselves."

The vision shifted, panning out to show them a group of people with glowing eyes and hands raising a house by the power of will.

"No one will go hungry."

More people, these dressed like the druids, tending fields lush with crops.

"Everyone will be taught how to use their magic."

Children gathered around an adult who was showing them how to manifest their abilities.

Sarah Jennifer choked out a sob when she saw the teacher looked just like Esme, breaking Ezekiel's concentration. The vision vanished, and everyone in the room applauded.

Ezekiel sat down abruptly. He wiped the sweat from his forehead and turned to look at her. "Sorry."

Sarah Jennifer shook her head. "Don't ever apologize for loving her. That was beautiful, Ezekiel."

Selah clapped Ezekiel on the shoulder. "Nice work. You might have a future as a mystic if you ever want to settle down." He turned his attention to Sarah Jennifer. "Your memories honor your friend."

Sarah Jennifer gave him a pointed look, resurrecting the barriers in her mind. "The downside of mental magic is, people with the ability can't resist the urge to root through your head."

Selah smiled ruefully, lifting his tankard. "Not something we mystics can help, I'm afraid. Why do you think we drink so much?"

"Your turn, Selah." Ezekiel pressed a hand to his head. "And I'd like another drink, myself."

The mystic grinned. "As you wish, my friend."

---

The night ended with Selah and Margit agreeing to accompany them back to Arcadia. Sarah Jennifer, Ezekiel, Linda, and Caitlin made arrangements to visit the mystics' mountain home the next day while Selah and Margit picked up their belongings for the trip.

Thanks to the mystics' brewing capabilities, the group set out from Craigston the next morning with clear heads and made their way to the pre-WWDE monastery where

Selah and his people lived.

Linda made a face when they reached the narrow mountain path that led to the monastery. "This won't do at all," she stated, her eyes glowing as she held out her hand.

She took the lead, reshaping the rock ahead of her into sturdy steps.

Selah marveled at the ease of the long climb as they followed Linda. "We need a rock mage here full-time, I think."

"Why?" Linda inquired, looking at the mystic.

"We have been slowly rebuilding the monastery over the last few years." Selah paused and rested his hands on his knees. "We needed a home out of the way of everyone else. It's extremely tiring being around people who don't guard their thoughts since we aren't able to switch that part of our magic off."

"Truth," Margit agreed.

"We can help with that," Ezekiel offered.

Selah grinned at Margit. "Perhaps our dream of seeing the temple built within our lifetimes is not so ambitious after all."

"Tell us about this temple," Sarah Jennifer asked. "Better yet, why don't you show us?"

"If we go just a little bit farther, we'll be able to see the building," Selah told her. They rounded a bend, and the crumbling ruins came into sight above them on the mountainside. Selah waved at a group of flat boulders on the inside of the path. "Here's as good a place as any for a rest. There's very little cloud cover today."

"Don't mind if I do," Caitlin enthused, plonking herself

down on one of the handy rocks. She took a long drink from her water bottle. "It's a hell of a hike up here!"

Margit took a seat next to her. "We're only halfway there."

Caitlin shrugged. "I didn't say it wasn't a nice hike. The view up here is amazing."

"It's beautiful," Mary-Anne agreed.

"It will be even better once we have the temple looking just the way we want it," Selah told them, his eyes turning white.

The ruins in the distance transformed before their eyes as he released his magic, weaving his vision for the rest of the group to see. The rough stonework was replaced by smooth painted plaster, and trees appeared to shade the open grounds. The simple square building had been expanded and enclosed in high walls over which a number of towers could be seen.

"Of course," Selah continued, "Now that there is so much magic in the world, there's no reason we can't make this a haven for all mystics."

Sarah Jennifer blinked as the vision dissipated. "You're going to stay up here all the time?"

Margit laughed. "No. We like to get out into the world every now and then. It's a good thing, too. Otherwise, the rearick would have nowhere to spend all that gold you're giving them for their amphoralds."

"Ember explained about the lack of farming in the Heights," Linda commented. "I was surprised to hear anyone still values gold as currency. We're more used to barter."

"Get used to hard currency again," Selah advised. "Many

of the communities west and north use gold and silver as currency."

Linda nodded. "I'll keep that in mind as we expand trade for Arcadia. I suppose we have to go back to the old ways if that's what everyone else is basing their economies on."

"Barter came before hard currency pre-WWDE," Sarah Jennifer countered as they crested the last incline before the monastery. Selah and Margit went ahead, leaving them to wait in the empty courtyard. "I suppose it was only a matter of time before local economies evolved this way. Having said that, I expect trade will close in after a few decades of the Defense Force being gone and transport between continents being limited to shipping routes."

"What do you mean?" Caitlin asked.

Sarah Jennifer considered her answer before replying. "Everyone has either goods or services to offer, right? Well, when creating an economy that works for everyone, there has to be a standard currency that can't be affected by the availability of those goods or services dropping off. Neither can it be based on the most valuable thing like, say, cocoa."

"Cocoa is pretty valuable," Caitlin agreed. "Why can't it be a currency?"

"How much wheat, or fish, or the manual labor it takes to produce those items is a pound of cocoa worth?" Sarah Jennifer asked. "How much cocoa can each nation produce? What happens if the cocoa crop fails? Gold is plentiful, but it's not the most useful product."

She held a finger up as Caitlin made to argue. "Unless the world returns to an age of electronics, which is highly unlikely. Yet, people value it, along with other precious metals. Linda, you need to get together with other leaders in the area to discuss setting a standard for gold, silver, copper, and to ensure amphoralds remain off the table except as a commodity."

Linda nodded. "Adrien said the same thing. He thinks everyone will come to rely on amphoralds for power, and if they do, the rearick will overtake the whole world with their wealth. He says no one group should hold that much power."

Sarah Jennifer hated to admit it, but... "Can't say I disagree with him, as friendly as the rearick are. Wealth can do funny things to people. Once they start accumulating it, they realize that they have to keep on accumulating it. The next thing you know, there's a blossoming dictatorship."

"Blossoming like a canker," Caitlin grumbled. "I've seen it happen."

"We all have," Sarah Jennifer told her.

Linda's eyes returned to their usual blue as she released her magic. "It makes sense to keep barter for day-to-day transactions with our own people, but I agree with everyone else when it comes to trading with outside communities. Drunk me knew that when I went searching for the gold we brought with us."

She spied a half-built wall across the courtyard. "There's something we can do while we wait," she told Ezekiel.

Ezekiel grinned. "No time like the present to get started."

They wandered off, leaving Sarah Jennifer, Caitlin, and Mary-Anne to continue the discussion.

Sarah Jennifer sensed Caitlin was holding back something. "Penny for your thoughts?"

Caitlin raised an eyebrow. "A what now?"

"What's on your mind?" Sarah Jennifer clarified.

Caitlin's shoulders dropped. "Oh. That. I guess I'm thinking about what life's going to be like without Kain when you take him away."

Sarah Jennifer could have bitten at the loaded statement. However, she was experienced enough to know it came from a place of sadness on the much younger woman's part. "You're set on going back to Canada, huh?"

Caitlin nodded. "My brother is there. I miss Silver Creek. Can't imagine what everyone there is doing now that there's no Madness to scare the shit out of them. Might even be a girl could hunt and fish and just...I don't know, commune with the land the way a human being ought to, you know?"

Sarah Jennifer nodded. "I do. Did a fair amount of communing with the land myself before the Madness hit."

"How old are you, anyway?" Caitlin asked.

"Old enough," Sarah Jennifer answered. "Not as old as Kain."

"Or me," Mary-Anne cut in.

"That's not an answer," Caitlin complained.

"It's the only one you're getting," Sarah Jennifer replied with a smile.

Selah and Margit returned, carrying a bag apiece. Sarah Jennifer turned her smile on them. "Are you ready?"

"We are," Selah replied. "But we have a problem. Artemis isn't here."

"Well, where is he?" Ezekiel asked. "Can't you just..." He put his fingers to his temples. "And find him?"

Margit shook her head. "He's not in range. We need to find him. If he's gone into the Madlands again..."

"Where the remnant gather," Selah explained in response to Sarah Jennifer's questioning look.

This was going to take more than one Pod. Sarah Jennifer activated her Etheric comm and called for Enora. "Don't worry," she told the mystics. "We'll find him."

---

"Damn nomads," Ezekiel muttered under his breath as he brought the Pod around to sweep the next sector.

"What have you got against nomads?" Kain asked.

"Nothing personal," Ezekiel assured him. "You know why the remnant didn't get the cure along with everyone else, right?"

Kain shook his head. "Can't say I was paying attention. I just know they're cannibals, and for some reason, this Artemis dude likes living dangerously."

"It's like this," Ezekiel told him. "Back before the Affliction hit the Weres, there was trade in Were blood as a drug that prolonged life. Before the Weres, the leeches would target vampires."

"I can confirm that," Mary-Anne chipped in. "Had to outrun them a few times, the persistent sons of bitches."

Ezekiel nodded. "The nomads were the leeches' best customers. They passed down those stolen nanocytes to their children, who mostly all went Mad because the nomads didn't do a damned thing to control the spread of the Madness. They turned their Mad loose without a care. That's why you won't find anyone from Salem or the Defense Force who doesn't find the nomads a sore point. Their irresponsible behavior cost a lot of lives, and it was always the Defense Force that had to go in and take care of their messes."

"That explains a lot, actually," Kain told him. "So, what turned them into cannibals instead of them getting the cure?"

Ezekiel sighed. "Esme and Lilith weren't able to fully reverse the Madness in them. The nanocytes we used to cure them are based on the Matriarch's and kind of on mine, as well. I'm immune to the Madness; that's why I was able to help Helena and Mary-Anne last a bit longer by feeding them my blood."

Kain narrowed his eyes. "I didn't know that."

"I didn't know you then," Ezekiel admitted. "I didn't want to have to fight you if you decided to try to drain me to save Ma."

Kain turned in his seat to look at Mary-Anne. "You have some restraint, lady."

"I wasn't about to kill the only lead we had for the cure," the vampire retorted. "How could I face Caitlin if I did that? Keep going, Zeke. Although, I'm going to guess that the reason that Esme and Lilith couldn't restore the nomad descendants is the same reason it would be a bad idea for me to take a big old bite out of Pooch here."

Ezekiel pointed over his shoulder. "Ten points for the smartest vampire in the world. I'm not going to pretend I understand the finer details of nanocyte programming, but I do know that vamp and Were nanocytes are incompatible."

Kain put a hand to his chest. "And there I was thinking we clicked, Ma. Now I find out eating me would be the vamp equivalent of three Taco Bell trips in one day. It kinda makes me question everything."

Mary-Anne sighed. "I miss Taco Bell. And McDonalds. And Chili's. Denny's, too."

Ezekiel gave Kain a nonplussed look.

"Fast food and diners," Kain told him.

Ezekiel was about to reply when the comm squawked.

"We've found Artemis," Sarah Jennifer informed them. "He's penned in. Coordinates incoming. Meet us there."

The narrow valley was swarming with remnant. Linda threw up a hasty wall to block the remnant closing in as she and Artemis darted into an abandoned shack. She slammed the door and put her back against it as she tore a strip off her dress.

Artemis looked at the gaping wound in her side with dismay.

Linda ignored him, focusing on stemming the blood flowing from the wound. "Distract them," she told him. "Don't let them see we're in here."

The mystic nodded without saying anything. He crept to a hole in the wall, his eyes white as he cast a vision to confuse the remnant separating them from Sarah Jennifer and Adrien.

Unfortunately, his magic also confused Sarah Jennifer and Adrien, who had joined the group to search for the mystic. They paused as the shack vanished and the ground where it had been turned to lava.

"Is that…" Adrien hesitated to step on the cherry-red flow.

"Mind magic." Sarah Jennifer ignored the illusion. She opened her comm. "Enora, did you find a landing site?"

"I found an open space half a kilometer south of your location," the AI responded. "Selah and Margit aren't too happy about being made to stay aboard."

"They'll have to deal with it," Sarah Jennifer responded. "I don't need to have my focus split protecting noncombatants."

"Where are Linda and Artemis?" Adrien ground out, his eyes turning black as his magic surged just beneath the surface. "Whatever that mystic is doing, it's stopping me from finding her."

Sarah Jennifer sensed the pull on the Etheric coming from the shack some fifty feet ahead and pointed as she picked up her pace. "There. Dammit, she doesn't have a comm."

Adrien blasted a remnant with fire as he dashed toward the shack, yelling, "Linda!"

"In here!" The reply came from Artemis.

"I could use some help," Linda called. "That remnant got me pretty good."

Adrien's face drained of color. "How badly are you hurt?"

"Losing a lot of blood." Her voice was shaky. "I need a healer."

The remnant weren't cognizant enough to realize they were being tricked by Artemis' mind magic. They turned their focus on the people they could see, altering their course to attack Sarah Jennifer and Adrien.

Sarah Jennifer regretted leaving her Jean Dukes Specials aboard the airship. She pulled a shard of ice from thin air and launched it at the remnant nearest them.

"Incoming!" Ezekiel called over the comm.

The ground exploded in a shower of dirt as Ezekiel brought the Pod overhead and fired at the remnant.

The next moment, Kain and Mary-Anne jumped out of the Pod, scattering the remnant as they landed. Kain was in his Pricolici form, and Mary-Anne had vamped out.

Sarah Jennifer breathed a sigh of relief as she covered the last few feet to where she thought the shack was.

Adrien was already there, yelling at Artemis as he felt for walls he couldn't see.

"Artemis, drop the illusion," Sarah Jennifer commanded. "We can't help if we can't get in."

"No!" Artemis shouted. "There's too many of them! I don't want to die!"

"Then you shouldn't have fucking come out here!" Adrien roared. "Linda!"

Linda didn't answer, which drove Adrien into a greater rage. "*I'm* going to kill you if you don't let us in!"

Ezekiel ran from the Pod when it landed, his eyes blazing red. He cut through the mystic's magic and dropped the walls of the shack with a wave of his hand.

They all saw Linda lying on the dirt floor in a puddle of her own blood.

Adrien screamed in fury and fear. He rushed to Linda's

side and scooped her into his lap, looking up at Ezekiel. "She's not breathing! Heal her!"

Ezekiel dropped to his knees beside them, his hands glowing as he reached for Linda.

"Behind you!" Kain shouted.

Sarah Jennifer turned as three remnant rushed them. She had no time to call on her magic before they were on her. She jabbed her fingers into the throat of the first and kicked him in the face as he folded. The next she grabbed and swung into the third, giving herself room to maneuver as the first recovered and came at her again. She snapped his neck, leaving herself open to the other two.

Mary-Anne and Kain had their hands full with the other remnant. Sarah Jennifer flung her arms wide, shaking off the grip of the remnant who had jumped onto her back and sank its teeth into her shoulder.

She reached over her shoulder and grabbed the remnant by the hair. It screamed in rage as Sarah Jennifer tore it free and slammed it onto the ground.

Sarah Jennifer blocked with her arm as the third remnant attacked, stamping on the head of the one who had bitten her as she shifted her stance. Her shoulder burned where the remnant had taken a chunk out of it. Realizing she wasn't fighting a Mad, she shifted to her wolf form on the spot and shrugged out of her discarded clothing, her shoulder knitting back together in seconds.

She snapped at the remaining remnant, driving it back enough to give herself room for a leap at its throat. She landed front paws first on its chest, knocking it to the ground. Somewhere in the background, she was aware of Ezekiel and Adrien screaming and Kain's snarls. She blocked it all out, tearing out the remnant's throat with a toss of her head.

More came, unperturbed by the deaths of the others. Sarah Jennifer was bitten on the flank as she attacked another head-on. She danced away and turned to bite back. The remnant piled on, burying her under the weight of their bodies. Sarah Jennifer twisted and clawed at them, biting and tearing her way clear.

Her breath came in ragged growls as she dived onto the writhing pile. She hadn't fought much in wolf form since the risk of infection when fighting Mad was too high. Still, it came naturally to her. She relied on her instincts, her wolf senses telling her where to go and how to move.

The remnant scrambled to escape her, to no avail. Her mouth was full of blood, and there were still remnant to kill. She leapt and ripped into the soft flesh of a remnant's ankle, severing its Achilles tendon. She tore out its throat and moved on to find the next, her whole world reduced to the need to remove the threat the remnant posed.

# CHAPTER TWENTY-FIVE

"Sarah Jennifer."

She didn't hear Kain.

"Sarah," he repeated, "It's done. Ezekiel needs you."

That snapped her out of hunting mode and back to the moment. Ezekiel's soft sobs drew her attention.

Kain held out her shirt, turning his head to look away. "Here."

Sarah Jennifer took the shirt in her jaws and shifted back before shrugging it on. She turned to the remains of the shack and saw Ezekiel kneeling on the floor by Linda's body, surrounded by red light. Adrien had his hand raised, his eyes black and his lips pulled back in a snarl while Artemis choked for breath.

She ran to the shack. "Let him go, Adrien. This isn't you."

"He doesn't deserve to live!" Adrien retorted. "Linda is dead because of his cowardice!"

"That doesn't give you the right to take his life," Sarah Jennifer told him.

Kain and Mary-Anne joined them in the wreckage, neither of them knowing what to do. Artemis continued to choke, his face turning blue.

Sarah Jennifer had no choice. She punched Adrien.

His knees buckled, and the black light faded from his eyes as he crumpled unconscious to the ground. Artemis gasped as the restriction on his airway vanished.

Sarah Jennifer cut the mystic off before he could thank her. "The only reason you're not dead right now is that Adrien has lost enough today. He doesn't need being a murderer on his conscience as well. Get out of my sight."

Artemis backed away slowly and slunk out of the remains of the shack.

"Not so fast," Mary-Anne told the mystic, grabbing him by the collar. "I'm going to make sure you don't get killed on the way to the ship. Kain, you coming?"

Kain nodded. "Yeah. You want us to take him with us?" he asked Sarah Jennifer, pointing at Adrien.

"That would probably be best. He's not going to be happy with me when he wakes up." Sarah Jennifer's eyes were on Ezekiel as Kain slung Adrien over his shoulder. "Pick up Caitlin and Jaxon from Craigston. We'll take the Pod back to Arcadia."

Ezekiel noticed none of the exchange. He rocked on his haunches as he continued to pour his magic into Linda. The air around him was static with the intensity of his effort.

Sarah Jennifer's heart fell. Another death was too much to bear for either of them. However, Ezekiel needed her help to keep it together. She took a knee, shuddering as the magic passed through her, healing the injuries she'd taken during the fight. She put her hand on his shoulder. "She's gone, Ezekiel."

"No, I can bring her back," he stated through clenched teeth, refusing to meet her eyes. "I won't give up."

Sarah Jennifer's bum knee gave up its eternal complaint as he ramped up his magic. She felt the cartilage regenerate, her magic reacting to Ezekiel's outpouring and her acceptance of the unfairness of loss. It would have been easy to rail and cast blame, but losing Esme and Linda in such a short time was a shock to the system that forced her to realign her thinking.

She gently pulled Ezekiel away from Linda and wrapped him in a tight hug. His magic faded, and he began to sob. She knew he loved Linda. He hadn't acknowledged how much he cared even to himself.

Ezekiel curled up on the ground with his head in Sarah Jennifer's lap. "I know, sweetheart," she murmured, stroking his hair as he cried. "I know. Let it all out. I'm here."

They stayed that way until long after the sun had set and the red sky grew dark, the stars obscured by the BYPS grid. Eventually, Ezekiel sat up and wiped his face. He leaned over and gently brushed Linda's eyes closed. "We need to take her back to Arcadia."

Sarah Jennifer nodded. "I'll get the Pod."

---

Another funeral, another gathering of the leaders from around the connected world. Adrien had stepped up to give Arcadia the leadership they needed in Linda's absence.

He took the chancellorship with a heavy heart as Ezekiel prepared to leave the city.

Sarah Jennifer pulled him aside after Linda's wake. "I want to make sure you can handle this," she told him as they walked the corridors of the academy.

The muscles around Adrien's eyes tightened, and he pressed his lips together. "I will do my duty by the people. Whatever it takes to provide stability for Arcadia."

Sarah Jennifer felt for the young man. "You've lost a lot. Lean on your friends, Adrien. Alexander, Selah, Amelie. The masters will support you in building the academy, and the rest will come in time."

The slump in Adrien's shoulders lessened. "I will honor Linda in my every decision. Arcadia will become a place of beauty and learning. I have Saul to help with day-to-day government decisions. Alexander will manage the forest and the druids. Selah and Amelie will teach their magic to those who show aptitude, and I will pass on everything Ezekiel has taught me about physical magic. I will institute commerce with towns and cities far and wide and welcome everyone Ezekiel sends here."

Sarah Jennifer laid a hand on his shoulder. "Linda would be proud of that. Her goal was always to support Ezekiel in spreading the knowledge of magic across the world."

Adrien nodded. "That's why I have decided to chair the academy." He continued to talk about his hopes for the expanding city as they entered Linda's former office and sat on opposite sides of the desk. "How long until you leave?"

"Two days," Sarah Jennifer told him. "I'm headed up to

the BYPS later today to switch off the grid. After that, I'll recall the Pods from Mars to transport everyone, and my people will finish collecting any pre-magic technology still on Earth."

"The Defense Force is really leaving." Adrien sighed. "I have to admit, it feels a little intimidating knowing we won't be able to call on them in times of trouble."

"You will establish your own ways of taking care of any trouble that arises," Sarah Jennifer assured him. "You should get with Saul to talk through what law enforcement in Arcadia is going to look like. You're too close to the Danelands not to think about protecting yourselves."

Adrien snorted lightly. "We are already seeing a large number of Danelanders coming into the city. They are welcome as long as they adhere to the rules. Saul suggests we incorporate some of them into the city guard."

Sarah Jennifer nodded. "Not the worst idea. Integration is key to building a stable society, as you know."

"It made all the difference when we merged Bad Salzig with our neighboring towns before the melt pushed us inland," Adrien agreed. He broke off, looking pensive.

A knock on the door interrupted whatever he had been about to say.

"Come in," Adrien called.

A woman Sarah Jennifer didn't recognize came in. "Adrien—" She saw Sarah Jennifer and closed her mouth.

"Ah, Monica," Adrien smiled, "I was hoping I would see you today. Sarah Jennifer, meet Monica LeFevre, my minister for trade."

Sarah Jennifer got to her feet. "Good to put a face to the name."

Monica's face flushed.

"Wait for me in the meeting room downstairs," Adrien told her.

She inclined her head in Adrien's direction and closed the door behind her.

Sarah Jennifer got to her feet. "I'll leave you two to work. I have Enora waiting to take me to the BYPS."

Adrien nodded. "Before you go, I want to thank you for what you did out in the Madlands. You stopped me from making a huge mistake."

Sarah Jennifer sighed. However prickly Adrien was, he wasn't a bad person. However, his reaction to Linda's death had shown her that he had the potential to go either way. "Adrien, promise me something?"

"What?" he asked.

"There are going to be times when the darkness in the world rises. When that happens, I want you to remember that our choices, *your* choices, are what will guide people toward the light."

Adrien's brow furrowed. "I... Yes, Major."

"That's all I can ask." Sarah Jennifer extended a hand across the desk.

Adrien shook with a rueful smile. "I guess this is goodbye."

Sarah Jennifer smiled. "Goodbye, Adrien, and good luck for the future."

She left the office and made her way out of the city to find Ezekiel. She found him in the training fields, working on the martial arts-style forms he had developed with teaching magic in mind.

Ezekiel didn't notice her at first. She leaned on the

fence and watched as he continued moving through his kata, crossing his arms over his chest and pushing them out with a wall of flames, then dipping into a low stance and stamping his left foot to bring a pillar of rock shooting out of the ground.

"Ezekiel," she called softly.

Ezekiel completed his move before walking over to where Sarah Jennifer was leaning. "Hey. Just practicing. What do you think?"

Sarah Jennifer smiled. "I think the time I spent teaching you self-defense wasn't wasted. This is how you're going to teach magic?"

Ezekiel nodded. "Yeah. I'm finding my students can focus their will better when they have set techniques to work through." He tilted his head in curiosity. "I thought you were switching the BYPS off today?"

"I am," she told him. "I was wondering if you wanted to come up there with me?"

Ezekiel grinned. "I'd love to. As long as you're not expecting me to be of any use with taking down the grid."

Sarah Jennifer laughed, pulling him into a one-armed hug. "No. Esme left me everything I need to get it done."

"In that case, I'm in," Ezekiel told her, returning the hug.

Sarah Jennifer called Enora as they made their way to the fields where the Defense Force was in the middle of striking the camp they'd been living in for the last few weeks.

Ezekiel caught her arm as they neared the edge of camp. "There's something different about you. Wait, you're walking just fine."

"That's because my knee is healed," Sarah Jennifer told him. "You provided the magic. I dealt with my emotional issues. It's all good."

"Does that mean you're going to quit avoiding Kain?" Ezekiel teased.

Sarah Jennifer shrugged. "I haven't been avoiding him. In case you hadn't noticed, we've all been busy."

"Now's your chance to prove it." Ezekiel pointed out Kain, Caitlin, and Mary-Anne working along with the Weres to dismantle the multitude of tents filling the open space. Many of the men were stripped to the waist as they worked under the strong spring sun.

Sarah Jennifer made a snap decision and waved Kain over.

Caitlin catcalled him as he jogged to Sarah Jennifer and Ezekiel. "What's up?" he asked.

"Wondering if you'd like a preview of space?" Sarah Jennifer told him, suddenly feeling shy.

Kain grinned. "Oh, hells, yeah! Meet you at the airship. Need to grab my shirt."

Sarah Jennifer had been trying not to notice he wasn't wearing one. "Caitlin and Mary-Anne are welcome to come along, too," she called as Kain ran back to where he'd been working. She gave Ezekiel a sharp look when he chuckled. "You'd better not be reading my mind," she told him.

Ezekiel raised his hands in submission. "Not me, honest!"

Sarah Jennifer ruffled his hair. "Fair enough."

The *Enora* was ready to go when they got to the temporary airstrip on the other side of the field. Kain was alone when he showed up. "Caitlin didn't want to go, and Mary-Anne won't leave her," he told them in answer to Sarah Jennifer's inquiry.

Sarah Jennifer nodded. "Just the three of us, then."

"Four," Ezekiel modified. "Enora will be there, too."

Sarah Jennifer smiled, her spirits rising for the first time since Linda's wake. "That's a given. You two haven't been out of Earth's atmosphere before. I was thinking we might swing around the local area while we're up there."

Kain looked up at the sky. "What are you counting as local?"

Sarah Jennifer's smile widened into a grin. "Oh, you know. The moon, Mars. I need to pick up the Pods."

Ezekiel grinned. "Sounds like a plan."

---

Sarah Jennifer worked out the flight plan with Enora while Ezekiel and Kain took care of the vital task of making coffee and snacks.

"This feels like the last hurrah," the AI commented wistfully as the airship lifted off.

"It's not all bad," Sarah Jennifer countered. "Just think of how good it will be to relax for the next couple hundred years." She thought about her grandparents and how much good the fifty-year vacation they'd taken before returning to the pack to begin hers and Sylvia's training had done them. The pack wouldn't be resting on their laurels, having the directive to be ready for any incursion coming from outside the Solar System, but they would have their own version of utopia as a backdrop for their training.

She wished Sylvia was coming with her, but her twin was set on remaining here on Earth. They had the IICS to keep in touch, and she could visit anytime. It would have to be enough.

"We're about to arrive at the primary satellite," Enora informed Sarah Jennifer, putting an end to her daydreaming.

Ezekiel and Kain came into the cockpit as Sarah Jennifer finished giving the access code.

Kain laughed. "I didn't peg you for an AC/DC fan," he teased.

Sarah Jennifer felt her face redden. "Would you believe I'm not?" she replied as the BYPS EI confirmed her authority to access the satellite.

Kain grinned. "I don't know. Kinda sounded like you were getting into that. I like your version better than the original without the mention of the Matriarch."

"Some genius decided those lyrics were the perfect access code," she told him.

Ezekiel slid into the co-pilot's chair and handed Sarah Jennifer a travel mug. "Well, I don't suppose aliens would know the altered lyrics you just sang."

Sarah Jennifer got to her feet, taking her coffee with her. "True. Okay, you two hang tight while I head over to the satellite."

"How long will this take?" Ezekiel asked.

"I shouldn't be more than an hour." Sarah Jennifer paused in the doorway. "I've got my comm if you need me."

She stopped by her cabin on the way to the drop bay and collected the thumb drive she'd found in Esme's cabin along with instructions on how to use it, then made her way over to the satellite in the roamer.

Being up here without Esme filled her with nerves. Sarah Jennifer took a seat on the high-backed stool and extracted the written instructions Esme had left her.

She unfolded the paper and stared at the neat, looping script. She hadn't read through the instructions yet, afraid that seeing Esme's elegant handwriting would trigger a tsunami of grief she couldn't afford to indulge while so much on Earth was still left to be resolved.

All she felt was the absence of her best friend. She missed her voice, her dry humor, and her pragmatic approach to the cascade of shitty situations they'd spent the last two decades working through for the sake of everyone else.

"I miss you," she murmured. "I wish I could tell you that I've taken my head out of my ass and decided to give this thing with Kain a chance. You would be so proud of how far Ezekiel has come. Truth, I'm beyond glad to be leaving for Mars. Not so I can forget you, but so I can do what you asked and stop holding myself back."

She plugged the thumb drive into the console and followed the steps Esme had written out. Then she returned to the *Enora* while the EI took care of the rest.

Ezekiel and Kain were playing cards in the crew lounge when she came up from the drop bay. The wallscreen showed the grid, which was still up for the moment. Sarah Jennifer glanced at the screen before taking a seat at the table.

Ezekiel dealt her into the next hand without asking. "How'd it go?"

"No problems," Sarah Jennifer told him. "What are we playing?"

"Rummy," Kain told her. "Kiddo here has a bad habit of mind reading when we're playing poker, and I don't feel like losing my ass today."

"'The only fair fight is the one you lose,'" Ezekiel intoned.

Sarah Jennifer shook her head. "I don't think Bethany Anne was talking about poker when she said that."

Ezekiel lifted a shoulder. "How do you know she wasn't? Winning is winning."

They all turned to look at the screen when the red light emitted by the BYPS grid flickered and then vanished. Sarah Jennifer laid her cards face-down on the table. "Enora, confirm the grid is down."

The AI replaced the view of the stars. "Confirmed."

Sarah Jennifer smiled. "Then take us out."

## CHAPTER TWENTY-SIX

Sarah Jennifer led the way as they went back to the cockpit.

Enora's avatar filled one corner of the viewscreen. The rest showed the expanse of space. Kain let out a low whistle as Enora moved out of Earth's orbit and the planet came into view at the bottom of the screen.

"It's beautiful, right?" Sarah Jennifer took her seat. "I came up here sometimes just to remind myself there was a whole world outside of my problems."

"Beautiful doesn't begin to describe it," Kain admitted. "I feel so small."

"Wait until we get out past the moon," she told him.

Ezekiel returned to the co-pilot's seat, his expression thoughtful. "It puts everything into perspective, that's for sure. Can I get some maps before you leave?" he asked Sarah Jennifer. "I'm going to be traveling a lot to search out the magic users. It would help if I knew where the people were."

"Sure thing. Enora can put something together for you."

Sarah Jennifer pointed at a reddish dot in the distance. "One thing at a time. We'll be getting to Mars within the hour. Make the most of the trip. This is literally once in a lifetime for you unless you get tired of shepherding Earth and decide to call me to come get you."

Ezekiel nodded, his eyes glued to the viewscreen.

Kain was also quiet as the void rushed by. Sarah Jennifer used the time to call ahead and inform Brutus they were on their way to retrieve the Pods.

Mars soon came into sight. Sarah Jennifer had a moment of her mind not registering what her eyes were seeing as the *Enora* got close. The saltwater lakes had filled and joined to create oceans, the band of forest around the equator had exploded in a riot of green and yellow, and she saw cloud formations that told her the climate control system had been put into Phase Nine—regular weather systems. But what made her heart leap was the square splodge of pink sticking out on the Reynolds Plain.

"Promessa," she whispered.

Once again, Kain let out a low whistle. "Fuck me. You weren't kidding about the changes to this place."

Sarah Jennifer frowned, then recalled Kain's age. "What were you expecting?"

He shrugged. "Not this, that's for sure. It's so...*green*."

"And blue," Ezekiel added. "It looks like Earth, only... alien in some way."

Sarah Jennifer chuckled at the awe in their voices. "Honestly, it's come along a ways since I was last here. Even I'm impressed."

"I wish we could stay long enough for me to visit the city," Ezekiel told her. "But I don't know if I could leave if I saw everyone. I need to get back to Earth. It's where I belong."

Sarah Jennifer nodded. "I don't want to go down there yet either. We'll do what we came here to do, and we'll get back to Arcadia."

"I have instructed Galileo to send up the Pods," Enora informed them. "You have a call, Major."

"Who is it?" Sarah Jennifer asked.

"The Queen," Enora replied.

"I'll take it in my cabin," Sarah Jennifer told her. "Let me know when the Pods are ready."

Bethany Anne was already onscreen when Sarah Jennifer entered her office. "I got a notification the BYPS has been switched off. Can I assume the Madness is no more?"

Sarah Jennifer gave her a brief rundown of the events since her last report. "People are starting to manifest magic," she finished almost forty minutes later. "I'm getting ready to move the remainder of my people out to Mars."

Bethany Anne's mouth turned up at the corner. "Yeah, about that. Why Mars? Why not continue rebuilding on Earth?"

"You want magic to develop naturally." Sarah Jennifer perched on the edge of her desk and folded her arms. "The BYPS isn't infallible; we've seen the proof of that. Mars. It still sounds so exotic." She smiled. "I'll send video in my next report. We're going to be happy here."

"You did build a colony there. It would suck six ways to Sunday if you didn't at least like the place." Bethany Anne returned Sarah Jennifer's smile. "The war out here is heating up. I don't hate the idea of having the Defense Force nearby."

Sarah Jennifer turned away from the viewscreen. "It's more than the need to remain nearby. We brought the planet to *life*. Magic and technology are going to go their separate ways while people learn to have faith in themselves. Earth will need protection from space; that's a given. We have the technology to make sure no entity coming here with the intention to conquer can succeed, thanks to you."

"There are going to be hard times ahead," Bethany Anne told her. "The people could use you down there."

Sarah Jennifer lifted a shoulder. "Old argument, one we've gone around and around on over the years, and I still believe the same. They would grow to rely on us. The Defense Force would only end up policing the world if we stayed. Factions would form. That's not the world either of us wants."

Bethany Anne sighed. "No. It's not."

"Ezekiel has the fight in him to guide humanity into this age of magic. We each have our own path to walk." Sarah Jennifer paused. "It would be better if we could make it a clean break."

Bethany Anne raised an eyebrow. "What are you suggesting?"

"Is there a way to make everyone forget about us?" The request came from her heart without thought.

Bethany Anne didn't answer immediately. "I don't think that's necessary. History becomes a dream, children's stories. They will forget you soon enough without my intervention. You're sure about Ezekiel? What about Lilith?"

"People follow Ezekiel," Sarah Jennifer reasoned. "He'll teach them that faith is what powers their abilities. Lilith is safe."

She touched her knee, healed at long last. The red planet filled her inner vision, its possibilities filling her mind. This was the safe haven she'd dreamed of for the Weres. A place to build a defensive line from which they could protect Earth.

"My place is up here. With my family."

A knock on the door distracted Sarah Jennifer before she could further articulate her thoughts. "Come in," she called.

Kain opened the door. "Enora says the Pods are all in place." His eyes flicked to Bethany Anne on the screen, and he inclined his head respectfully before giving Sarah Jennifer another glance and ducking out of the cabin.

Bethany Anne glanced at Kain as he left the cabin. "Who was that?"

Sarah Jennifer couldn't help but smile. "Kain."

Bethany Anne tilted her head. "He loves you. You feel the same?"

"I could." Sarah Jennifer snorted softly. The Queen's perception was as deep as always. "He almost died after the battle of Rift Valley. I knew even then. I don't know what the future holds for us, but I know I'm willing to be there for it."

Bethany Anne folded her arms, tapping a finger on her elbow. "You'll be there if Earth needs you." It wasn't a request.

Sarah Jennifer nodded. "*Always.*"

Ezekiel was overawed when she returned to the cockpit and relayed the parts of the conversation that pertained to him. "The Matriarch knows who I am?"

Sarah Jennifer fought her impulse to give him a shake. "This is your chance to teach the world to believe in their own power. The people of Europe need homes, centers of learning where they can explore Bethany Anne's gift with guidance. You need to keep your eye on Arcadia."

Ezekiel's face crumpled with distaste. "I've had enough of living under strictures that I don't intend to put them on anyone else."

Sarah Jennifer just smiled. The passing of his youth hadn't lessened his chafing reaction at the mere mention of authority. "Don't be a stubborn dumbass. This is your world now. Yours to shape. Do me and Esme proud, kiddo."

Ezekiel nodded. "I will. I swear."

"That's all I can ask." Sarah Jennifer turned to Enora on the viewscreen. "Back to Earth, Enora. It's time to wrap things up there."

***

Kain left on the *Enora* to take Caitlin and Mary-Anne back to Canada while Sarah Jennifer made her final trip to Arcadia to coordinate the withdrawal of her forces. Ezekiel remained stoic while the Pods were loaded and the Weres boarded.

As the last Pod lifted off, Sarah Jennifer looked up to see the *Enora* coming in from the west.

Ezekiel came to stand beside her, his expression thoughtful. "This is it. Goodbye." He held out his arms for a final embrace.

Sarah Jennifer wrapped him in a tight hug. "You've got this, Ezekiel. I have so much faith in you it's unreal." She sighed, thinking about the difficult conversation waiting for her when she got to Mars.

Ezekiel squeezed her. "Esme would be proud of you, you know."

Sarah Jennifer released him. "I was thinking the same thing about you while I was taking the BYPS down."

"Will you have a memorial for her after you've told the pack what happened?"

Sarah Jennifer nodded. "I'm going to name our version of Central Park for her. I don't want us to ever forget what she did for humanity. What about you?"

"I thought about what you said, that we need to forget the Defense Force ever existed. I'm going to honor Esme and Linda my own way." His eyes misted over as he worked to contain his emotions. "I'll spend most of my time in Arcadia until I know Adrien has things running right. Then I'm going into the world to find people who need a teacher. I'm going to found more cities and work to bring them all together."

The *Enora* landed, and the hatch opened. Sarah Jennifer glanced at the airship. "That's my cue to say goodbye, kiddo. I'm going to miss you."

"Same," Ezekiel managed around the lump in his throat.

"Watch out for Laughter returning." She took a small box from her pocket and handed it to him.

"What's this?" Ezekiel asked, taking the box.

"The only tech I'm leaving behind. An Etheric comm." Sarah Jennifer put a hand on his shoulder. "Keep it hidden, and don't tell anyone you have it. I'll have one eye on Earth, but I won't intercede unless there's no other option. If the threat from the Kurtherians resurfaces and it gets to be too much for you to handle, call me."

She pulled him into one last hug, then turned and headed for the airship before she started crying.

Kain was sitting in the co-pilot's seat when she walked into the cockpit. "How did it go?" he asked.

Sarah Jennifer brushed his shoulder with a hand on her way to her seat. "About as expected. How about you?"

"It was emotional, I won't lie," he answered. "But this is the right choice. Caitlin knows that. We parted on good terms."

"Are you ready to leave?" Enora asked.

Sarah Jennifer nodded. "Take us out, Enora. Next stop, Promessa."

---

Kain took himself for a walk around the city to give Sarah Jennifer space while she broke the sad news about Esme and Linda to the pack. He had a credit app on a datapad that he'd been issued on arrival by a Were he'd been introduced to as Ace.

His goal was to familiarize himself with his new home. He strolled along the streets, marveling at the thoughtful blend of technology with rustic architecture. His datapad had the location of the apartment he'd been assigned on the outskirts of the city center, yet he found himself gravitating toward the green space at the heart of Promessa, drawn by the scent of nature. He wanted to be alone to process the enormity of his decision, to get a feel for the people he hadn't met, and absorb the mood of the city.

He'd traveled plenty in his youth, more before WWDE, so city life wasn't new to him. However, he'd never been in a large city that somehow still felt like a small community. Everyone knew everyone, and he was greeted numerous times by people wanting to introduce themselves.

As he approached the park's gates, he was hit with a sense of dissonance, of the familiar in an unfamiliar setting. "She wasn't kidding about modeling this on Central Park," he murmured to himself as he walked through the open gate.

The pavers were pink, and the trees were a mixture of biological and artificial, but the paths ran in familiar routes, and the waterways were right where his mind expected them to be.

A group of children ran across his path, some in human form, some on four paws.

"Jody, no fair!" one of the girls squealed at the gangly wolf who tackled her.

Kain smiled, wondering if one day he would get the opportunity to be a father. He couldn't help imagining a couple of rugrats with his coloring and Sarah Jennifer's eyes. He chastised himself for having it so bad. She had definitely warmed to him, but not to the point he should be picturing what their children would look like.

He continued walking, following his nose to a scent he never thought he'd smell again. But there it was: fried onions, brine, and mystery meat. The smell was coming from a little cart whose awning promised the finest fast food in the city.

"Hotdogs," he murmured. "No freaking way."

Kain stopped to buy two with everything from the vendor before veering off the path into the tree-shaded undergrowth. He didn't have far to walk before finding a shady spot under an oak that looked like it had been there for a hundred years. He settled down with his back against its trunk and ate his hotdogs in contemplative silence.

His parting from Caitlin, Mary-Anne, and Jaxon had been more difficult than he'd admitted to Sarah Jennifer. He was certain she understood, however, having had her own goodbyes to say.

Feeling full after the food, he leaned back against the tree and closed his eyes, imagining what his life here would look like a year from now. The Defense Force wasn't for him. He had no wish to spend his life in the military. However, neither did he wish to while it away floating along the edges of society like he had done for so long.

*Give yourself a break*, he told himself. *The Madness didn't exactly provide any opportunities to settle down and make something of yourself.*

He knew how he wanted to spend his nights, but that was entirely down to Sarah Jennifer. She was never far from his mind. His sense of self-worth wasn't tied up in his usefulness, yet he knew he wouldn't be happy unless he was contributing something to the colony.

So, what was he going to do with his days? He had a yearning to work with his hands; he knew that much. Did they need carpenters here? Maybe all that was taken care of by the printworks he'd passed. Then again, mass-produced furniture lacked the loving touch of, say, a crib carved by hand.

There he went with the baby thoughts again...

Another familiar scent wafted toward him. He opened one eye and grinned as Sarah Jennifer walked through the trees.

"How'd you find me?" he asked.

She pointed at the datapad on the grass beside him. "Easy enough to ask Galileo someone's location."

Kain sat up. "I'll keep that in mind. How did it go with the pack?"

Her eyes clouded with sadness. "Hard. We're going to hold a memorial service in a few days." She held out a hand. "Come on a hike with me? I need to run."

Kain took her hand and let her pull him to his feet. "Lead the way."

"You'll want to shift. It's a long way."

"I don't want to scare anyone," he told her. "I'm good until we get out of the city."

"Your choice," she replied with a smile. "No one here is going to freak out at the sight of a Pricolici. Here, I packed for us both."

Kain took the adjustable harness she held out and examined the setup. "This is ingenious."

"It's based on the one Sarai designed for me." She turned to show him the smaller version she was wearing. "We have water and food and climbing equipment for the rock face."

"We're going climbing?" He hefted the harness on and fastened the buckles.

Sarah Jennifer nodded. "There's a ridge in the mountains fifteen miles from here that looks out over the plain. We'll be the first humans to set foot there."

She ducked behind a tree and came out a couple of minutes later in wolf form with her clothing bundled and attached to her harness.

Kain waited until they reached the tree line that marked the city limits before shifting. Together, they ran through the arti-forest, across the plain, and over and around the rock formations beyond the agricultural sector all the way to the foot of the mountains before they shifted back.

Sarah Jennifer pulled out her water bottle and sipped. She looked at Kain, whose attention was on the sheer cliff in front of them.

"You don't do things by halves, do you?" he commented, shading his eyes with a hand as he looked up.

Sarah Jennifer laughed. "You'll figure it out eventually. I'm an all-or-nothing kind of woman." She stowed her water bottle and emptied the largest pouch on her harness. "How experienced are you with free climbing? I brought a bunch of equipment to help you out with the ascent."

Kain grinned. "I come with equipment built in." The next moment he was standing in front of her in Pricolici form. He wriggled his claws at her before leaping onto the rock face. "Watch me go, Princess."

Sarah Jennifer's eyes narrowed, her mouth curving dangerously. "Oh, so it's a competition you want?"

Kain looked back at her, his eyes flashing with joy. "If you think you can keep up, then put your money where your mouth is."

Sarah Jennifer shrugged her harness back on. "It's *on*, Player. Last one to the ridge has to cook dinner!"

"You brought dinner?" Kain laughed. "Careful...that almost sounds like we're on a date."

Sarah Jennifer grinned. "Maybe we are. Let's see how you handle the mountain before I decide."

She sprang for the rock face as Kain pushed off with his feet and leapt for the next handhold.

Kain had brute strength in his favor, but Sarah Jennifer had traversed some of the roughest terrain post-WWDE America had to offer and had experience on her side. The race was pretty even, and their easy banter flowed as they progressed past the sheer cliff and tackled the long incline leading to the ridge.

Even with their enhancements, it was a solid four hours later when they reached the ridge. Sarah Jennifer hauled herself over the edge and unclipped her harness. She dropped flat on her back, her arms spread wide, breathing heavily.

Kain flopped onto the grass beside her a moment later, and they lay in silence as the sun dipped behind the mountain.

He turned onto his stomach to face her once he had his breath back. "Guess dinner's on me."

Sarah Jennifer rolled over and rested her chin on her hands. "Shouldn't be too difficult. I brought MREs." She sat up and reached for her harness. "I hope you like pasta. We have spaghetti and meatballs. Well, meat*less*balls. They're plant-based."

Kain raised an eyebrow, his mouth quirked to the right. "How is that date-appropriate? Don't you know the way to a man's heart is through his stomach?"

"Actually, the best way to a man's heart is through the

fifth left intercostal space at the midclavicular line." The grass tickled her forearms, sending a shiver across her skin. "Besides, did you want to set up a field kitchen?"

Kain laughed. "Spaghetti and meatlessballs it is, then. So, it is a date?" He didn't bother to hide the hope in his voice.

Sarah Jennifer looked into his eyes and nodded. "Yeah. This is a date. Let's watch the sunset while we wait for the food to heat."

Kain didn't care what dinner was. He only had eyes for Sarah Jennifer.

Sarah Jennifer flushed, nervous again. "Kain... It's been a long time since I had a date."

"It's easy. You just scoot over here, and we watch the sun go down." He lifted his arm, his easy grin putting her nerves to rest.

"That I can do." Sarah Jennifer smiled and moved to sit beside him.

Food forgotten for the moment, she leaned into his warmth and focused on the stars appearing in the gradually darkening sky. The moons shone brightly overhead, turning the grass silver. Across the plain, the lights of Promessa twinkled in the distance.

Sarah Jennifer slipped her arms around Kain and tilted her head to look into his eyes.

"You good?" he asked, his voice low.

Sarah Jennifer nodded, smiling. "Yeah. Yeah, I am."

All these months, she'd held him at arm's length, afraid to listen to her heart, afraid to take the risk it might get broken again. But tonight, here on their new homeworld, she couldn't deny the feelings that had grown stronger with every day she'd watched him be the man she wanted by her side.

He hadn't pushed, hadn't assumed she would capitulate to their mutual desire. He had just been there for her and everyone else around him, supporting, strengthening, and shining his light on every situation they'd found themselves in.

Even now, he held his desire in check. She saw it in his eyes. He wanted to make her his world.

Sarah Jennifer made her choice. She chose *him*, now and forever.

She lifted her hand to cup his face, and without a word, they kissed under the light of the moons.

# EPILOGUE

Bethany Anne had her own failsafe in mind. No one but Michael knew she was here on Earth, which was just how she wanted it.

The sound of her heels echoed in the giant borehole she'd had dug into this mountain a lifetime ago as she made her way to Lilith's cavern.

*My Queen, you honor me with your visit.*

Bethany Anne smiled at Lilith's tone. Somehow the Kurtherian managed to convey her empathy with that digitized voice. She laid a hand on the casing of Lilith's prison. "I wish it were a social visit. Sarah Jennifer wants me to make everyone forget her."

*I have been part of her consciousness for over thirty years,* Lilith told her. *She yearns for peace, for love and family.*

"Everything she's been denied up until now."

*I will miss her greatly,* Lilith admitted.

"I'm not going to do it." Bethany Anne told her. "You deserve to keep your memories. Just keep them to yourself."

*I appreciate your trust, and I am glad that Sarah Jennifer has a chance to move on with her life.*

Bethany Anne was prepared to go to great lengths to make sure Sarah got her chance. "Do you have a secure compartment in here?" she asked, scanning for a suitable receptacle. Her eyes landed on a ziplock bag containing washers and nuts.

A section of the wall slid back at Lilith's command, and Bethany Anne glanced inside. "That will do."

*What are you intending to hide?* Lilith inquired, confused.

"A Hail Mary. To be used only if the world is about to end." Bethany Anne emptied the bag and opened it on the bench to catch the blood that poured from the gash she cut into her wrist. "Tupperware would have been better than this," she grumbled as the cut healed.

Lilith observed in silence, awed that she was to be entrusted with the Queen's power.

Bethany Anne sealed the bag and placed it inside the compartment, reading Lilith's thoughts in the mindspace. "Ezekiel is young, and frankly, he's an arrogant little prick at times. He doesn't need to know about this until the world has knocked the chip off his shoulder."

*I understand.* Lilith was quiet for a moment. *What about Laughter? She will be back.*

"I have Hyrrheim's coordinates," Bethany Anne told her. "Laughter's facility will be a smear in the dirt by the time the Bad Company is done with that place. They owe Laughter an ass-kicking, and they don't like to be in debt."

*FINIS*

I have a whole list of thanks to give but let me start by thanking you for sticking with us all the way to the end of this series. Sarah Jennifer may lack the snarky attitude that defines many of the heroes who make up this universe but she makes up for it by having the biggest heart. It was my absolute joy to see her finally let go of the past and open up to love.

I have to confess, this was the most challenging to write of the three books, and not because it had crossover with so many other series' from around the KGU*. While SJ was working to open up her heart, mine was in bits as I dealt with one of the hardest times in my life. Starting over is never easy. I'm so grateful for the good people in my life who rallied around to make rebuilding less painful. You all know who you are. I love and appreciate you more than I can ever say.

This book also marks the end of my Kurtherian adventure for now. While I still have some input on helping Michael with Checkmate, I'm excited to be focusing on a new project in my writing. This is a whole new world! I'm taking my time to develop the story and putting everything I've learned about craft in the last few years into practice. If you like superhero action and techy stuff it will be right up your street.

It will be a little while before I have books to share in this new series. I'm sure Michael will tempt me with another shiny in the meantime...

Back to Sarah Jennifer. This isn't quite the end for her. I'm handing the Defense Force back to Michael and he will pick up around 70 years along from where I left off. The idea of having the pack placed on Mars was to have that first line of defense for Earth. I deliberately kept the development of the Mars location minimal to give him room to play. If you are all caught up on Endgame then you'll know what's coming. (No spoilers here!)

Thank yous!! First, to Michael and Lynne. We have family we're born into, and we have family we choose. To Kelly, Micky, and Elaine. Friends like you three are hard to come by. To Dan Willcocks for being such a good sport about me rearranging parts of his book. To Craig Martelle for kindly taking time to add a little bit to the scene where SJ calls her grandparents. To everyone in JIT who helped with the final polish of this book. If any oopsies snuck through they are all down to me.

Once again, thank YOU for reading and supporting this series. Until the next time I write author notes, much love, and HAPPY READING!

Nat

___

\* <u>Crossover with other series' within the universe.</u>

Age of Madness:

- The Caitlin Chronicles: Kain, Caitlin, and Mary-Anne.

Age of Magic:

- Rise of Magic: Ezekiel, Lilith, Olaf, Mika, and Adrien. (Also Linda, although she was only mentioned in passing.)

- A New Dawn: Selah, Margit, and Artemis.

- Tales of the Feisty Druid: Alexander.

Age of Expansion:

- The Kurtherian Endgame: Bethany Anne.

- Bad Company: TH and Char.

Age of Empire (TKG):

- Reclaiming Honor: Royland and Cammie.

Thank you for not only reading this story but also the author notes from Nat and I in the back!

**It's all about AI – Or is it?**

If you have read any of my other recent author notes, you know I'm playing with GPT-2 and hoping to play with GPT-3.

What are they? Essentially AI (Artificial Intelligence) tools from OpenAI.

Since I don't have access to GPT-3 (C'mon, OpenAI! Don't you know I'm a (*rather minor*) Science Fiction author here?!)

Petty jealousy of those who have access aside, I have found a couple of companies who are using GPT-3 to provided services (for a fee).

One of those is Conversion.ai, and the other is Resemble.ai.

I love chocolate chip cookies. *I just can't eat them.*

So, I played with the older version (GPT-2) last week

with chocolate chip cookies. This week, I'm going to do the same, and I suspect two results:

1) I'm going to wish I had cookies.

2) You are going to want to eat chocolate chip cookies (if you like them at all.)

**The Premise**

I start a minor statement and let Conversion AI make up the blog post header and two (2) starting paragraphs for a blog post.

Then...

I let Resemble AI change it to a voice file, and I provide the results.

I input "I like chocolate chip cookies" into the Conversion AI interface, and it provides two blog post suggestions. I grab "Five ways to perfect your chocolate chip cookies."

Next, I go looking for the tool that will write my whole blog post. I come away dejected...they don't have one.

*Dammit.*

Okay, so I find a template that will provide me a starter paragraph for the copy, and I test it using my super-duper new header above.

Here are the two results (AI results unedited):

*Result 1*

Most people have their own version of the perfect chocolate chip cookie recipe. From the type of flour to how much sugar and butter is used, everyone's got a different theory on what makes the best cookie. That's why we've collected these five tips that can help you make your cookies as good as they can be!

1) Using cold butter in your dough will give it a flaky texture and add some extra flavor.

2) Avoid over-mixing the dough or else it will become dense and tough instead of light and chewy.

3) One cup of each type (all-purpose, whole wheat pastry, bread flour) yields chewier cookies with big air pockets, while all-purpose flour alone results in crispier ones

### Result 2

It's a well-known fact that chocolate chip cookies are the best kind of cookie. But, like any dish, they can be perfected with the right ingredients and techniques. To help you get started on your journey to perfecting your favorite treat, we've come up with 5 ways for you to try!

*(Editor note: My teeth ache. I SO want to edit that paragraph.)*

1) The creamier way: replace some or all of the butter in this recipe with unsweetened applesauce or mashed banana. This will make them less dense and more moist (but still crispy!).

2) A little salt never hurt anyone: Add ½ teaspoon kosher salt to dough before baking for a salty crunch.

3) Nutty but not too nutty: swap out half of the granulated sugar for light

Of the two solutions, I prefer the first option. So, I went over to Resemble AI for text-to-speech and found out that the free plan (which provides you 2,000 characters a month to play with) is a bit of a pain in the @#%.

No problem, I persevered.

I figured out how to download the full audio (I think. I am presently waiting for the results.)

While I'm waiting, they have upgraded the interface since the last time I played with their tool. They have allowed you to break up the text into bite-sized pieces, and you can change the parameters (such as what artificial voice you wish to use, if there is emphasis on the sentence language and phoneme, etc.)

Okay, I went back to Resemble AI and figured out I broke the free version. They want me to use a smaller amount of text to play with the product. This won't allow me to provide an example here (well, obviously, this is a fiction book, not an audiobook), but I will go see what happens when I give it less than five hundred characters of text.

And the answer is?

https://app.resemble.ai/services/embed?pod=0eebf3ec

If you don't have the ability to listen, I would personally rate this as a strong C. It passes, and if I had no other options, I would GLADLY listen to something like this.

That is a subjective comment, of course.

As Natale, I, and many science fiction authors move forward with creating stories based in the future, we have to be careful.

Why?

Because the present is catching up to us. We might have to realize that we are now writing contemporary science fiction, *not future.*

Ad Aeternitatem,

Michael Anderle

**They say that behind every great man is a great woman...but what if that woman is a Werewolf?**

Available now at Amazon and through Kindle Unlimited.

*This digital box set contains ALL 11 books of the best-selling Terry Henry Walton Chronicles series from Craig Martelle and Michael Anderle.*

**Nomad Found**

Can Terry Henry Walton help bring humanity back to civilization?

He finds that he needs help and starts building his Force de Guerre, a paramilitary group that will secure this new world from those who would take and destroy.

When the enemies of peace appear before the FDG is

ready, Terry partners with a werewolf to fight a battle that he must win.

**Nomad Redeemed**

Sawyer Brown is no more, but he was just the minor opening act...

Terry Henry and Charumati (Char) have to deal with her Alpha coming back, the new refugees getting settled in the town and .. Beer!

With the FDG doubling in size, Terry Henry needs to bring about a little organizational structure to the group.While also deciding how to have that conversation with Char about her lineage...

Not sure how that is going to go, Terry Henry had better figure it out, or he is going to be up to his armpits in Werewolves and won't be sure if he can depend on his one ace-in-the-hole.

Or not.

**Nomad Unleashed**

The heat is unrelenting. The Wastelands are coming for New Boulder. Nature's a total bitch.

And then there's Werewolf heat.

Terry Henry Walton has to come to grips with the reality of his situation.

Civilization cannot return to humanity without help. More help than even an enhanced human can give. Terry and Char take their relationship to a new level before they head out to find a new home to save the people of New Boulder, to rally the survivors that the world is coming back...

And for themselves.

**Nomad Supreme**

Terry and Char cross the Wastelands returning to New Boulder carrying a message of hope. They'd found a better place. Could they move the whole town there, and would it be safer?

They have a lead on Terry's white whale, a secure military facility.

What will they find and can they break in?

**Nomad's Fury**

Settled into their new home of North Chicago, Terry and Char find more enemies than they suspected. Faced with their greatest threat, they put the FDG into action against a Forsaken who's surrounded himself with a small army of loyal humans. With Akio's aid, they go to war.

**Nomad's Justice**
**Nomad Avenged**
**Nomad Mortis**
**Nomad's Fury**
**Nomad's Force**
**Nomad's Galaxy**
**Nomad's Journal**

Available now at Amazon and through Kindle Unlimited.